Just the two of them.

Alone.

Get a grip, she told herself. It's only a friendly dinner. And certainly *not* a date.

Kara struggled with the urge to go home, but then Michael answered the door wearing a pair of jeans, a crisply pressed white shirt and a smile that reached the golden hue of his eyes.

He'd showered. And shaved. His eyes swept over her body in an appreciative caress. "Come in."

Kara moved into the small cottage. A fire crackled softly in the living room, and the easy sound of something classical played on the stereo.

Just friends. Neighbors.

"Can I pour you a glass of wine?"

Wine?

He flashed her a warm, friendly smile, and she wondered if she'd made more out of the offer than he'd intended.

We're just newfound friends having dinner. What harm could there be in that?

Dear Reader,

While taking a breather from decorating and gift-wrapping, check out this month's exciting treats from Silhouette Special Edition. *The Summer House* (#1510) contains two fabulous stories in one neat package. "Marrying Mandy" by veteran author Susan Mallery features the reunion of two sweethearts who fall in love all over again. Joining Susan is fellow romance writer Teresa Southwick whose story "Courting Cassandra" shows how an old crush blossoms into full-blown love.

In Joan Elliott Pickart's *Tall, Dark and Irresistible* (#1507), a hero comes to terms with his heritage and meets a special woman who opens his heart to the possibilities. Award-winning author Anne McAllister gets us in the holiday spirit with *The Cowboy's Christmas Miracle* (#1508) in which a lone-wolf cowboy finds out he's a dad to an adorable little boy, then realizes the woman who'd always been his "best buddy" now makes his heart race at top speed! And count on Christine Rimmer for another page-turner in *Scrooge and the Single Girl* (#1509). This heart-thumping romance features an anti-Santa hero and an independent heroine, both resigned to singlehood and stranded in a tiny little mountain cabin where they'll have a holiday they'll never forget!

Judy Duarte returns to the line-up with *Family Practice* (#1511), a darling tale of a handsome doctor who picks up the pieces after a bitter divorce and during a much-needed vacation falls in love with a hardworking heroine and her two kids. In Elane Osborn's *A Season To Believe* (#1512), a woman survives a car crash but wakes up with amnesia. When a handsome private detective takes her plight to heart, she finds more than one reason to be thankful.

As you can see, we have an abundance of rich and emotionally complex love stories to share with you. I wish you happiness, fun and a little romance this holiday season!

Karen Taylor Richman
Senior Editor

Please address questions and book requests to:
Silhouette Reader Service
U.S.: 3010 Walden Ave., P.O. Box 1325, Buffalo, NY 14269
Canadian: P.O. Box 609, Fort Erie, Ont. L2A 5X3

Family Practice

JUDY DUARTE

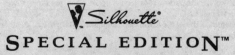

Silhouette®

SPECIAL EDITION™

Published by Silhouette Books

America's Publisher of Contemporary Romance

To Bob and Betty Astleford, who gave me a strong, loving foundation that became a springboard to reach my dreams. You taught me the values I hold dear and set a fine example of love, marriage and parenthood. I love you, Mom and Dad.

In memory of Regina Ann Ronk, who blessed my life and my writing. *Philippians* 1:2-3.

 SILHOUETTE BOOKS

ISBN 0-373-24511-4

FAMILY PRACTICE

Visit Silhouette at www.eHarlequin.com

Printed in U.S.A.

Books by Judy Duarte

Silhouette Special Edition

Cowboy Courage #1458
Family Practice #1511

JUDY DUARTE

An avid reader who enjoys a happy ending, Judy Duarte always wanted to write books of her own. One day, she decided to make that dream come true. Five years and six manuscripts later, she sold her first book to Silhouette Special Edition.

Her unpublished stories have won the Emily and the Orange Rose writing contests, and in 2001, she became a double RWA Golden Heart finalist. Judy credits her success to Romance Writers of America and two wonderful critique partners, Sheri WhiteFeather and Crystal Green, both of whom write for Silhouette.

At times, when a stubborn hero and a headstrong heroine claim her undivided attention, she and her family are thankful for fast food, pizza delivery and video games. When she's not at the keyboard or in a Walter-Mitty-type world, she enjoys traveling, romantic evenings with her personal hero and playing board games with her kids.

Judy lives in Southern California and loves to hear from her readers. You may write to her at: P.O. Box 498, San Luis Rey, CA 92068-0498. You can also visit her Web site at: www.judyduarte.com.

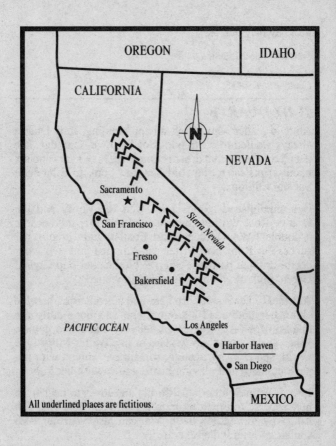

OREGON

IDAHO

CALIFORNIA

NEVADA

Sierra Nevada

Sacramento

San Francisco

Fresno

Bakersfield

PACIFIC OCEAN

Los Angeles

Harbor Haven

San Diego

All underlined places are fictitious.

MEXICO

Chapter One

"Dr. Harper, now that your wife is in prison, what are your plans?"

Barely out of his black Jag, Michael Harper tensed his jaw, slammed the car door and shoved past a cocky reporter and a heavyset cameraman. Ever since the trial, the press continued to dog him.

Why wouldn't they leave him alone? The whole damn mess was yesterday's news, at least as far as he was concerned. He'd been cleared of any wrongdoing, Denise was in prison, and their divorce had been finalized three months ago.

"Just one question, Doc. Has your practice suffered because of the scandal?"

A camera flashed in Michael's face, and he clenched his fist, fighting an urge to grab the photographic equipment and sling it to the ground. "No comment."

He strode toward the private stairwell that led from the underground parking garage to his second-floor southern

California office, hoping to shake more than the dank odor of concrete, gasoline fumes and exhaust. Why the interest in him? In his practice, his life? He hadn't done anything, just been an unwitting victim.

The thought of himself as a victim turned his stomach, knotted his gut. Michael Harper, son of the Raleigh-Harpers of Boston. Distinguished graduate of Harvard Medical School. Renowned cardiovascular surgeon. His life had been charmed from birth. Perfect.

Until now.

Damn you, Denise. Michael swung open the metal door and slammed it behind him. He wasn't sure how much more of this he could take. Sure, the whole sordid mess had taken a toll on him. His former wife who had also been his office manager had carried on a lengthy affair with a high-profile politician. That was tough enough to handle.

But she'd laundered drug money through his office, then made illegal contributions to her lover's campaign. There'd been a thorough investigation, and Michael had been cleared of any wrongdoing. Still, the embarrassment was hard to live down. Hard to forgive. Impossible to forget.

The press continued to dog him, Dr. Michael Harper, who had nothing to do with any of this. Even those sleazy tabloids had found him a newsworthy topic. Apparently, the public enjoyed hearing about a wealthy surgeon cuckolded by a bad girl and a notorious politician. But quite frankly, he was ready to escape the limelight.

Forever.

When he reached his office, he unlocked the door and stepped inside. He wasn't sure why he even bothered to come in today. Habit, he supposed, but it wasn't necessary. Due in part to the depositions and trials, both federal and state, he'd cut back on his patient load until it was nearly nonexistent.

"Michael?" Bertha Williams, his office manager, asked. The woman had come out of retirement to fix the god-awful mess his ex-wife had made of his books. "Is that you?"

"Yes, it's me." Michael followed the smell of fresh coffee and the sound of an electric percolator to the break room.

In years past, Bertha had hovered over him like a mother hen, fixing him a hot lunch when he'd been too busy to eat or too concerned about a patient to realize he'd skipped a meal or two. She handed him a steaming cup of coffee, then eyed him carefully. "Did you forget to shave again? Or is that an attempt to shake your wholesome, all-American look?"

"Neither." Michael stroked the day-old bristles on his chin, then shrugged. "Maybe it's apathy."

"Humph." She clicked her tongue, crossed her arms and shook her head. "You're looking bad, Michael. Not overworked, but under too much stress."

"I'm all right, just tired of all the fuss."

Concern simmered in her hazel eyes. "You're a surgeon, dedicated to your profession and respected among your peers. I've seen you work with only an occasional game of golf as a diversion. It may have been enough in the past, but not now. I think you should consider a vacation."

A vacation? Impossible. "I need a permanent break from the press and media, but there's a host of reporters staking out my jet at the Santa Monica Airport. They're just waiting for me to show my face."

"You could take a drive up or down the coast," Bertha suggested. "Maybe find a secluded house on the beach."

Ocean breezes. Sunshine. Long, solitary, mind-cleansing walks on the sand. It sounded too good to be true. Michael shook his head. "I can't even go downstairs to the parking garage without meeting an entourage of reporters.''

Bertha furrowed her gray brow and drummed her fingers on the table, then she brightened. "Take my car. It's parked out front today. Of course, it won't be at all like driving that fancy black Jaguar of yours.''

Michael smiled. He doubted anyone would expect to see him drive an '89 Ford Taurus out of here. Maybe her idea had merit.

Bertha stood. "I'll get the keys. Then I'll check with Dr. Hanson about taking the few patients you have scheduled this week.''

"No, I don't think it will work. I'd have to go home and pack—"

"Oh, pshaw. You've got a shaving kit and change of clothes here. And anything else can be purchased along the way. Michael, you need a break, if not a full-scale vacation. Take some time to yourself, and maybe then you'll be ready to come back to work.'' Bertha dug through her oversize handbag and handed him a set of keys.

Two hours later, Michael drove south on Pacific Coast Highway. He wasn't sure where he was going, but as long as the press hadn't followed him, he'd be content to watch the sun set over the ocean, maybe even try surfing again. He hadn't taken time to relax in years. He hadn't really needed to.

A small, nearly obscure sign identified the upcoming town as Harbor Haven. The name had a pleasant, out-of-the-way sound. He flipped the blinker then turned left. A haven was just what he needed, especially if it provided peace and quiet.

He passed several pastel-colored storefronts—Bailey's Bait Shop, Connie's Bookstore, and the EZ Suds Laundromat. On the other side of the street, he spotted a mom-

and-pop grocery store. Harbor Haven wasn't really a town, he realized, but rather a small secluded enclave.

Down the road, a sign advertised Campbell's Seaside Cottages, and an arrow pointed to a side street on the left. Michael followed the directions until he spotted a group of quaint little beach houses, all white with latticework trim. Only a bright yellow number distinguished one from another. A pink, flashing neon sign hung in the window of the largest cottage and announced, Vacancy.

He swung into a graveled parking lot, empty except for two kids and a mixed-breed dog playing with a soccer ball. Carefully avoiding a small, sandy-haired boy and an older redheaded girl, Michael pulled the Ford into a parking space.

As he turned off the ignition, he noticed the Rolex on his wrist. Not exactly sure why, he slipped off the expensive gold watch and placed it in the empty ashtray. Today, he was just a regular guy who drove an old Ford. Certainly not anyone famous or newsworthy.

As he swung open the door and stepped from the sedan, the soccer ball came flying toward his feet, resting underneath Bertha's car.

"Sorry, mister, I'm not too good at kicking yet." The little boy's soft brown eyes pleaded for understanding, and he pointed toward the broken-down fence that lined the back half of the parking lot. "The ball was s'posed to go over there."

Michael stooped to retrieve the soccer ball, then tossed it toward the boy. The girl, wearing white shorts and a pink sweatshirt, struggled to hold the dog. When their eyes met, Michael did a double take.

It was easy to see how he had mistaken the petite woman for a child—but only from a distance. Up close, her maturity struck him as obvious, and when she smiled, her wholesome beauty stunned him.

The breeze stirred up the smells of salt and seashore

and played havoc with her curly red hair, as did the sunlight, highlighting the color of autumn leaves and, for only a moment, reminding him of Boston. And the park where he had played as a boy.

She swatted at the springy strand that whipped across a lightly freckled nose. Large, expressive eyes, the color of the sea, enhanced a small, delicate face. She eased her hold on the dog until it lunged toward Michael with its tongue flopping. Snagging the bright yellow collar, she jerked the black overgrown puppy back. Michael wasn't sure the petite woman could control the monstrous animal, but she did.

"Gulliver," she scolded. "Behave yourself, or I'll put you in the backyard."

"I didn't mean to spoil your fun," Michael said. "As soon as I rent a cottage, I'll move the car."

"Hey, that'll make you our neighbor." The boy smiled. "I'm Eric, and this is Kara."

He hadn't meant to speak, to introduce himself. This quest had only been for solitude, a time to form a game plan of sorts. He'd toyed with the idea of relocating his practice from Los Angeles to Boston and hoped taking time off would help him decide.

When she flashed him a shy smile, warmth slowly poured over him, like aged cognac from a crystal decanter. And the words spilled out without any effort on his part. "My name's Michael."

Kara Westin nearly stumbled over the panting dog, but when she regained her footing and glanced into the amber-colored eyes of the man who'd just introduced himself, her heart jumped, and her breath caught in her throat. She wrestled the urge to gawk at the stranger standing before her.

Tall and broad-shouldered. Handsome, too. Hair, golden brown—sun-bleached, most likely. He had that lanky, water sport aficionado look. Jet skis, surfboards, sailboats.

Vacationing? she wondered. This late in the fall? The tourist season was over, which she found disappointing. A people watcher by nature, Kara missed the daily activity that provided fodder for the journal she kept.

She extended her hand in greeting before he did. "It's nice to meet you, Michael. How long will you be staying?"

"I'm not sure. A few days, maybe a week."

Kara eyed him carefully, trying to garner a sense of who her temporary neighbor might be. She found him hard to read. That, in itself, told her she should be wary. Her instincts about strangers had usually been on target. But this particular man wasn't giving her intuition very much to work with.

"Where are you from?" she asked, unable to keep herself from prying.

"A couple of hours up north. I had some time off and thought I'd just travel along the coast."

Kara, glad the dog had finally settled down, eased her hold on Gulliver's collar. "Sounds like you've got an adventurous spirit."

He slid her a half smile. "I've been accused of being staid and boring, but never adventurous."

"That's too bad." Kara wondered how a man who looked to be the epitome of outdoor fun could consider himself dull. It didn't seem possible. "Life can be tough if you can't find time to enjoy it."

"Kara's just about the most funnest person you'll ever know," Eric interjected. "She's always got a cool idea. She can make the yuckiest things kind of neat."

"I'm not into fun," Michael said. Topaz-colored eyes studied Kara a bit more intensely than she liked. It seemed as though he was trying to read her, just as she had tried with him. She found it unsettling until he turned and smiled at Eric. "I just came here to walk on the beach. Think. Have some alone time."

And then Kara saw it, that glimmer of something in his eyes that told her more about the man than he told her himself. She recognized sadness, and although he'd only allowed her a brief glimpse, it was there. She was sure of it. Michael, whoever he was, had come to Harbor Haven to ease his pain.

Her heart went out to him, just as it did for every orphan she met—human or animal. Of course, she didn't need to adopt another lonely stray into her world. Her time was spread a bit too thin, as it was.

When she wasn't working at the Pacifica Bar and Grill and saving every dime she could for graduate school, she was helping Lizzie make a home for the children.

"Well," she said, dismissing her analysis of the good-looking stranger, "Harbor Haven should give you all the fresh air and sunshine you need." She pointed toward the office built on the front of Lizzie's cottage. "You'll find Elizabeth Campbell inside. She's the owner."

"Thanks," Michael said. Then he strode toward the office, leaving Kara and Eric to their game of soccer.

"Okay, Kara," Eric said. "Let's finish our practice. What does the book say we need to do next?"

Kara smiled at the boy whose childhood had been interrupted by tragedy, knowing it was their commonality that led to their friendship and camaraderie. She, too, had been orphaned, but she didn't have family to look after her. "I left the book on the picnic table. Let's go read the next chapter."

Eric dashed ahead, still favoring his left foot. Last year a tragic car accident had damaged his hip and thigh. The orthopedic surgeon said Eric might never regain the full use of his leg. Kara hoped he didn't need any additional operations. The poor kid had been through enough already.

"Out of my way, Gulliver," Eric said, as he tried to maneuver around the loping dog. "You're supposed to watch and get the ball when we miss the goal. Only people play soccer."

Kara wished she'd played soccer herself, as a kid. She hadn't, of course, but the public library had oodles of books on sports, and she was determined to learn along with Eric. Instead of putting them at a disadvantage, reading and studying together had a lot of positive effects—the least of which was developing a close, loving bond with each other.

Eric, who had virtually no reading skills six months ago, was now browsing the library with enthusiasm. He saw education as a means of achieving anything he wanted, including fun on the school playground.

And that's exactly what Kara had hoped would happen. It was her own plan of action. That's why she struggled so hard to put herself through junior college, then on to a four-year degree. It had taken her six years to do it, but she'd achieved it without any student loans or financial aid.

As a child, she'd been a ward of the state for as long as she could remember, dependent upon the charity and handouts of others. But not any longer. Everything she owned, every oddball, mismatched piece of furniture, secondhand pair of shoes or outfit had been provided by her own labor. Self-sufficiency made her feel as rich and proud as a queen. And she would never take a dime from anyone else, never feel obligated to anyone again.

"Oh, Gulliver," Eric said, as he and the gangly dog collided. The boy's bad leg gave way, and he fell to the graveled parking lot and skidded on his hands and knees. "Ow."

Oh, no. Not his leg, Kara thought, as she strode to Eric's side, hoping the injury was minor. Lizzie hadn't been too happy about Eric playing outside, let alone soccer. Too dangerous, she'd said. But Kara figured the woman was more concerned the courts would find fault with her and take Eric and his baby sister away. It hadn't been easy for a seventy-five-year-old woman to gain custody of her grandchildren, but the boy's heroism in the midst of tragedy had made him a celebrity of sorts.

Several televised reports and a heart-stunning newspaper editorial had led to an outpouring of support. Telephone calls to the television stations jammed their lines for days, and a slew of letters written to the editor of the newspaper demanded the children's need for a loving family member to take them, no matter what her age. The judge, swayed by public sentiment, granted Lizzie temporary custody of Eric and Ashley, the baby sister whose life he'd saved.

Still, the guardianship Lizzie held was tenuous. Kara, having been jerked about within the system herself, knew firsthand how temporary custody and foster care could be. When it became necessary for the kids to have a more permanent home, she hoped the press would back her attempt to adopt the kids she'd grown to love. She had Lizzie's blessing, but the court would make the ultimate decision. And at this time in her life, she had little to offer the kids except love.

"Are you all right?" she asked.

Eric struggled to stand, tears running down his dusty cheeks to a quivering bottom lip. "That dumb dog—"

"Gulliver didn't mean to knock you down," Kara said. "He thought you wanted to race and play."

"I know, but it really hurts, Kara."

She scooped the boy up in her arms, then carried him toward the cottage he shared with Lizzie. "We'll get you cleaned up and bandaged. You'll be good as new in no time."

"It stings, really bad."

"I know it does, honey." Kara carried Eric to the office steps, then adjusted him in her arms so she could open the door. "I don't think we should let Gulliver play soccer with us anymore. He's too big and rough."

Eric blew at a scrape on his palm, then glanced at Kara. "But that would hurt his feelings, like when the kids at school don't pick me to be on their team."

Kara sighed. "You're right. I guess we'll have to figure out something else." She knew how cruel some kids could be. *Freckle-face strawberry. Raggedy Kara Ann. Don't play with Kara—she's got cooties.*

Sometimes the sounds of childhood crept back to haunt her. She stilled them by remembering the kindness some of her teachers had shown—teachers like Miss Green who had shown compassion for a homeless girl by keeping a comb and brush set in her desk drawer.

Every morning, Kara would stop by the classroom where she could wash her face and comb her hair before the first bell rang. Most days, Miss Green would have an extra barrette or ribbon. The teasing seemed to ease after that, which was probably why Kara was still obsessed with cleanliness. She might not have any clothes that weren't hand-me-downs or secondhand purchases, but she owned an array of soaps, body lotions and hair products that would put a teenage girl to shame.

As Kara nudged the door with her shoulder, Lizzie looked up from her desk. "Land sakes, what happened?"

Michael watched her every bit as intently as Lizzie, but she hoped to get Eric into the bathroom with as little fuss as possible. Things like this seemed to cause Lizzie's already high blood pressure to skyrocket.

"Nothing that a little soap, water and bandaging won't help," Kara said, hoping to sound cheerful.

"But his leg," Lizzie cried. "The doctors said to be careful."

"He's fine. Don't worry, Lizzie. Sit down before you have a heart attack."

Michael was at Kara's side in a moment. "Here, let me help," he said, taking Eric from her arms.

She appreciated his assistance, which would allow her hands the freedom to care for the wounds. "The bathroom is this way. If you'll just set him on the counter, I can do the rest."

Kara led Michael down the hall, but when he placed Eric upon the pink-tiled counter, he didn't turn and leave. Instead, he carefully checked each wound. His gentle assessment surprised her. Most men had a rather macho side, at least those she'd met while working at the Pacifica Bar and Grill. An image of Jason Baker came to mind, a man who had once thought Kara should be thrilled that a guy of his wealth and social standing should want to date her.

Hon, she could imagine him saying, *just rub a little dirt on it. It'll toughen up that wimpy kid.*

"Do you have any antibacterial soap?" Michael asked, pulling Kara from her musing.

Unable to spot any on the countertop, she stooped to search the cabinet under the sink where Lizzie kept bathroom supplies. Finding soap in a clear, plastic bottle decorated with cartoon characters, she stood. "You don't have to help me. I can take it from here."

"It's no trouble," he said.

She watched him work carefully, all the while talking to Eric about soccer and school, taking his mind off the cleaning of gravel embedded in his right knee. Then Michael paused, glancing at one leg then the other. Noting the extensive scars and disparity in musculature? Kara wondered. If so, he didn't comment, which was good. Eric was self-conscious of the difference.

"You're pretty good with fixing skinned knees and hands," Kara said, trying to make conversation. "What else are you good at?"

He looked at her with another one of those unreadable

expressions, then their gazes locked for only a moment, but long enough for her to feel a flutter in her stomach and a warmth in her breast.

What else are you good at? Good grief. Had she said that? It sounded so suggestive, and she certainly hadn't meant to...

"I mean," she said, "any other talents?"

"None to boast about," he answered. His amber eyes never left hers, and the room seemed to close in on them.

Boy, it was hot in here. Kara blew out her breath. "Ready for some gauze and tape?" she asked, trying to still her awkwardness.

"Yeah," Michael said, returning his attention to Eric.

When Eric had been bandaged, Kara reached to take the boy from the counter and set him on the floor, but apparently Michael had the same idea. Their hands brushed together, and they both jerked back in response.

Kara, her fingers still tingling from his touch, felt her cheeks warm. Darn that telltale flush. She didn't want him thinking she felt embarrassment or anything else. He was a stranger, just passing through. And she had a lot on her plate these days. A brief—

A brief what?

For goodness sake, was she even thinking an odd encounter in Lizzie's bathroom with a stranger was a prelude to anything at all?

She'd been reading too many romance books.

And if she'd learned anything at all, happily ever after only happened in fairy tales. It had been a tough lesson, but one she wouldn't ever forget. She would never allow a Prince Charming to rescue her and set her up in a castle in the sky.

Kara Westin could take care of herself.

Kara carried Gulliver's leash and stepped out on the porch, intent on taking her usual sunset walk south of the harbor. It had become an evening ritual, ever since she'd first moved into the Haven.

The quiet hour before dusk was her favorite time of the day. She relished the tranquillity as the sun sank low in the pink and gray streaked sky. It gave her time to think, to plan, to dream.

Resting her hands against the lattice railing, she watched the waves crash upon the shore. Sometimes, when things were really quiet, she envisioned herself on the deck of a huge ship, sailing across the sea to a land of plenty and promise. Kara didn't have many possessions, but she did own a vivid imagination, something she found priceless.

A lone gull sounded in the distance, and she searched the horizon. Instead of the bird, she spotted Michael, her new neighbor. He sat, alone and pensive, perched on the rocks that lined the jetty.

Who was he? Why had he come after the other tourists had gone home? She wanted to honor his privacy, but to do so meant she would remain on the porch instead of walking barefoot in the sand. Perhaps she could wave, acknowledge his presence, then continue on her own. She didn't need to strike up a conversation or bother him.

She stepped from the deck and strode toward the fence behind Mr. Radcliff's house. Kara and Mr. Radcliff were the only two permanent tenants of Lizzie's cottages. The elderly man had been kind enough to allow Gulliver to stay in his yard, since Kara's house didn't have a fence. Kara, in turn, fed and cared for the dog and kept Mr. Radcliff's yard clean.

Lizzie thought Mr. Radcliff rather stodgy and persnickety, but Kara disagreed. Losing his eyesight had surely made the old man act that way. Besides, Kara liked to focus on the good qualities people had, and as far as she was concerned, Mr. Radcliff had plenty. He'd been the first to suggest a trust fund be set up for Eric and little

Ashley. And he'd organized the Gray Brigade, a group of senior citizens who had besieged the local paper with phone calls and letters to the editor in support of Lizzie's request for custody.

Mr. Radcliff was kindhearted, even if he was a bit cranky at times. Lizzie referred to him as another of Kara's adoptees, which, in a sense, he probably was. Of course, Kara made it a point not to coddle him, but she did take him dessert some evenings. And whenever his hometown newspaper arrived in the mail, she made time to read it out loud to him.

After she snapped the leash on Gulliver, Kara and the dog took off toward the shore, a bit more quickly than Kara had intended. "Come on," she warned the dog. "Take it easy. I want to walk, not race. And if you don't stop jerking ahead, you'll pull my arm from its socket. Then who will exercise you?"

Gulliver, apparently not the least bit intimidated by Kara's threat, didn't show much restraint as they neared the stretch of beach where Michael rested upon the rocks, one knee bent, the other extended. He seemed so lost in his thoughts that she doubted whether he noticed her watching him. Or whether he even cared.

He picked up a small stone, studied it carefully, then tossed it into the surf. The breeze ruffled his golden hair, and the sun glistened off a bristled cheek, making him look like an eighteenth-century sea captain who'd lost his ship and crew. Kara's imagination took hold, and she envisioned him marooned on a desert island, forlorn and helpless.

So pensive, so alone, she thought. So sad. Why did she always gravitate toward the downtrodden? Little boys who'd been orphaned, motherless babies, lonely old men and women, stray dogs.

Surely, she should leave him alone, allow him some privacy.

But like the call of the gull, his solitude cried out and beckoned her.

Chapter Two

Michael watched the sun dip low in the sky and found some peace at last. So far, so good, he thought. No one had recognized him or badgered him with questions he hadn't even taken time to consider himself. For that reason alone, this quiet little hideaway might be just what he needed.

A bark caught his attention, and he glanced over his right shoulder where Kara walked her dog along the beach. No, he corrected, the monstrous dog walked her.

She caught his gaze and, perhaps assuming he wanted company, tugged on the leash to encourage the dog closer to the rocks. The breeze teased her autumn tendrils of hair, and the brightness of her smile seemed to challenge the setting sun. Like a pixie, she enchanted him. He studied her longer than was polite.

"Hello," she called. "Gulliver and I are going for a walk along the beach, care to join us?"

Gulliver, she'd called the dog, and the image of a tiny

Lilliputian queen trying valiantly to capture the giant brought a smile to his lips.

"What's so funny?" she asked, swiping at a fiery strand of hair whipping in the ocean air.

He doubted telling her she reminded him of a Lilliputian would sit well, even if he bestowed the respectful title of queen, so he changed the subject. "Looks to me as though that dog wants to drag you down the beach."

"I'm stronger than I look," she said with a grin. "Tougher, too."

Michael smiled again, finding it hard to believe that the redheaded pixie was either. He'd seen his share of strong women, hard women. Spending a few moments with one who was entirely different than others he'd known suddenly seemed appealing. He stood and climbed from the rocks, brushing the sand from the backside of his khaki shorts while he made his way toward her. "Maybe I should hold the dog."

She shrugged as though his offer didn't warrant much consideration, but a dimpled cheek and dancing green eyes told him she found something amusing in his words. "Suit yourself," she said, handing him the leash.

As she transferred control of Gulliver, the dog danced and pranced before nearly dislocating Michael's shoulder. "Hey, settle down, boy." Then he glanced at the woman walking at his side and wearing a smile as light and easy as the ocean breeze.

"Gulliver loves to run on the beach," she said, the lilt of her voice as fey as her appearance. "But I'm trying hard to train him to be well mannered."

She had her work cut out for her, Michael thought. The dog still needed a lot of discipline, but he didn't mention it. "How long have you been working with him?"

"Since I found him about three weeks ago," she said,

stooping to reach for a shell resting on the sand. She blew on it, then held it out for him to see. "Pretty, isn't it?"

He nodded, although he would have stepped right over it himself.

She flashed him another effervescent smile. "I collect things."

"Besides stray dogs and strangers?" he asked, unable to resist teasing her a bit.

She tucked the brown and yellow speckled shell into the front pocket of her shorts. "There's enough loneliness in the world."

He wondered whether she had experienced loneliness firsthand, or if she just had a compassionate heart. Both, he surmised. The sudden curiosity about her surprised him. "Mrs. Campbell said you've been helping her with the kids."

Kara nodded. "At first, it was a neighborly thing to do, like reading to Mr. Radcliff. But I fell in love with Ashley and Eric. And we've become a family of sorts. When Lizzie can no longer take care of them, I'd like to be their guardian. Their mom. And I'll take care of Lizzie, too."

It seemed a noble thing for her to do. He couldn't imagine his ex-wife being so tenderhearted that she'd take in a couple of orphans. Denise hadn't wanted any of her own kids.

Why hadn't he spotted her true character until after it reached up and smacked him between the eyes? In a way, he only had himself to blame for the entire mess.

"How long have you known the Campbells?" he asked, trying to put the past aside.

"Ever since the accident."

"Accident? What happened?"

She sighed, then looked at the ocean. "Eric, Ashley and their parents were driving home late at night when they were involved in a hit-and-run collision. Somebody sideswiped them, causing the car they were driving to spin out of control. It hit a concrete guardrail and burst into flames. The parents died upon impact, according to the coroner.''

The wind whipped a strand of hair across her face, and she brushed it from her cheek. "Eric was seriously injured, but instead of panicking, he released his baby sister from the car seat and carried her from the burning vehicle. A highway patrolman who came upon the scene found Eric holding Ashley on the side of the road, tears running down his face, trying his best to calm the crying baby. The city council proclaimed him a hero. It was in all the papers.''

Michael vaguely recalled reading about it, but lately, his mind had been on his own trials and tribulations. A small voice urged him to take care, to avoid rubbing elbows with anyone who might stir up media curiosity, but he pushed it aside. The accident had happened nearly a year ago, if he remembered correctly.

"Mrs. Campbell mentioned she had custody of her two grandchildren," he said.

"Lizzie had to fight hard for it, though. She's nearly seventy-five years old, and her health isn't the best. A wave of public sentiment swayed the judge to grant her temporary custody. I help as much as I can, when I'm not working or in school.''

School? She had a youthful appearance, yet a wisdom in her eyes. He wondered how old she was. Yet what did it matter? So what if she was at least ten years his junior. She was just a woman he'd met while on vacation, certainly not a potential date. Still, she had tweaked his curiosity.

"Where do you go to school?'' he asked, wanting to know more about her, about how she spent her time, what goals she had set.

"I graduated from Cal State San Marcos last June. I've

been accepted into graduate school, so I'm working hard to save enough money to go.''

''What's your major?''

''Liberal arts. I want to be a teacher and plan to get a master's degree in education.'' She flashed him another fey smile, and he had no doubt she would charm children and parents alike. He'd seen her with Eric. She'd make a great teacher.

''How about a student loan?'' he asked. ''Then you wouldn't have to work at all.''

She sobered. ''No. I've had enough public assistance in my life. I want to put myself through school, even if it means working at the Pacifica Bar and Grill until I can save enough for tuition.''

He missed the smile, the lighthearted tone of her voice. And he wondered where she'd hidden them. And why.

Be clinical and detached, he reminded himself. *This woman is none of your business.*

''Oh, look,'' she said, pointing to a round piece of blue plastic up ahead. ''A Frisbee.''

She darted toward the circular toy and bent at the waist to retrieve it, giving Michael a tantalizing glimpse of a perfectly rounded derriere and two shapely upper thighs that peeked through the flared hem of her shorts. He swallowed hard, trying to ignore a surge of desire. Kara might be small in stature, but she was woman through and through. An enticing woman, although he had the feeling she wasn't aware of how striking she was.

''Want to play?'' she asked, eyes bright.

Play? With her? In a heartbeat. But not Frisbee. Gulliver jerked on the leash, drawing Michael to reality. ''I'm afraid I haven't played on the beach in a long time. I doubt my aim is worth a darn.''

''We'll just have to see about that,'' Kara said, waving the blue toy as she carried it to him, all the while flashing him a dimpled smile.

A seagull cried overhead, then swooped toward the sand, pecking at a bag of potato chips left on the beach.

Spotting the gull, Gulliver yipped in excitement, then leaped up and jerked against the leash. In an effort to chase the bird, the fool dog circled Kara, throwing her into Michael. Then, as Michael reached to steady her, Gulliver wrapped the leash around their legs.

Off balance, Michael and Kara fell to the sand, while the dog slipped from the collar and ran down the beach, leaving the humans lying in the sand, arms wrapped around each other.

Michael couldn't help but stroke her arm, soft and sleek from a peach-scented lotion that wafted and swirled around him. "Are you okay?" he asked, senses reeling from the feel of her, the sensation of lying next to her.

"I'm fine," she said, her voice husky and velvety, unlike the lighthearted tone he'd found attractive before but far more mesmerizing.

Waves crashed upon the shore, and their hearts pounded in unison. His eyes caught hers and locked in a soul-piercing stare, a gaze that communicated something they both felt but couldn't voice. A tingle of awareness, a jolt of hunger.

Afraid he could remain locked in her arms forever, Michael rose up on an elbow, unwrapped the leash from around his legs, then stood. "Let me help you up."

Her hand gripped his, and he pulled her to her feet. Brushing sand from herself, she chuckled softly. When she glanced at him, eyes crinkling in mirth, he spotted a dried piece of seaweed dangling from her hair.

He removed it, slowly and gently, allowing himself to touch the soft, springy curls that intrigued him. Her breath caught, and he knew she felt the undercurrents of desire as he had, but she quickly laughed it off. In an effort to break the tension, he supposed.

He'd be wise to do the same, to let the awkward moment pass. "Your dog ran down the beach. Should we chase after him?"

"No," she said. "He'll come back home. He always does."

She bent to retrieve the Frisbee she'd dropped in the melee, giving him another glimpse of a shapely backside. He raked a hand through his tangled, windswept hair and blew out the breath he'd been holding.

"Let's play," Kara said, taking the toy and loping down the sand. So unlike any of the socialites Michael had known, her playful spirit taunted him.

She sent the Frisbee flying toward him.

Michael snagged the circular toy and sent it back.

"Hey, not bad," she said, flicking her wrist and shooting the blue disc in a wide arc.

For the first time since the scandal had disrupted his orderly world, Michael found himself laughing. Bertha had been right. What he needed was a vacation, something to take his mind off his troubles.

As Kara leaped to snag the blue plastic plate, her sweatshirt lifted, giving him a glimpse of a small, ivory-skinned waist. A waist his hands could easily encircle and his fingers ached to caress.

He'd never been one to take sexual relationships lightly, yet he couldn't help but wonder whether a brief affair might help him shake the rejection he still felt after his ex-wife's betrayal. It seemed like a logical prescription to him. And certainly more pleasant than allowing his emotional side to weigh him down.

"Hey," he called to the bright-eyed pixie. "How about having dinner with me tonight. I'll pick up a couple of swordfish fillets we can grill." And a bottle of wine, he reminded himself.

"That sounds like fun," she said. "I have to help Lizzie put the kids to bed. It's kind of an evening ritual. Can we make it about eight?"

"Sure," Michael said. That would give him time to run to the drugstore and purchase some condoms. *Just in case.*

It had been a long, long time since he'd tried to romance a woman. He wondered whether he still had the touch.

Kara stood before Michael's door, her fist raised, ready to knock. She watched a moth frantically try to penetrate the yellow globe of the porch light.

Was the glow a welcome or warning? She couldn't be sure. What was she doing here? Why had she agreed to have dinner with him? To be neighborly, she reminded herself. But good grief, Lizzie was a neighbor. Mr. Radcliff was a neighbor. Michael was a stranger.

Oh, sure, he had a warm smile and a gentle touch, but that was all the more reason she had no business having dinner with him. Just the two of them.

Alone.

Get a grip, she told herself. *It's only a friendly dinner. And certainly not a date, for goodness sake.* Dates had always made her uneasy, but when the last one ended in humiliation and tears, she'd vowed to steer clear of men and romantic notions.

Her stomach knotted at the memory of the family dinner party Jason Baker had taken her to. When he'd first asked her, she'd declined, not wanting him to think she was serious about him. But he'd prodded her until she agreed. *I want you to meet my family,* he'd told her. *You'll like them.*

But he'd been wrong.

When she arrived at the house, she'd been unprepared for the formality, the suspicious evaluations, the snide remarks.

You remember Kara, don't you, Mom?

Oh, yes. The cocktail waitress.

At first, the accusations had been silent—a haughty grin, rolled eyes. Then a few heartless comments and innuendoes were made about Kara and her cunning attempt to snag a wealthy husband.

Marriage? To Jason Baker? She hadn't given it any thought at all. And after she'd met his family, particularly his snobbish, sharp-tongued mother, she knew she'd rather die than have anything to do with the man or his family again.

The dinner had turned into a social inquisition, and Kara, nails clawing her palms, had excused herself and slipped out before dessert was served. No, she would never put herself in that position again. Nor would she date someone whose parents considered themselves socially and financially superior to her.

She'd probably date again. Someday. When she had Ashley and Eric living in her own home. Those precious children were her priority, not romance and glitter.

She placed a hand on the doorjamb of Michael's cottage and closed her eyes, reminding herself of the precious good-night kisses she'd just given and received. The gentle sway of the old oak rocking chair, the scent of baby powder, a dribble of milk on baby Ashley's tiny chin. A sleepy-eyed grin that sported two little white teeth had filled Kara's heart with enough love to last a lifetime.

After laying the baby in the crib, Kara had sat on the edge of Eric's bed and read him another chapter of *Charlotte's Web*. She'd listened to his prayers, cupped his cheek and kissed him good-night. The ritual was as pleasant and restful for her as it was for the brave little boy she had come to love.

Kara slowly opened her eyes, then scanned Michael's porch. Two lawn chairs flanked a small outdoor table. A beer can and a magazine rested upon the glass tabletop. *The Aviator.* Why would Michael be reading that? Was

he an aspiring pilot? She'd never been one to judge a
man by the car he drove, but an old Ford didn't seem
like the kind of vehicle a pilot would drive. But what did
she know about pilots? And what did she know about
Michael?

She struggled with the urge to turn and go home, to
call him with an excuse as to why she couldn't come to
his house tonight, but she'd agreed to join him for dinner.
She couldn't back out now. He was expecting her.

Once again, she reminded herself this wasn't a date.
And it certainly wouldn't turn out like the dinner party
at Jason Baker's house. Garnering her courage, she
knocked on the door.

Michael answered, wearing a pair of jeans, a crisply
pressed white shirt and a smile that reached the golden
hue of his eyes. He'd showered. And shaved.

She rather missed that salty, sea dog air he'd worn
before.

His eyes swept her body in an appreciative caress.
"Come in."

He appeared genuinely glad to see her, and it both
pleased and unnerved her. Impulsively, she turned and
snatched the magazine and empty can from the table and
thrust them toward him in an effort to put some distance
between them, between him and her thoughts. "You left
these outside."

"Thanks." He took them from her and stepped aside,
holding the magazine and soda can against his chest.

Kara moved across the threshold and into the small but
tastefully decorated cottage Lizzie had just refurbished.
A fire crackled softly in the living room, and the easy
sound of something classical played upon the stereo.

Just friends. Neighbors. Yet the romantic ambiance
told her otherwise. As did the light, musky scent of aftershave. Her heart fluttered to a zip-a-dee-do-dah beat.

"Can I pour you a glass of wine?"

Wine? For a moment, Kara wondered if Michael's expectations for the dinner were different than hers. She certainly hadn't planned on a romantic encounter, and she quickly sought his eyes, hoping to see he hadn't, either.

He flashed her a warm, friendly smile, and she wondered if she'd made more out of the offer than he'd intended.

She slowly ran her hands down the sides of her long, loose-fitting cotton skirt. *We're just newfound friends having dinner. And maybe a few laughs. What harm can there be in that?*

"Sure," she said. "Wine sounds great."

Chapter Three

Michael stood like a starstruck teen as Kara entered his temporary home. Her simple cotton dress fit like a curtain flowing in the breeze. The soft peach fabric lay against ivory-colored skin blessed with a faint scatter of freckles, setting off that fiery shade of hair. When had plain cotton stood out as lovely, breathtaking?

Denise, his dark-haired, provocative ex-wife, had worn a lot of red and black, Lycra and silk. She'd chosen colors and tight-fitting material to make her stand out in a crowd. But had Michael been mingling in a banquet hall with elegant and notable guests, he wouldn't have been able to keep his eyes from the petite redhead who smelled of peach blossoms and taunted his senses with a plain, wholesome appeal. Had she chosen a dress to match her scent in an attempt to tantalize him?

She cocked her head and looked at him in a strange and fidgety way. Had he made her nervous? He hadn't meant to.

Wine. He'd asked her if she wanted some, and she'd said yes. "Why don't you take a seat on the sofa? I'll bring you a glass. Is chardonnay all right?"

"Sure." She swept into the living room, the gentle sway of her hem brushing small but shapely calves, and took a seat.

Michael placed the magazine on the counter and tossed the empty can into the trash. He withdrew a bottle of chilled wine from the refrigerator, pulled the cork and poured two glasses. As he handed one to Kara, he noticed how close she sat to the armrest of the sofa.

He'd meant to wine and dine her, to provide a sensual evening. To suggest they see how far this attraction went. But he'd never intended anything that wasn't completely mutual. That had never been his style, not even when he was an intern and a few of the other young doctors were intent upon hitting on every good-looking nurse—whether she was willing or not.

His studies and his job had been too important for him to take lightly. Not that he'd remained celibate. He hadn't.

While he tried to conjure up a way to ease the awkward moment, she nodded toward the Formica countertop where he'd placed the magazine. "Are you interested in airplanes?"

Did he dare tell her he had thought about selling his Citation, maybe making another purchase? No need to prompt any personal questions. Yet the way she lifted an auburn brow, cocked her head to the side and flashed him an interested smile caused him to digress in a way he hadn't intended. "Planes have always interested me, ever since I was a kid, but I never took the time to pursue any training."

"I'll bet it's fun, seeing the world from high above the ground." She sighed, then gave a wistful shrug. "I've never flown before, but I've always wanted to. I used to hang out in the library when I was a kid. I'd read travel magazines and imagine myself taking exotic trips. Reading has to be the most exciting thing in the world."

More than actually experiencing the world? Kara seemed to enjoy life in a way most people never did. Playing soccer with a kid, finding a shell in the sand, throwing a forgotten Frisbee through the ocean air. If anyone deserved an exotic trip, it was the effervescent young woman sitting on his sofa. "Do you still read?"

"Every chance I get." Imagination lit up her face and seemed to dispel her nervousness. "I've been to the far ends of the earth, by dogsled, biplane, clipper ship. You name it."

He felt a compulsion to take her someplace she'd only read about but reeled in the urge. Her enthusiastic, playful nature was having an unusual effect on him. And God knew he was clinical, rational, certainly not a fly-by-the-seat-of-his-pants type. "I've got the grill on the back patio. Do you want to sit outside while I prepare the fish?"

"Sure." She flashed him a dimpled smile, then stood. "Can I help?"

"You can keep me company."

On the back patio, a harvest moon rose high in the evening sky, watching them with mystical intent. Ocean air, crisp and fragrant, mingled with the smell of grilled swordfish and charcoal. Michael stood over the barbecue, watching the fillets sizzle over the hot coals, yet he couldn't keep his eyes from casually glancing at the woman who watched him work.

Kara sat in a plastic patio chair, her feet barely resting on the deck. He found it nearly impossible to keep his attention focused on the task at hand, which didn't seem at all natural. Kara wasn't his type, wasn't of his world, yet it didn't seem to matter tonight. She intrigued him. "Have you always lived in Harbor Haven?"

"No. I've lived here for nearly a year and a half. That's about the longest I've been in any town, but I'm not a wanderer by nature. It's just the way things worked out."

"So why here? At Campbell's Seaside Cottages?"

"One day, while having lunch at the Pacifica, Lizzie offered to rent me a cottage at a reduced rate if I would help her out with some of the more physically demanding chores. I've always been on a limited budget, so I jumped at the chance to save some money." She smiled and shrugged. "But Lizzie became more of a friend than a landlord and, when the kids moved in, we became a family. I can't imagine being anywhere else."

He watched her, the way she tilted her head, the way the patio light sparkled like glitter on the auburn strands. "You don't seem like a homebody to me," he said, even though she didn't seem to be an adventure-driven nomad, either. "You have a playful spirit."

"I've never really had a home, not one in the classic sense of the word, but I do now. I've taken great pains to make it warm and cozy. I've refinished a maple dining room set someone placed on the side of the road with a Free sign taped to it. Mr. Radcliff, the old man who lives between us, let me use his sander. I did a fairly decent job of refurbishing it, if I do say so myself." She tucked a strand of hair behind her ear, appearing to grow more comfortable, and flashed a teasing wink. "And you ought to see the tree house Eric and I are working on."

"A tree house?" Michael laughed. "I'd like to see it sometime."

She cocked her head to the side, sending him another dimpled grin. "Of course, you have to ring the bell to be allowed admittance."

"Of course," he said, falling prey to the playful notion.

Kara took a sip of wine. "How about you? Where are you from?"

"Originally, Boston." He didn't want to lie but wasn't about to divulge any more information than necessary. As far as he knew, Kara hadn't realized his identity. Not that he'd really kept it secret, but he'd come to Harbor Haven to escape, not attract more attention to himself. Landing in the public spotlight was the last thing in the world he wanted to do.

She drew up a knee, placing a small foot on the rim of her seat and tenting the long sundress she wore, then rested her hands on her knee. Nothing showed, not a peek of skin, yet he found the move so revealing, so utterly sexy, he stood beside the barbecue like a befuddled teen. He snatched his wineglass from the patio table and took another taste—a long, deliberate taste.

"I've never been to Boston. What's it like?" Her eyes lit up in anticipation, much like a child's in a candy store, while she awaited his response. He didn't have the heart to tell her his memories of the family home didn't warm him the way she might imagine.

"Boston is historic," he said. "And seasonal. Snow in winter, new leaves and blossoms in spring, hot and humid in the summer, colorful foliage in the autumn. I'm sure you'd like it."

"Tell me about the holidays."

Holidays? What kind of question was that? They had the usual; it wasn't like Boston was a continent within itself. "What do you want to know?"

She shrugged her shoulders, then her eyes widened. "Christmas. Did your family have a wonderful Christmas?"

Michael didn't like the reminder of stiff, formal holidays. It seemed as though his mother had insisted he and his father wear suits for the entire month of December. Droves of the elite swept into the house, but never more than was expected, more than was polite. "We always had snow, if that's what you meant."

She laughed. "I would expect a white Christmas in Boston. Tell me about your tree."

Somehow, Michael doubted she wanted to hear that his mother hired professional florists to come in and decorate not only the tree but the entire house in holly, ivy, baby's breath, bloodred roses, Irish lace and gold trim. He wished she'd go back to searching the library for answers to her questions. It wasn't a memory he relished thinking about. "Our tree was always tall and green. Smelled like pine."

"You're no fun," she said, waving him off with a hand.

He wasn't a fun person. His job was a serious one. His life had always been one of commitment, responsibility. Clinical detachment. He held other lives in his hands. Emotional detachment was necessary for their survival. Vital for his own. "I told you before, I'm not considered a fun-loving person."

"Christmas is a magical time of the year. You're supposed to remember the wonder of it all, the excitement, the heartwarming things."

How could he tell her his Christmases hadn't been heartwarming, hadn't been magical? They were pretty much like the rest of his life, only more lavish, more formal. "Why don't you tell me about your holidays?"

"There's not much to tell," she said with a sigh. Then she brightened and pointed a small but elegant finger at him. "But that doesn't mean I'm not planning on having the biggest, most wonderful Christmas ever. This December will be my first with Lizzie and the kids. We're doing it up special—cranberry and popcorn trim on the tree and a real tree, not one of those store-bought models."

"It sounds great," he said, easily imagining it would be, if Kara had anything to do with it. He almost wished he could be there, see the magic she would set into motion. Before changing the subject, he glanced down at the swordfish steaks. Done and ready to eat. He speared each one and set them on a plate. "Come on," he told her. "Dinner's ready. Do you want to eat inside or out?"

Kara glanced at the nearly full moon overhead, then at the small glass-topped table and two wrought iron chairs Lizzie had purchased for the patio. She flashed her host a smile. "Outside, of course. I'll help set the table."

She was on her feet and heading for the kitchen when she heard the roar of Jason Baker's modified Ford pickup outside. No one else in this town had an engine that blasted that loud. It announced his arrival before he turned into the drive. Her first concern was that he would wake up Ashley and Eric. Her second, that he had come to see her.

When he honked his horn, as though Kara and the entire neighborhood should run to greet him, it took all her gumption not to march outside and give him a piece of her mind.

"Who's that?" Michael asked, striding toward the living room window. He peered through the wood-slat blinds.

"Jason Baker, I imagine." Kara slowed her steps, not at all wanting the arrogant jerk to know where she was. He'd been pestering her lately, ever since she'd told him she wouldn't date him any longer. Not that she'd actually dated him before. As far as she was concerned, a Saturday matinee and a humiliating dinner party didn't mean they had a budding relationship.

"He's knocking at your door." Michael stepped away from the blinds and gave Kara a cautious glance. "I'll put the fish in the oven."

"Don't you dare. It's bad enough that he comes by

the Pacifica where I work, but I'm not going to encourage him to start dropping by my house."

"What does he want?"

Kara shrugged. Who ever knew what Jason wanted, other than public attention and a flock of female admirers? "Maybe he wants to lay on the charm and convince me I made a mistake by not going out with the richest guy in town."

Michael lifted a brow. "He's rich?"

"Well," Kara said, "by virtue of his birth. His parents own the EZ Suds down the street and a chain of five or six others in the county. As far as I know, he's thirty years old and his only job has been to play hard, especially at the gym. His parents give him a pretty hefty allowance."

Michael slid her a slow, easy grin. "Sounds like he's the pick of the litter."

"He's the whole litter. Jason's an only child—Daddy's boy and Mama's baby."

Tires squealed and gravel crunched as Jason pulled out of the drive, obviously unhappy to find Kara away from the house.

Michael opened the refrigerator and pulled out a salad he'd made. "Sounds as though he thinks you're his girlfriend."

Kara rolled her eyes and sighed. "That's the problem. He's the *only* one who thinks that."

"Here." Michael handed Kara the salad bowl. "You can carry this out to the table. I'll bring the plates and silverware as soon as I locate a candle."

"A candle? I think we'll be able to see. The porch light puts off a nice glow."

"The candle is for ambience," Michael said. "Besides, it will keep the bugs away."

Kara laughed. "Well, then bring on the ambience."

The fish was cooked to perfection. And the salad was

so light and tasty the dressing couldn't have possibly come from a bottle. Kara couldn't remember the last meal she'd enjoyed so much. "Dinner was delicious. Where did you learn to cook?"

"In college. My roommate's parents owned a restaurant. He made it look so easy, I decided to try a few simple dishes myself. I don't get a chance to cook very often, and my wife—" He paused, and a pained expression crossed his face. Had he not meant to tell Kara he was married? Had something happened to her? "We ate a lot of meals out."

The fact that he had arranged a dinner, one that had subtle hints of a romantic ambience, caused an uneasiness to surface. She furrowed her brow. "I had no idea you were married."

"Was married," he said. "The divorce was final three months ago."

"Any kids?" Kara asked, suddenly realizing there was a lot she didn't know about this man.

"No, thank goodness. The divorce was messy. I'm glad I was the only one to suffer through it. I don't know what I would have done if I would have had to explain things to a child."

Kara reached out a hand to touch his forearm in comfort but wasn't prepared for the surge of heat her compassion had unleashed. Her stomach did a somersault, and she quickly withdrew her hand.

But it was too late.

Their eyes locked, and something passed between them. Understanding and friendship, she hoped, but it was more than that. It was something she'd never felt before—a strange kind of push-pull. Something that felt as though it was too much and not enough at the same time. "It's too bad things didn't work out for you."

"The divorce was for the best."

"Still, I'm sorry."

He placed a warm, gentle hand on top of hers, in comfort, she supposed. "Don't be sorry, Kara. It takes the magic out of your eyes."

"The magic?"

He slowly, as though reluctant, withdrew his hand from hers. "There's something special and effervescent about you. It dances in your eyes."

If he was trying to put the moves on her, it was working in a way she hadn't anticipated, hadn't encountered before. Every reasonable bone in her body begged her to retreat, but some mysterious inner voice urged her to listen. To draw closer. To see if she could find magic in his eyes.

"Thank you."

He caught her chin with the tip of his finger. "That wasn't a line. You have a wholesome vitality I've rarely seen."

Before Kara could summon the words to speak or the strength to look away, a souped-up engine roared into the small neighborhood. An amplified stereo blared as the vehicle entered the gravel parking lot. The door opened and shut, but the engine continued to run, and the sounds of heavy metal blasted throughout the sleepy neighborhood.

Jason was back.

Michael didn't usually dislike people he'd never met, but in Baker's case, he'd make an exception.

The wave of anxiety that crossed Kara's face made Michael want to stomp outside and chase that damned idiot away. What kind of guy pursued a woman who wasn't interested? He had half a notion to call the police but kept his seat.

He reached across the table and took Kara's hand. Her fingers clutched his, and he felt the need to keep her safe. To chase all the bad guys away.

What a crazy thought. He was no hero. He was just a doctor. A man who held his emotions in check. A man who, by necessity, held himself at a distance. A man who didn't need to become involved with anyone for a long time, if ever again.

As tires spun in the drive and Jason peeled out in a show of frustration, Kara released his hand and smiled. "I guess I'd better go."

Before Kara had come for dinner, Michael had entertained thoughts of having her spend the night, but now his intent was more to protect her than to pursue the passion that flared between them. Not that desire for her had left him, by any means. If anything, he found her more attractive, more precious. "I don't like the idea of you being over there alone."

She scooted her chair from the table and stood, then gathered the plates and silverware they'd used and carried them to the sink. "Jason's not dangerous. He's just bothersome. If he comes back, I'll pretend I'm not home."

"If he comes back, I'll be outside before he climbs from the truck." Michael grabbed the empty wine bottle, laced the stems of the goblets between his fingers and followed her to the sink. "Don't worry about the dishes."

"All right," she said, fidgeting with the dish towel that lay on the counter. She looked at him, eyes catching his and drawing him into their depths.

He cupped her cheek to offer comfort. To convey friendship. Or so he told himself. His thumb made a slow, gentle circle on her skin. Her eyes widened, and her breath quickened. Not in fear or discomfort, he surmised, but in a surprised reaction similar to his own.

Not intending to force the obvious attraction, he placed a light kiss on her forehead in an affectionate manner— friendly and brotherly. That's what he'd meant it to be, what he had convinced himself was appropriate. Sure, early on, he'd thought about a passionate evening, even had a new box of condoms tucked into the drawer in his nightstand, but he'd thought the decision to have sex would be mutual. Seducing Kara wasn't his intent.

His face lingered above the spot on her forehead where he'd kissed her. The melon scent of shampoo taunted him, as did the subtle peach fragrance she wore, tempting him to distraction. He lifted his head and stepped back, his eyes watching her reaction to his neighborly gesture.

Her lips parted, more in surprise than in an effort to prompt him for another kiss, one more than neighborly. In spite of the fact that he had no intention of taking advantage of her, the desire to taste her sweetness was more than he could ignore.

He tried to brush a light kiss across her dusky lips, but as he lowered his head, he drew her close. She whimpered softly and leaned into him in a move so natural, so gentle, he had no idea why it unleashed such a powerful desire for her touch, her embrace.

She tasted like sunshine and moonbeams, snowflakes and raindrops. Mountain meadows and morning dew—everything that was right with the world. But before he could take the kiss further, catch a glimpse of the places passion could take them, she pushed her hands against his chest and broke the soul-stirring spell.

"I'm sorry," she said, her voice husky and soft.

Sorry? She was sorry? He was the one who had kissed her. The one who had planned a seduction, of sorts. "You have nothing to be sorry for."

She stepped away from him, pink-tinged cheeks, a tell-tale, sensual flush along her neck and chest. "I don't know why I let that happen."

Let that happen? Shoot, Michael doubted either one of them could have kept that from happening, not once their lips touched and the power of what they felt had been unleashed.

"Do you have a boyfriend?" he asked. "I mean, other

than Jason.'' The question surprised him, since it really wasn't any of his business. Yet for some reason, it seemed to matter a great deal.

She appeared to ponder his question or maybe her answer. The slow response caused him an odd sense of discomfort.

''No,'' she said, as though choosing her words slowly. ''I've never really stayed in one place long enough for any kind of friendships to develop. And now that I've settled in Harbor Haven, I don't have time for a relationship like that. I've got too much at stake to become involved with anyone right now.''

''What do you mean?''

''Lizzie's health isn't good. Her doctor has already told her to cut back on the stress in her life. I try to help whenever I can, but we're not sure how much longer she'll be able to care for Eric and Ashley. I'd like to adopt them, but I'll need to prove myself worthy to the courts. And that could be difficult.''

''Why?'' She was good with Eric, and Michael assumed she'd be good with Ashley as well.

''I'm a twenty-four-year-old single waitress. I don't have a family of my own—no parents, aunts, uncles. And after graduation last June, I don't have much money left in the bank.'' She shrugged. ''The list goes on, but I'm pedaling as fast as I can, trying to put myself in an admirable position.''

''I think your objectives are commendable.''

''Thanks, but the courts might not be so understanding. They still prefer two-parent families with steady incomes.'' She brushed a strand of hair behind her ear and sighed.

Michael knew there was a lot more to providing for kids than financial stability, but he doubted the court would agree with him. But what did most people know about spending holidays in an exclusive boarding school?

Or having a chauffeur deliver a fourteenth birthday gift to camp? "I think kids belong with people who love them and have time to spend with them."

"Me, too," she said. "Well, I'd better get going."

Even though Michael wanted her to stay, wanted to see how far their attraction would go, he knew pursuing any kind of relationship with Kara was out of the question. She'd made it clear that the kids were her priority. And he certainly didn't need to get involved with anyone right now. Especially not someone who dreamed of warm, intimate, down-home family holidays. Or Christmas trees with handmade decorations.

She paused at the door. "Dinner was delicious. I had a nice time. Thank you."

"You're welcome." It hadn't turned out to be the sensual kind of evening he'd originally planned, but it had worked out for the best. Still, he couldn't seem to shake the memory of the toe-curling kiss they'd shared.

"Maybe we can do it again before you have to leave."

Do it again? The kiss immediately came to mind, even though he knew they were discussing dinner and friendly conversation. He hoped she hadn't read his mind, but when she blushed, he realized her thoughts had drifted in the same direction as his.

She offered him a shy smile. "I was referring to dinner."

"I know."

He was amazed by her innocence and determination yet realized she had her own battles to fight in Harbor Haven. And he had a hell of a mess to go home to—a practice he needed to rebuild or move across the country and an ex-wife who continued to write him letters of apology for the gut punch she'd given his pride. No, he and Kara had nothing in common. And their differences were legion.

He took her hand and opened the door. "Come on, I'll walk you home."

"I told you I'd be okay," she said, lifting her chin in determination.

Michael gave her hand a gentle squeeze. "I know you'll be just fine. But I'll feel better knowing you got inside the house all right."

Then, as he led her onto the porch, he left his front door open wide.

Because he'd be right back.

Because the lamp from his living room would help light their path.

And because he needed a reminder that he had a home to return to.

Chapter Four

As Kara and Michael made their way along the darkened path that lined the cottages, an evening breeze stirred the scent of night-blooming jasmine. The wind also tousled Kara's hair, but she was more concerned about the way that unexpected kiss she'd shared with Michael played havoc with her mind.

The comfort he'd provided had left her senses buzzing, her skin tingling. Oh, sure, there was a certain amount of solace in his eyes, in his embrace. But there was also a fire in his touch, a mind-robbing passion in his kiss.

What had she been thinking? She had no business kissing a stranger, a vacationer. It was bad enough she'd have to stand before the judge as a young, unmarried woman applying for custody of Eric and Ashley. She certainly didn't want the court to think she was juggling her own needs and those of the children. The well-being of Eric and Ashley came first, above all else.

"Watch out," Michael said, steering her away from

an outstretched branch of a scraggly hibiscus plant that grew along the walkway between her home and the darkened cottage belonging to Mr. Radcliff.

She made a mental note to trim the floral shrub, then glanced at Michael. She could barely make out his features, only the shadowed outline of an angular profile. Yet she was very much aware of his protective nature. His kindness. He appealed to her, and the attraction she felt pushed the limits of friendship.

How could this stranger stir feelings she'd never had before, she'd never imagined? He had to be much older than she, well into his thirties, no doubt. A transient vacationer who wouldn't be in town for very long. Certainly not long enough to establish a friendship, let alone something more than that. Something lasting on which she could pin her hopes and dreams.

Silly romantic fantasies had dogged her throughout a lonely childhood, but she quickly swept any such notions aside and focused her thoughts on the only family she had really known—Lizzie, Ashley and Eric. Kara would never leave them, never place them second in her life.

As they reached the porch of her cottage, Michael's steps slowed. He scanned both sides of her house. "Where's that dog of yours?"

"Gulliver?" she asked. "He stays with Mr. Radcliff, since he has a fenced yard and I don't."

"He's not much of a watchdog. Why isn't he barking?"

Kara smiled. "Gulliver is still a puppy. And besides, he sleeps in the house. I don't think I've ever heard him bark at anything other than a seagull."

Michael released her hand and cupped her cheek. "If you get scared, or if you need anything at all, give me a call."

"I don't have your number," she said with a smile.

He paused, as though caught off guard. "I never expected any calls. Never wanted any. I forgot to ask Lizzie what my telephone number was.''

Kara laughed. ''I had a nice time, Michael. Go on home and relax. I won't need to call you.''

A furrowed brow indicated he wasn't convinced by her bravery, but he sported a grin. ''Good night, tough guy.''

She swatted his arm. ''I'm tougher than you think.''

Kara watched him walk to his cottage and hoped her words rang true, because the only thing she really feared was losing Ashley and Eric to someone the courts decided could offer them a better home.

But would that someone know how much Ashley liked graham crackers and peaches? How she liked to stroke the satiny part of her blanket whenever she got tired? Would that someone cherish the time spent reading bedtime stories to Eric? Or admire the way he struggled to overcome his disability?

Kara didn't think anyone else could love those kids like she did. Those precious children meant the world to her, and she'd do anything to be their legal mommy, to provide them with the loving home they deserved.

The next afternoon, while he was drinking a ginger ale and thumbing through another aviation magazine, a pounding on the front door jarred Michael from his reading.

Eric, wide-eyed and trembling, stood on the front porch. ''You gotta come quick. Ashley hurt herself and is gonna die. She's bleeding really bad and crying. We don't know what to do. You just gotta come.''

''Let's go.'' Michael followed the boy to Lizzie's house. The door was open, and he strode inside.

Kara sat on the sofa, holding a cloth against the baby's head. Blood had seeped through the white cotton as well as Kara's fingers. Lizzie glanced up, face pale, hands clasped tightly in front of her.

"Ashley pulled herself up to the coffee table, then took a tumble," Kara said. "She caught her head on the corner. We need to go to the hospital."

"Did she lose consciousness?"

"No."

"Here," Michael said, stooping before the whimpering baby. "Let me see."

"I can't remove the cloth, her wound is bleeding too much."

"Face cuts bleed a lot. They're usually not as bad as they appear."

"She's got a nasty bump, too. Head injuries scare me."

Michael lifted the cloth from Ashley's brow. "Hey, pumpkin, that's the hazards of standing alone and trying to be a big girl." He gently probed the swollen knot and assessed the gash on her head. "She'll be fine, although you might want to have the cut stitched. I could put a butterfly bandage on it, but it's a bit deep."

Kara glanced at him, her face pale, her eyes searching his. "How do you know so much about first aid?"

Michael probably should have told her he was a surgeon, but so far she hadn't questioned him about who he really was, about things he'd rather not discuss. "I work at a hospital. I've seen plenty of knots, cuts and bruises. Believe me, Ashley's fine."

Eric made his way to Michael's side and placed a hand on his knee. "I knew you could help my sister. That's why I ran to get you. You fixed up my skinned knee and made it not hurt any more. You're practically a real doctor."

Kara smiled and tousled Eric's hair. "He sure is nice to have around in an emergency." Then she turned those teal-blue eyes on him. "Thanks."

"I told you before, give me a call if you need me."

"We didn't call you," Kara said with a dimpled grin.

"I don't know your phone number, and Lizzie can't remember where she filed it."

He smiled and brushed his hand over Ashley's downy soft curls. "Then I guess it's a good thing I'm just two houses away."

Kara turned to Lizzie, who sat in an overstuffed easy chair near the window, fanning herself. "Are you okay?"

"Well, I am now. All that blood. Ashley crying. I suppose it is just a minor injury, but my blood pressure still doesn't know that."

"Why don't I take her to the hospital and have the cut stitched," Kara said. "You'd better stay home and rest."

Lizzie pulled herself to her feet, "If I don't go, how are you going to get there? Take the bus?"

The bus? That was silly. Michael could offer to drive her, but he would rather avoid any hospital settings. He might be more recognizable there.

"Can't you just drive Lizzie's car?" he asked. The baby had settled down. The wound had stopped bleeding. Kara appeared to be relaxed.

"I can't," Kara said.

"Why not?" he asked.

"I never learned to drive."

Michael's jaw must have dropped when he heard her words, because Lizzie explained. "Kara hasn't had the same opportunities as some young people. She has never owned a car, so she's never been able to practice. I keep thinking I'll take her out driving, but I guess we haven't taken the time."

"It's no big deal," Kara said. "I walk a lot. And the bus system works great."

The bus. Michael bit back a scowl. Shoot, it wasn't as though he were a fugitive. The worst that could happen would be having reporters find him and harass him again. If that happened, he'd just leave town.

He raked a hand through his hair. "I'll take you to the

hospital. Just give me a minute or two. I'll go get my keys."

As Michael left the room, Lizzie let out a slow sigh. "He is the nicest young man. Aren't we lucky to have someone who knows first aid living next to us?"

"Yes," Kara said. "Do you think he's a doctor?"

"Driving that old blue Ford?" Lizzie made a noise with her lips. "Doctors are rich. I'll bet he's just a hospital orderly."

"You're probably right," Kara said. She placed a kiss on Ashley's head. "But still, it's nice to know that someone around here has some medical skill. Maybe I'd better sign up for a first aid class through community services. Michael won't be here forever."

"No, he won't." Lizzie placed her hands on the armrests of the chair and slowly rose to her feet. "Too bad. He would make a nice neighbor."

Yes, he would, Kara thought. She, too, was glad to have him near. On one level. Under the surface, she knew having Michael next door would be a trial of sorts because each time she looked at him, she remembered the feel of his hand on her cheek, his lips on hers, the taste of him. It was a distraction she didn't need right now.

Before she could respond to Lizzie's comment, Michael returned with his car keys and Eric on his heels. "Are you ready?"

"Oh, dear," Lizzie said. "You'll need a car seat. We'll have to take it out of my back seat and put it in yours."

"Why don't I just drive your car, Lizzie?"

"Oh. That would be easier, wouldn't it?"

Ten minutes later, Michael pulled into the hospital drive. He dropped Kara and Ashley off at the ER entrance, then parked Lizzie's car in the visitor's lot.

This was a new experience for him. Usually, he pulled

into a reserved spot. There was a special status given to doctors, even more so to surgeons. He'd never realized how special until he entered the double doors of the ER like any one of the others waiting their turn.

An older woman and her male companion sat quietly and thumbed through weathered magazines. Michael wondered if they were actually reading the words or just going through the motions.

A young man in baggy jeans paced the floor, walking on the shredded hems of his pants. Michael figured he'd walk off the excess length of his jeans before the afternoon was up. He glanced at the clock. Two thirty-five. This would probably take forever.

He counted the people in the room—fourteen—then shook his head. Back in med school, he'd spent an ungodly number of hours during his long shifts in the ER— hours on end, days with little sleep. Still, the time had passed quickly. A string of emergencies, one crisis after another, kept him going. The hours passed quickly.

Two thirty-six. At this rate, he and Kara would be here all day.

He spotted her at a small window, balancing Ashley on her hip and pulling out insurance cards and a permission-to-treat form Lizzie had signed. He thought about joining her at the window, but didn't. Instead he studied the figures in the room. He saw loneliness, worry and boredom etched on the faces before him. One man slammed down a magazine, then stomped out the door. Michael felt as though he'd like to do the same thing, but before he could give it any thought, Kara made her way toward him.

"I've signed her in," she said, trying to twist her head from Ashley's reach. The little girl grabbed a handful of the red hair and jerked. Kara merely tugged the strands from Ashley's grip, leaving several hairs behind. "The receptionist said they'd call us when it's our turn."

Our turn? Michael scanned the room, then nodded. They took a seat near the telephone.

Two thirty-seven. He made another assessment of the gash on Ashley's forehead. Three stitches, maybe four. Four hundred dollars and half a day wasted. Oh, well. What did he have to do, anyway?

"Would you please hold her?" Kara placed the infant on his lap before he had a chance to ask why. "I need to call her doctor. With all the excitement at home, I forgot."

"Sure," Michael said. He rested Ashley's diaper-clad bottom on his knee. She was a pretty little thing. Not much hair, but big brown eyes that would drive the boys wild in a few years.

The baby thrust a fist at him, two strands of Kara's hair still held tightly in her fingers. "I know you like the color. Me, too. But if you continue to pull it out like that, Kara won't have any more for us to admire."

Ashley laughed as though they'd shared a private joke.

Michael hadn't held babies very often. Not like this. Ashley blew bubbles through pursed lips, and he couldn't help but smile. "You were squawking pretty good a few minutes ago. Had everybody in panic mode. Did it hurt that bad?"

The baby let out a happy shriek, the high-pitched sound surprising the smile from her face.

"I didn't think so."

When Kara returned, she reached for the diaper bag before Michael could put the baby in her arms. "Are you hungry, little one?" she asked, handing Ashley a bottle of milk.

Ashley eagerly snatched the bottle and slunk down in Michael's arms. She kicked one heel against his knee while happily mouthing the nipple. A dribble of milk eased down her chin, and he caught it with the tip of his finger. She smiled at him, as though grateful for his assistance. This was a strange experience for him. Sure, he'd held kids. Sick kids. Recovering kids. But not like this. Not in a day-to-day way.

The tap of Ashley's heel upon his knee slowed to a stop, and she closed her eyes and slowed her sucking. When her lips loosened upon the nipple, a flurry of tiny bubbles rushed into the remainder of the milk, filling the half-empty bottle with a lacy froth.

Imagine that, the little kid was sleeping in his arms. A little angel—with a tummy full of milk and a knotted gash on her noggin.

He held her like that for a long time, watching the gentle rise and fall of her chest. Amazing, he thought. The little girl rested in peaceful slumber, but he, too, found a sense of peace. Relaxation. Well-being. Something he'd been searching for on the jetty by the harbor. When Ashley woke up, this mellow mood in which he found himself would pass. But he'd touched the clouds for a moment and discovered a hint of the peace he'd been after.

"Michael?" Kara tapped his shoulder and pointed to a nurse in the hall. "It's our turn to go."

Michael sheepishly glanced up from his musing, only to see many of the same people still waiting. "How did you manage to take cuts?"

She smiled. "Dr. Weldon was visiting a patient on the fourth floor. When I called his service, they had him paged."

Of course, Michael thought, as he got to his feet, careful not to wake Ashley. That made sense. He followed Kara, who followed the uniformed nurse to one of several cribs provided for the youngest ER patients.

"Dr. Weldon will be right in," the nurse said. "Since the baby's sleeping, why don't you just hold her until he comes. They'll be poking and prodding her soon enough."

Michael glanced down at little Ashley. It seemed a shame to wake her, but he knew the routine. And the procedure. She'd be strapped to a papoose board that would restrict her movements, and she wouldn't like it at all. He held her close, wishing he could spare her the pain and discomfort and knowing he couldn't.

Dr. Weldon approached Kara and drew the curtain around the crib, providing what little privacy the ER could offer. Weldon had a paternal, grandfatherly appearance, with bushy white hair, a bit of a potbelly and ruddy cheeks. "Well, well," he began in a patronizing fashion. "What happened?"

"She pulled herself up on the coffee table, then lost her balance. She hit her head on the corner."

"Did she lose consciousness?" he asked.

She's all right, Michael wanted to say, but he kept his mouth shut. This wasn't his case. It wasn't his kid. He was just the neighbor who'd brought Kara and the baby to the hospital. Keep it simple. Stay detached.

"No, but she sure did cry," Kara said. "You should have seen the blood. She about scared the liver out of me and Lizzie."

"I'll bet she did," Weldon said. He made a cursory exam of Ashley's wound then looked into Michael's eyes. He lifted a white bushy brow and took on more of the grandfatherly persona Michael had first recognized. "I'm Dr. Weldon." As his eyes caught Michael's, recognition flickered. "You look familiar. Have we met?"

"I don't think so," Michael said.

"Michael isn't from around here," Kara said. "But he has first-aid training. He works at a hospital."

"Is that right?" Weldon said, his eyes clear and piercing, like those of a headmaster at an exclusive, all-boys boarding school. Like those of old Iron Bones at Brynwood Hall, where Michael had been sent at the age of eight.

Michael had the strange urge to shuffle his feet and hang his head like an errant schoolboy on the verge of expulsion. Instead, he straightened. Hell, he wasn't hiding from anything. What did it matter if the older doctor knew who he was? As a rule, doctors had a code of ethics when dealing with each other. Michael doubted Weldon would rush out and call some tabloid reporter and offer an interview for a price. "My name is Michael Harper, but I doubt we've ever met."

The perusal was over as quickly as it began. Dr. Weldon did an admirable job stitching Ashley's wound, in spite of the tears of protest—both Ashley's and Kara's. Michael had to smile at Kara's stricken expression as the doctor deftly sutured Ashley's face as good as any hotshot plastic surgeon could have done. Weldon's training undoubtedly came from years of experience.

The elderly doctor released Ashley from the papoose board that had secured her, allowing Kara to comfort the crying baby, who was more angry at being confined than in pain from the wound or its suturing.

"How is Lizzie feeling?" Weldon asked Kara as he removed his gloves.

"All right, I suppose." She held Ashley close, cooing to her and patting her back like a seasoned mother. "She complains about the number of pills you've got her taking."

"She needs them all," Weldon said. "I'll swing by on my way home tonight. I want to take her blood pressure when she's at home and relaxed."

Michael had wondered whether Ashley's doctor was a pediatrician. Now his question had been answered. He was a general practitioner. And probably a darn good one. The kind they didn't make anymore.

"Thank you, Doctor," Kara said.

"That's what I'm here for," Weldon replied. Then he

turned to Michael, those wizened blue eyes ever vigilant. "I still think you look familiar, son."

Michael shrugged. "Maybe I remind you of someone else."

"Maybe. I'm sure it will come to me after you go." Weldon turned his eyes to Kara. "I'll see you later this evening."

"All right," Kara said.

Weldon's eyes swept Michael one more time, then he strode out the door, white coat flapping in the breeze—unleashing, so it seemed, the familiar scent of hospital disinfectant, the sounds of rubber soles upon the freshly waxed tile, ballpoint pens gliding across clipboards, gurneys rolling down the corridor. The sights and smells of the ER swirled around him, snaking into his memory and shaking his conscience. He belonged in a place like this, not on a lazy seashore.

Michael tensed. "I'll bring the car around," he told Kara.

She nodded.

As he strode from the ER, he tried to shake the feeling of being caught. Caught doing what? Taking time to himself? Making a game plan regarding his career?

Did he fear being recognized by Dr. Weldon?

Or being chastised for a dereliction of professional duty?

Guilt tugged at him, and try as he might, he found it hard to shake. He had a surgical skill other heart surgeons hadn't perfected. It was a skill and technique he wasn't using. How could he think of taking a vacation? Of wasting his time strolling on the beach?

But how could he provide the best medical care to his patients when his mind was preoccupied with the reporters who hounded him, who hung out by his car in the parking lot, who waited to pounce on him in the hospital cafeteria, who followed him home in the evenings?

He supposed part of their fanatical interest in him was the fact that he came from an ultra-wealthy family, that he'd achieved notability on his own talents and merits and not by virtue of his birth. The last tabloid had suggested he was now the most eligible bachelor in the country.

But if Michael had learned anything, it was that he wasn't marriage material. Hadn't Denise said as much? His career meant too much to him. His patients would always have priority over his wife.

As he pulled Lizzie's small, compact car to the front entrance of the ER, Kara carried Ashley through the automatic door. Beyond the opened portal, he could see a white-uniformed nurse pushing a gurney.

Someday soon, he would return to the medical world in which he belonged. After he'd thought through the choices facing him.

Kara opened the car door, then pushed the front passenger seat forward so she could squeeze herself and Ashley into the back, where the baby's car seat was secured. Michael enjoyed watching the athletic maneuvers she had to make, the gap of her neckline, the glimpse of a white lacy bra strap, the rounded handful of flesh that filled the lacy cup.

What was the matter with him? Kara Westin, with her youthful spirit and compassionate heart, was more than a one-night stand—and definitely off-limits, especially for him.

Michael Harper had no intention of staying in Harbor Haven any longer than the short R and R he had allotted himself.

Chapter Five

They'd only been home from the hospital for two hours when Eric came running to Michael in another state of alarm.

"Oh, boy, you'd better call the fire department!"

Michael laid the newspaper he'd been reading on the porch and stood, his senses alert for a whiff of smoke, a flame, a sign of fire. "What's the matter, son?"

"A cat got stuck in our tree, and I told Kara we'd better call the fire department 'cause I watched a show on TV and the firemen got a cat out of a big tree. But Kara said we shouldn't bother them."

Michael glanced around, looking for Kara and not spotting her. "Where is she?"

"That's the problem," Eric said. "Kara climbed the tree to get the cat, but now we gotta call the fire department for sure, 'cause Kara and the cat are both stuck up in the tree. And it's gonna take a pretty big truck and ladder to get them both out of there before they starve to death. Or something worse.''

Michael tried not to laugh. Poor Eric was so concerned, but Kara stuck in a tree? The image struck a humorous chord he didn't know he had.

He placed a hand on the boy's small shoulder. "Before we bother the busy fire department, why don't you take me to where she is.''

"Okay,'' Eric said. "But you gotta swear you won't tell anyone where I'm taking you. It's a secret.''

"Cross my heart,'' Michael promised. He followed the boy behind the cottages and down a sandy path to a copse of trees. Just past the perimeter, he spotted a large old sycamore with steps nailed up the side of a thick trunk. Above a rustic tree house, Kara straddled a limb, holding on to the branch where a tabby cat rested.

"Well, I'll be darned,'' Michael said. Wasn't that just like Kara? Her heart had put her in jeopardy. How many women would do that for a stray animal?

"Okay,'' she said, "it was dumb to climb up here. But someone had to save the poor little cat.''

Michael laughed. "And now someone has to save you.''

Kara's cheeks warmed. She didn't need a mirror to know they were bright red. "This isn't funny.''

"Actually, it is.'' Michael began to climb the awkwardly nailed steps. "How sturdy did you make this thing?''

"We didn't make it. We found it,'' Kara said. "It holds us just fine.''

"Yeah, well, you probably don't weigh a hundred pounds,'' Michael said, making his way to the Keep Out sign on the tree house door. "And I weigh considerably more than that.''

"I'm a hundred and five pounds," she said. "With my shoes on."

"And a purse full of change," he countered.

She really didn't feel like joking about this, not while hugging a tree branch and straddling another that could break at any moment. The inside of her knees stung where the bark had scratched. And her hands, gritty and sweaty, trembled whenever she loosened her hold.

As he reached the upper level of the tree house, he placed a foot upon the rooftop and carefully tested the structure before climbing higher.

Kara watched his body move with grace and agility. Sunlight glistened off the golden strands of his hair, making him appear godlike. Who needed a common fireman when she had Michael coming to get her? She stifled a grin.

"Surprisingly, this thing might hold me without collapsing," he said.

"I think it's pretty safe," Kara said. "I checked it out before allowing Eric to climb up here."

As Michael stood atop the tree house, he reached his hands to her. "Come on, I'll help you down."

Kara shook her head while squeezing her thighs against the tree limb and holding on tight. "No, wait. Let me get Buster."

"Buster?"

"The cat."

Michael sighed. In exasperation, she guessed, but there was a glimmer of amusement in his eyes. She reached for the cat, receiving a scratch for her valiant efforts, then managed to take the distressed feline in her arms. She held it close and whispered soft, reassuring words.

"Hand me the cat," Michael said.

She did, but the tabby fought the rescue attempt and jumped from his outstretched hands, springing to the rooftop on which he stood, then scampering down the tree to safety.

"Ouch." Michael rubbed a long, bright-red scratch upon his arm. "Ungrateful beast."

Kara couldn't help but laugh.

"Don't worry, you guys," Eric hollered from down below. "I'll get Buster." Then he dashed off to chase the cat.

Michael stroked the calf of Kara's leg, sending a flutter of tingles up her thigh. "Now it's your turn. I've got you, and I won't let you fall."

She closed her eyes, garnering all the courage she could muster, then slowly eased herself off the branch. The bark scratched along the inside of her legs and arms, scraping her skin until she landed safely on the rooftop with Michael.

He turned her around so that she faced him. "Are you all right?"

She nodded, although her legs felt like jelly and her hands were shaking. "I'm fine, other than a few scrapes and scratches."

"You're trembling." He ran his hands along her arms, from her shoulders to her elbows and back in a gentle caress. His gaze caught hers and took her breath away.

A charge passed between them, a jolt of heat. And a feeling other than compassion or concern and much more than a sense of relief. If she'd felt rubbery before, she was more unsteady now.

She placed her hands on Michael's waist to stabilize herself, but as she felt the solid, muscular cords of his waistline, her hands did a bit of stroking themselves.

He pulled her close, wrapping one arm around her shoulder and pressing her cheek to his chest with the other. He rested his chin on her hair.

She could feel the beat of his heart and the warmth of his touch. His musky scent mingled with the aroma of the sea breeze and dampened leaves. The effect was so natural, so earthy, so carnal that she wondered if he sensed it, if he felt it, too.

Lifting her eyes, she caught him watching her with an intensity that buckled her knees. Unable to help herself, she leaned into him, molding into his hard length.

He moaned softly before lifting her chin and lowering his mouth to hers. Their lips met, and hers parted. His tongue touched hers, slowly at first, and then with a fury that promised to take all she would give and offer it back to her tenfold. Kara marveled at the powerful hunger that threatened to consume her right where she stood—high above the ground.

In a tree house, for goodness sake. A place where childhood dreams were fashioned, imaginary alliances formed. A place where secrets were shared.

This tree house would never be the same again. And neither would she.

Kara placed her hands upon Michael's chest, feeling his heartbeat, the depth of his breathing. She pushed her hands against him, breaking the mindless kiss.

Of all the crazy, careless things she'd done in her life—

"Are you okay?" Eric asked. "Did Michael get you down? Buster must be all right because I can't find him anywhere."

"I'm fine," she told the boy, yet her pounding heart wasn't so sure.

"Good," Eric said. "'Cause Dr. Weldon just drove up here."

"Tell him I'm coming," Kara said.

"Okay, I will." Eric dashed off, leaving Kara to face Michael and the awkward aftereffects of a kiss that should never had happened. Where had her common sense gone?

"I don't know what got into me," she said, her eyes

flitting from the intensity of his stare to the leaves and branches all around them. "I hope you don't think—"

Michael cracked a smile. "You don't want me to think that you bring all of your boyfriends up here?"

"Yeah," she said. "I guess that's what I'm trying to say." Then she took a deep breath and tried to gather her thoughts. "You know, I was serious when I told you I didn't have time for a relationship right now. I can't let that happen again."

He ran a hand through the golden strands of his hair, then shook his head. "Kara, I don't have time for a relationship right now, either. Neither one of us can afford to let that happen again."

She nodded, glad that he agreed but at the same time strangely disappointed. Then she climbed down from the tree.

Michael followed Kara along the path away from the tree house. He'd never had a kiss affect him like that. And he sure as hell had never expected to find himself sexually aroused in a tree house, of all places.

Staid and boring. That was him. People kissed under mistletoe and made love in a bed. That was one of the things his ex-wife had complained about. Michael had no imagination.

But heck, he'd never been one to fantasize. He lived in the real world, the here and now. He hadn't even fantasized about Denise, although she'd thrown enough seductive ideas at him as suggestions—ideas that had never interested him. But one hell of a fantasy had developed when he'd held Kara in his arms high above the ground.

Nighttime. Crickets chirping. A full moon peering through a lace canopy of sycamore leaves. A satin comforter atop the tree house roof. Kara, her hair spread upon a goose down pillow, her arms outstretched—

Michael grumbled under his breath. Fantasies like that he could do without.

He spotted a white Cadillac parked in the graveled lot, the driver standing beside the car. Kara waved. "Hello, Dr. Weldon."

Not in the mood for small talk, or any talk at all, for that matter, Michael made his way toward his cottage.

"Harper," the doctor called. "Can I have a word with you?"

Great. Michael slowed his pace and turned. He caught a glimmer in the older doctor's eye. Recognition? Disapproval? Did it actually matter what the man thought? "What's on your mind?"

Weldon arched a white, bushy brow and smiled at Kara. "Would you excuse us, dear?"

"Sure," she said.

Michael watched Kara head toward Lizzie's house, but several times she tossed a gaze over her shoulder to the two men facing each other. He had a feeling he would have to deal with her questions later.

"Come on, son," Weldon began. "Let's take a walk."

As they followed the sandy path that led to the beach, Michael held his tongue, biding his time, waiting for the older man to speak.

"You said your name was Michael Harper, didn't you?" Weldon continued to walk, hands in the pockets of his gray slacks, eyes on the shoreline.

"That's right."

Weldon nodded, looking thoughtful. But Michael wouldn't mistake the man's down-home demeanor for a lack of intelligence. "You look remarkably like Dr. Michael Harper, the cardiovascular surgeon whose face has been plastered all over the nightly news for the past six months."

So much for a vacation. A chance to get away from it all. Michael slowed his steps. "I haven't been watching television, and I've stayed away from the newspapers. Am I still front-page news?''

Weldon matched his pace. ''I suppose so. People like to hear about the trials and tribulations of the rich and famous. Helps make them content with their own sorry lives, I suppose.''

Michael shook his head and surveyed the ocean, watching as a wave crashed upon the shore. ''I needed to get away for a while. News reporters, if that's what you want to call them, hounded me every moment. I couldn't concentrate on my work.''

''Well, I'm no psychologist,'' Weldon said, ''but I imagine your wife's affair with that corrupt politician must have affected your concentration, as well.''

A muscle in Michael's jaw twitched, and he glanced at the sandy path on which they stood. Denise had accepted cash for surgeries not performed, then written donations in support of her lover's campaign. When the affair and her illegal involvement came to light, Michael had defended himself. He'd been exonerated, of course, but not before testifying at a high-profile trial.

The defense had taken a lot out of him, while public scrutiny and embarrassment had caused him to falter, to cut back on his workload. His surgical skill depended upon a slow and steady hand, on an ability to concentrate his attention on the patient lying upon the operating table.

But that wasn't the only thing he'd had to deal with. The whole sordid affair had wounded his self-esteem, something he'd never had happen before. *Yeah, I'm Dr. Michael Harper, the guy who couldn't keep his wife satisfied.* But he'd put that behind him, as well, and he damn sure wasn't about to pour out his guts to a stranger. ''I dealt with it. We're divorced. Case closed.''

''Hey, I didn't drag you out here to pry into your business. But you're a respected surgeon and a darned good one. I'd hate to think you're having thoughts about giving it all up.''

Michael took a deep breath, gathering in the salty scent of ocean spray. "I'm not giving anything up. I just need some time alone." He shot an accusatory gaze at Weldon. "I need time away from the probing questions."

"I understand, and that's all I intend to say about the matter." Weldon placed a hand on Michael's shoulder. "But if you need someone to talk to, someone who's a good listener, I'm available. And I make house calls."

Michael gave the man a crooked smile. "Yeah, I see that."

"Well, I suppose I'd better check on Lizzie. I'm afraid her days of watching over these kids are coming to an end. I hate to be the one to blow the whistle, but if she doesn't rid herself of some of the stress she's taken on, I'm afraid she'll collapse."

"Kara wants to take over," Michael said. "She loves the kids."

Weldon nodded. "That she does. But she's young and may have a tough time convincing the court to let her have custody. She'd be hard pressed to support the children on her income."

Michael wanted to defend Kara, to say that a kid would be lucky to have a mom like her, a woman who would make Christmas something special, who would build a tree house.

Thoughts of Kara in the tree house took a lusty turn, an inappropriate progression he didn't want to contemplate. "From what I understand, there aren't enough people willing to be foster parents. The court should be happy to have someone volunteer."

"In most instances, but this case is different. You've seen yourself how the media focus can turn into a circus. Same thing happened here in Harbor Haven when Eric saved his sister's life and became an instant hero. I'd guess any number of people would come forward to take Ashley and Eric. Most of them would be compassionate sorts. Others would be more interested in the trust fund set up for the orphans.'' Weldon cleared his throat. ''Well, I didn't mean to chew your ear off.''

''It seems you're a good talker as well as a listener,'' Michael said. He cast the old doctor a grin.

''Well, either way, I'm just a phone call away. Lizzie has my number, and I'm in the book.''

''If I need someone to talk to, I'll give you a call.''

''All right. But don't stew on it too long. The sooner you get back to work, the better you'll feel. The media attention will shift. Some other poor fellow will find himself on the front page instead of you.''

''The sooner that happens, the better,'' Michael said.

As he and Dr. Weldon made their way along the sandy path to the cottages, Kara stood on her patio, watching them. Still curious, Michael noted.

She wore a turquoise and pink Hawaiian-print sarong that exposed a good portion of her thigh. She tugged at the hem when she spotted Michael, then proceeded to walk across the graveled parking lot.

Weldon headed toward Lizzie's cottage, but Michael slowed his steps and spoke to Kara. ''Where are you going?''

She nodded down the street. ''To work.''

In that skimpy little outfit? Not that she didn't look great. ''Are you walking?''

She shrugged her shoulders and smiled. ''It's not far.'' Again, she tugged on the hem, then started down the road.

''Come on,'' he said, taking her by the arm. ''I'll give you a lift. Just tell me where.''

''The Pacifica Bar and Grill. But you don't have to bother taking me. I always walk, since it's so close.''

''Is that the place along Pacific Coast Highway?''

She nodded.

"I saw it while I was driving into town. Are their burgers good?"

"The best," she said, fingering the narrow shoulder strap of her purse.

"Thick and juicy?"

She flashed him that impish smile and brushed a wind-blown strand of hair from her cheek. "With steak fries and all the trimmings."

"All right. Get in the car. I've got a hankering for some good old-fashioned food."

Michael didn't know why he'd insisted upon taking her to work. She was right, it wasn't far away. And he wasn't especially hungry, even though he had been craving a hamburger. So why *had* he insisted?

Maybe he didn't like the idea of her walking alone.

Maybe he wanted to spend more time with a woman who was different from his ex-wife. A woman whose kiss sent his senses skyrocketing. A woman who made him feel something more than clinical detachment.

He couldn't remember a woman ever making him feel the way Kara made him feel. Maybe no other woman ever had.

As Michael backed the Ford out of the lot and turned onto the road, Kara rested an arm on the passenger door, then glanced around the interior of the car. Nothing fancy, but certainly serviceable. It pleased her that he didn't have one of those extravagant, status-boasting cars. Some men needed the extra attention a nice set of wheels brought them. Men like Jason Baker.

She noticed a gold band hanging from the open edge of the ashtray. "What's this?"

"My watch," he said. "I forgot I'd tossed it in there."

An inquisitive spirit, she supposed, caused her to withdraw the watch and hold it in her hands. She examined the timepiece carefully, feeling the weight, noting the workmanship. Gold. Well-made. Not that she could actually tell the difference, but she'd seen Jason's watch, and it looked remarkably similar. The same brand.

Jason had been brash enough to explain to her how much it had cost and why he was important enough to have a possession of that quality. She hadn't been impressed, but she had taken special note of the details. The weight and style. "An ashtray is a funny place to store your Rolex."

He didn't answer right away, so she studied his profile. His eye caught hers, and he smiled. "Looks real, doesn't it?"

It could be a fake, she supposed, but for some reason she didn't think so. Yet, why would he lie to her? If he was trying to impress her, wouldn't he tell her the watch was real? Like Jason had? She assessed the weight and workmanship again. "It sure looks expensive."

"Do you like your job?" he asked. The fact that he hadn't responded to her comment about the quality of his watch didn't go unnoticed, but maybe it wasn't important.

"I really don't like being a waitress, if that's what you mean." She returned the watch to the ashtray where she'd found it. "But the pay is good—better than anything else I could do. Once I get my teaching credentials, I'll turn in this skimpy uniform. Until then, I'll make the best of it."

As Michael pulled into a parking space in front of the Pacifica, he rested his hand on the steering wheel and caught her gaze. "I think your goals are admirable, but I wish there was something else you could do to earn a living."

"Oh, it's not so bad. Most of the regulars are great people. And we serve food. The Pacifica is more like an oceanfront sports bar than a cocktail lounge." Kara smiled, then scanned the parking lot. She pointed at the beige sedan that belonged to Rose Crenshaw. "See that car?"

Michael nodded. "What about it?"

"That belongs to an eighty-three-year-old woman named Rose. She and her two friends come in every day at this time. They're the nicest ladies you've ever met. And real characters. You'll get a kick out of them. They make the afternoons pass quickly."

She expected a smile, something to show he understood how the customers who frequented the Pacifica made her days and evenings more pleasant.

"I think you should reconsider financial aid while you're in school," he said. "It would make life a lot easier for you."

"Life hasn't ever been easy for me, but I'm not so sure that's a bad thing. At least, not in the long run. I think it's strengthened me, made me determined to achieve something on my own. Something to be proud of."

"An education is an achievement you can be proud of. I don't see that taking a loan would negate what you've done."

"There's nothing wrong with student loans or financial aid. At least not for other people. But it's a personal decision for me. I grew up on handouts and state aid." She tried to offer him a smile. "When I turned eighteen, I swore I wouldn't take anything from anyone again. It's a promise I've kept."

He stretched an arm across the seat, his fingers lightly touching her shoulder. "It wouldn't be a handout. It's a state-funded loan for education. You'd pay it back."

She patted the top of the hand that rested on her shoulder, then opened the car door. "Thanks for the suggestion, but it's very important to me that I provide for myself."

As she climbed from the car, she realized Michael lagged behind, sitting in the driver's seat and watching her exit. She hadn't meant to stun him with her refusal to seek financial assistance. Since reaching adulthood, Kara had survived life's blows on her own. And she'd handled them with determination and grace. It seemed all of her friends wanted to offer help and advice. Rose and the girls had insisted she needed a husband, but she'd told the well-meaning women the same thing she'd told Michael.

She wasn't waiting for some hero to come swooping in on a white horse. Kara was a survivor—a heroine of her own making. She didn't need anyone's help.

Not the state's and not a husband's.

Chapter Six

As Kara climbed from the car, Michael remained behind, one arm extended across the seat, the other hand resting on the steering wheel.

He reached into the ashtray and pulled out the Rolex. What in the world had compelled him to lie about the damn watch? It wasn't like he was a deceitful sort. He'd always been honest in his relationships.

Not that he and Kara had a relationship.

But why had he lied about something so minor? What difference did it make whether the Rolex was real or fake?

As he slipped the watch into the ashtray, a quiet voice stilled his thoughts and jabbed a finger at his conscience. *Wondering whether people would like you without a medical degree and more money than you know what to do with?*

Michael had, in the past, had that problem, particularly with women. They seemed to like him all the more when they learned he came from old money. But Kara wasn't like other women, and their relationship, what there was of it, was based on friendship.

Grumbling and cursing his momentary lack of honesty, Michael jerked open the door, slid out of the car and pocketed the key. He shut the driver's door, then followed Kara into the bar and grill.

The Pacifica was nearly empty when Michael entered, but he sensed anticipation in the air. Three fans swirled overhead, creating a tropical island effect. A mural of brightly colored parrots, swaying palm trees and azure sea on the south wall couldn't compete with a bay window that faced the ocean and provided a fiery view of the sunset.

The only patron, an elderly woman with a pink-tinted hairdo, sat in a corner booth. She eyed him carefully as he closed the door and searched for a seat. He chose a glass-topped wicker table near the window.

The sea had always beckoned him. Even though he'd lived and worked only a mile from the beach, he hadn't always taken the time to fully appreciate it. Would life have been different had he taken time for himself? Time for his marriage?

It had been one of Denise's biggest complaints, but he doubted it would have helped. She'd never valued his commitment to his practice or his patients. She probably would have demanded more and more of his time. That might or might not be the truth, but he'd settle for the belief that he couldn't have done things much differently. Dwelling on regrets wasn't part of his nature. And the only real regret he had was marrying Denise in the first place.

His thoughts were interrupted when a tall brunette, sporting the same outfit Kara wore, handed him a menu painted on a teakwood paddle. "Can I get you something to drink?" She nodded toward the bar where a heavyset bartender stood. "It's happy hour. Well drinks are two dollars, and wine and beer on tap are a dollar fifty."

Michael ordered a Mexican beer with lime.

"Those are at the regular price," she said, as though she thought he might prefer a bargain.

"No problem." He studied the menu and wondered where Kara had gone. Before he could give it much thought, she strode through saloon-style bamboo doors that seemed to separate the bar and grill from the kitchen.

"I'm glad you're here," the brunette said to Kara. "I got a call from the sitter. My six-year-old is running a temperature, and I need to leave."

"Why didn't you call me at home?" Kara asked. "I would have come in earlier."

"I just got the message a few minutes ago." The waitress turned to Michael. "This is Kara. She'll be taking over for me."

Michael didn't tell the woman they'd met, that they were neighbors. And neither did Kara.

"I'll order your beer from the bartender on my way out," the waitress told him. Then she whispered something to Kara, but he couldn't hear what she said.

When Kara clicked her tongue and rolled her eyes, Michael couldn't help questioning her. "What was that about?"

"Jason came by looking for me earlier. Instead of acting dumb, Gordy told him I'd be in later."

"Gordy?" Michael asked.

Kara nodded her head toward the round-faced bartender. "He's new and didn't know I'm trying to avoid Jason."

"I don't like that guy harassing you."

"He's just annoying. I can handle him." She pulled a notepad from the hip pocket of her skimpy outfit, lifting the hem and giving him a more thorough glimpse of her thigh. "You wanted a burger, didn't you?"

For a moment, he wanted more than a hamburger. His hand itched to travel along the contour of her upper leg, to pull her close.

Damn his lusty thoughts. "Yes, I'll take a hamburger—well done and with the works."

"Fries?"

As a doctor, he knew better than to make a habit of eating a diet heavy in fats. In fact, he'd seen and repaired more than his share of clogged arteries, but he was on vacation. "Make it a double order."

"You've got it," Kara said. Then she made her way to the corner booth to speak to the elderly woman.

Rose, he thought she'd called her, but it didn't really matter. Michael had no intention of becoming friendly with the locals. He was, after all, just passing through. The more people he met or came into contact with, the more chance that someone would recognize him. The way Dr. Weldon had. It was best if Michael kept to himself.

The elderly woman smiled. A pink cloud of hair reminded him of cotton candy. He couldn't help but stare, and in spite of his best efforts, he found himself smiling.

The door opened, and two other women entered.

"Yoo-hoo, girls." Rose lifted a hand and wiggled her fingers at the ladies. "I ordered our drinks."

The girls, as old and spry as Rose, waved back. One was tall and thin with perfectly coifed steel-gray hair that resembled a football helmet. The other was short and plump with hair he doubted had ever been that black. They must keep the local beauty salon busy, he thought.

They joined Rose in the corner booth, where laughter rang out, along with several giggles. Michael couldn't hear their words, but the camaraderie and merriment were impossible to ignore.

Kara returned carrying a tray laden with drinks, including a long neck bottle with a lime slice wedged in the narrow rim. She stopped at Michael's table and handed him the beer. He thanked her, then nodded toward the corner booth. "Friends of yours?"

Kara graced him with a dimpled smile. "I'll have to introduce you. They're characters, but good people—the best."

"Kind of like a television sitcom, I imagine."

She smiled. "I don't watch much television, but they're novelties for sure. They come in at the same time each day, choose the same table and order the same drinks."

Michael looked at the tray she carried, noting a teapot, cup and saucer and a frothy ice-cream drink. The other was hard to miss. "Is that a martini?"

"For Iris. She usually downs two before they leave. Rose drinks the root beer float, and Grace has hot tea with lemon."

"Just the usual, huh?" Michael chuckled at the diversity of their preferences.

"I always give them the opportunity to change their minds, but they haven't altered that order since the first day I began working here. Excuse me while I drop off their drinks."

Michael watched her work, but instead of rushing to his table, she remained with the ladies long enough to laugh. He liked the soft lilt of her voice, the way she tossed her head. He wished he'd chosen a table closer. A sense of abandonment settled over him, making him feel like a reprimanded child who'd been banished to the outer reaches of the schoolyard, able to watch the fun and games but unable to participate.

Something the taller woman said caused Kara's cheeks to flush. She surreptitiously cast her eyes at him while the elderly ladies studied him, bright-eyed and giggly, like teenagers. No wonder Rose had called them girls.

Kara shook her head before leaving the women to chat among themselves.

"What was that all about?" he asked, when she stopped by his table.

"Rose, Grace and Iris refer to themselves as the Harbor Haven Fairy Godmothers. They've been trying to find me a prince for the past six months." She patted him on the shoulder, her cheeks still a bright red. "Not to worry. I told them not to get their hopes up, since you're just passing through."

"Do they try to set you up with every bachelor who comes in here?"

"And a few who are married. The girls are good-hearted, but they see a handsome face and get a bit carried away before they scan the ring finger." She smiled, then brushed an auburn curl from her cheek. "I've frustrated them to no end."

"Why is that?" Michael studied the fey princess before him.

"I find something wrong with every prince they find."

"I take it you're serious about not wanting to date," Michael said. It was a shame, he realized. Kara was the kind of woman who would be fun to date—playing Frisbee on the beach, sharing hot kisses in a tree house. He tossed away the thoughts as quickly as they surfaced. Neither one of them needed any entanglements now. They'd both said as much.

"The kids come first." She shot him a warm smile that touched his heart. "They always will."

Her words conjured a memory, one he'd nearly forgotten—a telephone conversation.

I'm sick and tired of playing second fiddle to the hospital, Michael. I want you to come home. I've been looking forward to the Banisters' party for months.

Denise, you knew I was a surgeon when you married me.

Yes, Michael, I knew what you were when we married, but not how obsessed with work you would become. You'd rather be at the hospital or on the phone with some lab, some other doctor. I'm your wife. Doesn't that mean anything to you?

It means something, but you have to understand. I have a twenty-eight-year-old man in recovery. I nearly lost him on the operating table, and I'm not leaving until he's out of danger.

For God's sake, Michael. The man's in recovery with a well-trained medical staff. You can have them cover for you. For once, put me and our marriage first.

I'm sorry, Denise. My patients will always come first.

The sound of a souped-up engine tore into his thoughts. The skid of a car rolling to a stop announced someone's arrival. How many people drove vehicles like that? Michael figured only one. Jason Baker, heir to the EZ Suds fortune.

Sight unseen, Michael hadn't thought much of the guy, but as a short, overly buff jerk swaggered through the door, the low opinion Michael had formed plummeted further. Baker wore a T-shirt that melded to a muscular frame created, Michael figured, more by steroids than by Nautilus equipment.

Michael lifted the beer to his lips, his eyes fixed on the man scanning the room.

When Jason's eye caught Kara's, barely controlled panic gnawed at her stomach. She tugged at the hem of the sarong the owner insisted all his waitresses wear. He called them uniforms, but the darn things were difficult to work in and too revealing for Kara's comfort. Tall, long-legged women could get away with short skirts, but not her.

She watched Jason saunter toward the table where she stood, the table where Michael sat. A flood of wishes poured over her—wishes that she'd called in sick today, that Jason hadn't come by, that Michael hadn't chosen to have a hamburger this afternoon.

Jason moseyed closer. "Hey, sugar babe. I've been looking for you."

In an effort to keep the conversation private, Kara moved toward the bar. "I don't know why. I thought I made myself clear the last time you stopped by."

Jason chuckled. "Fickle women drive me wild."

All women drove Jason wild. Kara couldn't believe she'd actually gone to a movie with him, but when she first met him, she'd felt sorry for him. He didn't seem to have many friends, although now she knew why. And he'd only grown more obnoxious when she told him she wasn't interested in dating him.

"I'm not going to change my mind about dating you, Jason. We have nothing in common."

"Sure, we do. I have money and you want it. I can take you places you've never been, show you things you've never seen. Buy you things—"

Kara jabbed a finger at his bulky chest. "I don't want you or your money. Can't you get that through your head?"

Jason grabbed her finger and squeezed until she winced. "Don't point your finger at me. It ain't polite." Then he eased his grip and grinned. "Bet you learned how to be stuck up and rude by working at a bar. Cocktail waitresses get hit on all the time. I guess they have to be rude sometimes. But Kara, I'm not just anybody."

Kara rubbed the knuckles of her hand, all the while glaring at Jason. "Please leave."

"I'm a customer, sugar." He ran a hand along the outside of her arm, causing her to flinch. His hand dropped as he eased onto a barstool. "Take it easy."

Kara sighed. The manager wasn't due in for another hour or so. If he were here, he'd throw Jason out, but for now there wasn't much Kara could do, other than make a scene. She preferred to let her annoyance pass. "What will you have?"

"That's more like it." He slid her a toothy smile that would make his orthodontist proud. "I'll have a Scotch on the rocks."

"Gordy," Kara said to the new bartender who was, she hoped, learning why the other employees helped her avoid Jason. "Will you pour a Scotch, please?"

"That a girl." Jason cupped her jaw, sending a dreadful rumble to her chest. "Kara, why don't you give ol' Charlie your notice. Give up this low-life job. I can get your old job back for you."

"I don't want my old job," Kara said, turning her back and stepping from his reach.

"It wasn't my fault you lost it," he said.

Kara brushed off his comment. It was his story, he could tell it any way he liked. She wasn't about to argue the point, but if he didn't stop coming into the Pacifica and bothering her, he'd be the cause of her losing this one, too.

"How about working for us down at the EZ Suds. We've always got an opening."

That didn't surprise her a bit. His parents held a tight rein on the entire chain of Laundromats and, from what she'd heard, they were very demanding of their employees. That's probably why the turnover rate was so high. Kara couldn't think of anything worse than working for the Bakers. Unless, of course, it was having dinner at their house. Her stomach still churned at the memory of that awful night.

"No, thank you," she told Jason as she stepped away, looking to escape him. "And whether you believe it or not, I like this job."

On her way to the break room, she passed through the kitchen, where Carlos stood over the grill. When he looked up, she nodded in greeting, intent on escaping Jason, if only for a minute or two. But how long could she remain in hiding from the annoying pest who appeared hell-bent on disrupting her life? Not as long as it took Jason to finish his drink and leave.

She walked to the water cooler and filled a paper cup. What had she done to deserve this?

A small, childlike voice quizzed her further. What had she done to deserve anything life had thrown in her path—never knowing her father, being taken from the custody of her mother, living in a slew of foster homes.

So what? she asked herself. That was the past, and there was nothing she could do about it except forge on, determined to make the rest of her life better than the first eighteen years.

And she had. It had taken four years, three moves and several different jobs to land her in Harbor Haven. For the first time in her life she felt as though she had a home, family, friends, a game plan for her future. No one, especially Jason Baker, was going to take that from her.

Kara tossed the cup into the trash and strode from the kitchen.

Michael was glad Kara had stepped away from Baker, and he hoped the guy would get the hint and leave. But something told him Baker was too stupid and too much of a jerk.

If Michael weren't so keen on keeping a low profile, he'd take the guy outside and talk to him. Suggest he jump into that souped-up vehicle, drive away and find himself a willing woman to date.

As Kara walked out of the kitchen, Baker grabbed her by the arm. ''Hey, Kara, what time are you off work?'' She tried to twist from his grip, but he seemed to squeeze harder. ''You're not avoiding me, are you?''

Michael tensed his jaw and narrowed his eyes. He'd

had just about enough of that jerk. The bartender stood gawking at the two. Why didn't he step in? Do something?

Kara managed to pull away from Baker's grip. "I'm not going out with you. Not today, not ever."

Jason slid from the bar stool and stood inches from Kara, but she didn't step back. His face reddened. "You don't need me or my money anymore, do you? Now that you've latched on to those orphaned kids with a big trust fund."

For a moment, a pained expression crossed her face, but her emotions appeared to rally, and she faced him like a Lilliputian queen. "That money belongs to Eric and Ashley. I wouldn't think of touching it, even if I could. I love those kids, Jason. That's something I doubt you could ever understand."

He laughed, a cold, sneering chuckle. "How could someone like you know anything about love? You don't even have a real family."

Kara's hands flew to her hips. "If you don't stop bothering me, I'm going to get a restraining order against you."

The cocky bastard's eye twitched, then he laughed. "Do you think that scares me?"

Michael had watched long enough. In spite of not wanting to draw any attention to himself, he couldn't stand by and watch Jason's harassment any longer. Michael was at their side in an instant. "Maybe you didn't hear the lady. She'd like you to leave her alone."

"And who the hell are you?" Jason asked. His muscles flexed under his T-shirt.

"I'm a friend of Kara's."

Jason's jaw tensed. He stood tough but had to bend his neck to look at Michael. "This don't concern you."

Michael wished it didn't, but it did, more than he cared

to admit. He didn't like Jason threatening Kara. "I'll press charges myself."

Jason crossed his bulky arms. "And who do you think you are?"

"A friend," Michael said.

Jason uncrossed his arms and gave Michael a shove, nearly causing him to lose his footing.

"Oh, for goodness sake, Gordy," Rose yelled from the corner booth. "Call the police."

Jason eased closer to Michael, cocked his head and thrust up his chin in a move meant to be intimidating. "The only one getting hauled off is you, pal. My dad's a big shot in town, and we've got ties with the local law enforcement. My family donates plenty in support. The cops aren't going to do squat to me. You, on the other hand, are a stranger."

If he allowed Jason to throw his weight around, those beefy fists and Popeye muscles could inflict some damage. Michael wasn't a fighter, but as a doctor, he knew several vulnerable spots where a blow could temporarily disable the guy.

And Jason's chin was tilted just right. With one swift jab, he could drop Jason to his knees—maybe to the floor. But Michael wouldn't hit him unless provoked with more than a sharp tongue.

Kara had called Jason harmless, but Michael had serious doubts about that. Jason Baker was a force to be reckoned with, even if she didn't think so.

In a move probably meant to sidetrack his opponent, Jason turned as though intending to walk away, then swung around, knuckles raised and ready to strike.

Michael doubled up his fist and, using his brain along with a bit of brawn, sent Baker flying backward and onto the floor with a thud.

While Michael made a routine physical assessment, Rose and her friends hovered over him and Baker.

"Is he dead?" Rose asked.

"No, just unconscious, but he has a knot on the back of his head and will probably wake with a headache."

Placing a hand on Michael's shoulder, Rose turned to her friends. "Now, this is what I call a prince, even if he's only vacationing."

"Well, he's definitely a dragon slayer," one woman said. "It's about time someone put Jason Baker in his place. Lord knows his father should have put his foot down years ago."

The older women mumbled their agreement while continuing to study the fallen heir to the EZ Suds fortune.

"Darn kid," one of them said.

"A big old bully, that's what he is," Rose corrected.

"And a show-off. What makes them do that to their cars?" the gray-helmeted woman asked.

Michael didn't know, but he thought it was time Jason learned what "leave me alone" meant.

As a siren sounded in the distance, he suffered his first pang of remorse. Didn't reporters have radios that picked up police frequencies?

The fact that he'd just become involved in an altercation didn't bother him too badly. As far as he was concerned, Jason Baker deserved what he got. But on the other hand, Michael dreaded having his name broadcast on the evening news and having his short bout of tranquillity interrupted.

He felt for the wallet in his hip pocket. At least he had his driver's license with him. If it came to a police interrogation, he'd be only too willing to let his identity speak for itself. And as for the media? He'd face that consequence if and when it happened.

If some snoopy reporter tagged along after the police, well, then, *c'est la vie*. If it came to that, he'd just have to pack up and leave town. In the meantime, he couldn't let Baker get away with bothering Kara.

Jason moaned as the police car pulled into the parking lot.

Chapter Seven

The troublemaker came to just as a uniformed police officer walked into the Pacifica. Baker sat on the floor and rubbed his head.

"What seems to be the problem?" the policeman asked.

Before anyone could speak, Jason spouted his name and recited a rundown of his clout with the district attorney's office and his friendship with various public officials.

The officer who arrived on the scene didn't seem impressed.

"I want that guy arrested," Jason said, pointing at Michael.

The police officer looked at Michael. "Care to tell me what happened?"

"I'll tell you what happened," Jason interrupted.

"Why don't we step outside," the officer said to Michael. He nodded toward the door. ''I'd like to hear your story first.''

While Michael walked outside, Jason continued to babble about the injustice done to him. It didn't seem as though anyone, not even the police officer, was paying him much attention.

''Do you have any identification?'' the policeman asked.

''Yes, sir.'' Michael withdrew his driver's license and gave it to the officer. ''I'm Dr. Michael Harper. Baker was harassing one of the waitresses and when he grabbed a hold of her, I stepped in. He took a swing at me, but my punch landed first.''

The policeman studied the photo on his license, then looked up and smiled. ''I've heard about you, Doctor.''

Michael tensed. Everyone, it seemed, had heard about him.

''I have a buddy who works for the district attorney's office in Los Angeles County. He told me how cooperative you were during the investigation.''

Michael shrugged. He had to open up his books to the investigators. Besides, he was trying to clear his name. ''There wasn't much else I could do.''

''You on vacation?'' He handed Michael his ID.

''Sort of. I've been trying to avoid the press.'' Michael slipped the license into his wallet. ''So far, no one seems to have figured out I'm the same Michael Harper they've read about. But I guess my bit of respite is over.''

''Jason Baker is the town crybaby. If he finds out, he'll make an issue out of it, I would imagine.''

''I'm sure the others inside will back my story. Baker started it.''

The officer nodded. ''I deal with Baker on a monthly basis, or so it seems. Let's go back inside.''

As they entered the Pacifica, Jason bellowed at the policeman. ''Are you going to arrest him or not?''

"I'm investigating the circumstances," the officer said.

After taking time with each of the witnesses, the policeman closed his notepad. "I think you'd better leave the premises, Mr. Baker."

"I don't care what anyone else says, this guy hit me for no reason." Jason crossed his arms and glared at the police officer. "And you damn well better not let him get away with it. You know who my dad is. One call to your captain, and you can kiss your retirement goodbye."

When it became clear that the officer didn't care who Jason or his father knew, Jason became belligerent and threatening, which didn't help his case. Neither did taking a swing at the policeman, who immediately called for backup.

In spite of Jason's proclaimed importance and his threat to have the arresting officers fired, the Harbor Haven police hauled him to jail.

Michael wasn't sure how long the EZ Suds heir would be detained, but he doubted the Bakers would let him stay incarcerated for long. For that reason, he remained at the Pacifica until Kara was off work.

He wasn't proud of the fact that he'd allowed himself to become involved in a barroom brawl, something that went against his nature. Hell, he hadn't been in any kind of physical altercation since grade school. But he'd do the same thing in a heartbeat if Jason tried to bully Kara again.

As Michael pulled the car into the cottages' graveled drive, Kara's porch light illuminated the interior of the Ford.

He glanced across the seat and found her looking at him, her expression pensive, eyes wide and laden with regret. "I'm sorry you got caught up in that."

Michael reached for her hand, amazed at how easily it slipped into his, how delicate her fingers were, how soft her skin was. He squeezed gently. "That guy isn't as harmless as you think. I'm going to help you file that restraining order."

Kara nodded. "I suppose you're right. Jason's getting out of control."

He reluctantly released her hand. "Come on, I'll walk you to your door."

"But I—"

He placed a finger on her lips to still her objection, then exited the car, intending to open the door for her. He wasn't sure why he felt so noble, so intent on behaving as a gentleman. He'd only meant to be neighborly, to see her home.

She climbed out before he could get to the passenger side, and they walked to her porch. The light bathed them in a soft yellow glow. Kara fumbled in her small purse, digging for a key, he assumed. She pulled out a stick of gum, a nail file, a wallet, a small tin of breath mints.

"It's in here—somewhere." She offered him a whimsical shrug before resuming her search and pulling out a single key. "Voilà! It's a feminine secret," she said with a wink, "learned early in life."

He grinned. "You mean, little girls acquire the art of packing a purse shortly after birth?"

She nodded sagely. "That's right, and we're bound by a code of ethics to keep that secret to ourselves."

When she flashed him a smile in that impish, fairylike way, something warm swept over him, causing him to react without thought, without the reason that usually dictated his every move. Unable to help himself, he cupped her face in his hands and lowered his lips to hers.

The kiss began gently, his hands upon her cheeks, hers placed lightly upon his waist. It should have ended like that, too, friendly and chaste, but a force he had not yet reckoned with began to pulse in his blood. His mouth opened slowly, and his tongue stroked her lips. She moaned softly before opening to him, allowing his tongue to enter, to slow dance with her own.

She tasted of peppermint, and he hungered for more.

The scent of peaches swirled around him, lulling him into a mindless place where passion raged. Like a ship at the mercy of the sea, he was a captive to her charm, her essence, her embrace. It was too much and, at the same time, not nearly enough.

A sense of urgency swept over him, and he pulled her close, felt her hands slide up his waist, over his chest, around his neck. Her fingers snaked into his hair, and a jolt of desire damn near sent him over the edge. This kiss, more powerful than the last, promised to be his undoing.

The key she'd held in her hand dropped to the plank floor of the porch, yet neither of them reached for it. Neither, it seemed, cared whether they'd find it later. There was a heat in that kiss, a power beyond imagination, something he'd never experienced before, something he already wanted again. And he wasn't about to let it go—not yet. Not while the blood coursed through his veins and throbbed in his groin.

She leaned into him against a demanding erection, and he had a notion to carry her into the house, lay her on the bed, make her his own. Instead, he thrust his tongue deep into her soft, peppermint-flavored mouth, ran his hands up and down the gentle curve of her back, cupped her rounded bottom and pulled her flush against him.

Kara had never felt such an intense reaction to a kiss. Heat pooled in her belly—and lower, stirring a swift sensation of emptiness that only Michael, it seemed, could fill.

What was happening to her? To her resolve to remain unattached, unfettered by a relationship? She meant to stop the kiss, to stop the mindless assault of his touch upon her senses, but before she could push away and break the spell, a dog barked.

Not Gulliver, she realized, but a dog down the street. It gave her the chance to regain some semblance of control, some sense of right and wrong. She dropped her hands to Michael's chest and slowly pulled away, reluctantly withdrawing her mouth from his. Nearly breathless, she gathered her thoughts in spite of a racing pulse. "I don't know what to say."

Michael raked a hand through his hair, then scanned the darkened cottages that surrounded hers. "I'm not one to behave like that in public."

"Neither am I," she said, realizing he was referring to a kiss that should have been kept in the privacy of one's bedroom. The truth struck her like an old screen door slamming in the wind, repeating the message and sending a warning.

The kiss they'd shared had been a bedroom kiss. And Kara had better get a grip on her waning decision to keep this relationship platonic, friendly. Neighborly.

"I'd better go inside," she said, the husky tone of her voice surprising her. "Thanks for bringing me home."

And for the kiss, she wanted to say, but she kept that absurd thought to herself. So what if she'd always wondered what secrets lovers shared, what a sexual relationship might be like. This evening, her curiosity had been satisfied, or so she hoped. Kissing Michael wasn't something she should let happen again.

"I meant what I said about filing that restraining order against Jason," Michael said. "I might not be around the next time he harasses you."

The reality of his words hit home. He might not be around next time because he was leaving soon. Going back to Los Angeles. Back to his own world. Out of her life and that of her chosen family.

"All right. I'll place some phone calls tomorrow and

find out the first step I need to take.'' She offered what she hoped was a friendly smile, then turned to the door. Her hand fumbled; the knob wouldn't turn.

''You didn't get a chance to unlock it.'' Michael stooped to search for the key she'd dropped.

Her fingers touched her lips, still swollen and tingling from the kiss they'd shared. She watched him hunt for the key and find it beside a potted plant. He stood, placed the key in the lock and opened the door for her.

''Good night,'' she said, her voice a near whisper.

''Sleep tight,'' he told her, before turning to walk away.

Michael heard the door close behind him and stifled the urge to look over his shoulder, to glance at her cottage before returning to his. What had gotten into him? Had Kara not stopped him, he might have carried her inside, made love to her until they both lay in a tumble of sheets, arms and legs wrapped around each other. Yet something told him once with Kara wouldn't be enough.

She had a hold on him, one that frightened him. He found his out-of-character behavior bewildering. Discomfiting. She played with his mind, creating fantasies and daydreams that had never surfaced—not since he had shoved them deep into his subconsciousness many years before.

Will you come to visit next month? See me play soccer? Meet my new friends? He swept the eight-year-old voice from his mind, but not before hearing his father's reply.

If your mother and I return from Europe in time. We'll be visiting friends in Monaco. You remember the Harringtons, don't you, son?

A dog, the same one that had interrupted the kiss he'd shared with Kara, howled in the distance, jarring his thoughts, protecting him from the memory he wanted to forget.

When he reached his porch, he fumbled in his pocket for his key. What was it about Kara that fascinated him? Her vivacious spirit? Her honest determination? Her compassionate heart?

Michael let himself inside then shook his head. Kara wasn't like any other woman he'd ever known. She was unusual, a novelty of sorts. That's what it was, what it had to be. She afforded him a pleasant escape. Isn't that why he'd stopped in Harbor Haven? For a temporary escape from reality?

He made his way to the bathroom and turned on the shower, allowing the water to heat until steam clouded the mirror. He stood before his foggy image, trying to catch sight of himself in the glass, hoping to recognize someone familiar. Who was Michael Harper? And what did he want to do with his life?

As he undressed, leaving the clothes he'd shed piled upon the floor, he continued to stare into the mirror. Where did he want to practice? Los Angeles? Or Boston?

Dr. Harper, now that your wife is in prison, what are your plans? That's what the prying reporters wanted to know. And why they'd hounded him for an answer.

A chill eased over his naked body as the irony struck him. Maybe the media's unrelenting attention and interference in his life, which had all but destroyed his privacy, bothered him for another reason. Could their rapid-fire questions have disturbed him because he had no answers for them?

Or because he had no answers for himself?

The next morning, after shopping for groceries, Michael spotted a flower vendor with a bright red and yellow umbrella-shaded cart parked along the sidewalk. He had no intention of stopping, but the vendor, an older gentleman with a paunch belly and a jaunty smile, apparently wasn't about to let him pass by without notice.

"We got lots of pretty flowers guaranteed to put a smile on that special lady's face."

"I don't have a special lady," Michael said to the jovial fellow who sported a red and blue baseball cap and rainbow-colored suspenders.

The man winked. "Too bad. Maybe if you buy some flowers, you'll find yourself one. I haven't seen a woman yet who doesn't love flowers."

Michael supposed they did, but other than Kara, he couldn't think of anyone to surprise. Kara, with her bright eyes and playful nature, would probably enjoy a bouquet. And the gift was sure to bring a smile to her face—one that lit her eyes.

Would giving her flowers complicate things? Maybe, but they'd both been clear about not wanting or needing a relationship.

He scanned the baskets in front of the cart and spotted a bouquet of peach-colored roses. The color reminded him of the peach scent Kara always wore. Unable to help himself, he bent to catch a whiff of the buds that were just beginning to open. The fragrance was intoxicating.

He reached into his pocket and pulled out a roll of bills held together by a rubber band, small denominations covering larger. Denise had hated the idea of him using a rubber band instead of a fancy money clip. She also thought the hundreds should be displayed prominently. He'd refused to use the solid gold clip she'd given him one Christmas.

The rubber band, a trick he'd picked up from a roommate in college, made it difficult for a pickpocket to slip money from his pocket without notice. He had explained that he didn't need to use a fancy money clip or flaunt large bills. She didn't seem to care whether he got mugged and thought his habit mocked the classy lifestyle she enjoyed. It was one of many complaints she'd had.

"How much for this bouquet?" he asked.

"Ten dollars," the vendor said. "I guess you decided you had a special lady, after all."

"She's just a friend," Michael said, quickly disregarding the memory of that last blood-stirring kiss that wasn't at all friendly. Lust, he reminded himself, was easily confused with emotion. Not having had sex for a while did things to a man.

To a woman, too, he supposed, remembering how the kisses had left Kara flushed and breathless.

"You'll be glad you bought these," the man said sagely. "Women like flowers."

Michael supposed they did, although he'd never brought a bouquet home for Denise—not because he was insensitive, but because she had an account with the florist. Twice a week, fresh floral arrangements would be delivered to their home, filling each room with color and a fresh scent. Michael had paid the monthly bill. Wasn't that the same thing as giving his wife flowers?

But standing before the brightly colored cart, inhaling the fragrance of the roses he'd chosen for Kara, Michael knew it wasn't the same at all. In fact, since his revelation in the shower last night, he'd come to grips with a few things he'd done wrong, a few signs he'd missed along the way.

Maybe this short vacation in Harbor Haven had done his soul good, had begun to heal some of the pain he'd suffered. Kara, in her own way, had started him on the contemplative quest. Maybe that's why the flowers had called out to him. It was his way of thanking her for pointing him in the right direction.

The vendor whistled a tune while he wrapped the stems of the roses in waxed tissue, then handed the bouquet to Michael. After paying with a ten, Michael wrapped the rubber band around his bills and tucked the small wad into his pocket.

''Thanks, son,'' the vendor said. ''Remember, it's the little things that impress a lady.''

Michael nodded at the unsolicited advice and continued down the road. He didn't have time for the little things in life. His time was taken up with another priority—his patients, the seriously ill he'd been trained to heal. Denise hadn't understood. Maybe most wives wouldn't be able to. For that reason, he was better off not looking for a woman who would want more from him than what he had to offer.

Not that he was in the market for a wife, but when the time came to settle down, he'd look for someone who worked in the medical field. A woman who understood the late night calls and mad rushes to the hospital. The hours and days it took him to deal with the loss of a patient he had so badly wanted to save. Countless times, he'd tried to explain it to Denise, but she'd never really understood. Moody and selfish, she'd called him.

It took a special person to be a doctor. Michael knew that. What he hadn't realized was that a doctor's spouse had to be an extraordinary person, too.

As Michael turned down the lane that led to the cottages, he carried the roses in one hand and the grocery bag in the other. The sun shone brightly for an autumn day, and the gulls called in the distance. He was glad he'd chosen to walk to the market. The fresh, salty air stimulated his thoughts. Soon, he'd have it all together, have his mind eased, his game plan set. And then he could head north, back to Los Angeles, back to his medical practice—older and wiser. Rested and ready to return to work.

He couldn't deny a strong physical attraction to Kara— an attraction he wouldn't let proceed to an affair, as much as his libido might try to convince him otherwise. He glanced at the roses he meant as a token of friendship, of appreciation. He hoped she didn't think he was hitting on her, as much as he'd like to. Kara wasn't that kind of woman. Besides, she was probably ten years his junior, a young woman on the verge of maturity, with eyes toward motherhood, family and a home—things he didn't need to be a part of.

Nah, he told himself, she wouldn't get the wrong idea. He'd give her the flowers as a friendly gesture, just to see her smile.

And she would smile, because that's the kind of woman she was—effervescent, happy. The fun-loving, sisterly kind men liked to be around.

Ten minutes later, he stood on Kara's porch, feeling awkward, like a self-conscious adolescent. And he wasn't at all sure why.

Chapter Eight

Kara was on her knees, cleaning out the oven, when a knock sounded at the door. Her joints creaked when she stood, and the topknot into which she'd secured her hair slipped to the side. She used the backside of her gloved hand to brush an errant curl aside and blew out a sigh.

Eric was in school, so she figured Lizzie and Ashley had come over, bringing her cookies or wanting to chat. Kara hated to tell her dear friend she didn't have time for her, but she was elbow deep into a dirty job and wanted to finish.

"Just a minute," she called. "I'm coming." She slipped off the grungy rubber gloves and washed her hands at the sink. On her way to the door, she glanced at a charcoal smudge on the front of the oversize white T-shirt she wore and sighed. She must look a fright, but Lizzie had seen her in worse condition.

She opened the door, but it wasn't Lizzie on the porch. Kara's breath caught at the sight of Michael, who wore jeans and a white collared shirt, open at the neck. He stood sheepishly, holding a bouquet of roses. Beautiful roses.

"Hello." She batted at the same lazy lock of hair that had challenged her while cleaning.

"I, uh, saw a flower vendor along Pacific Coast Highway and decided to surprise you." He flashed a lopsided smile and, when he handed her the bouquet, something squeezed her heart, making her step back.

Tears filled her eyes, and she tried to blink them away. No one had ever given her flowers before, other than Eric, who liked to bring her dandelions so they could blow the seeds and make wishes. Touched by the unexpected gift, she didn't know what to say.

Michael wrinkled his brow and pulled the flowers toward his chest. "I'm sorry. Did I do something wrong? I only meant this to be a friendly gesture, one that would make you smile—not cry."

"I'm the one who's sorry." She swiped a tear from her eye and offered a grin. "No one has ever brought me flowers before. I was taken aback."

Michael shrugged. "Well, we've both experienced a first. I've never brought anyone flowers before. Do you want them? Or should I give them to Lizzie?"

"Oh, no." Kara reached for the bundle of delicate buds and clutched them close to her heart. "I want them. Thank you."

Michael raked a hand through his hair. "I'm not very good with tears. How about a dry-eyed smile?"

Kara laughed. "I can't promise dry eyes, but the smile is real." She took a deep whiff of the roses and sighed. "They're absolutely beautiful and so fragrant."

"Are you going to place them in water?"

Kara glanced over her shoulder, then nibbled her bottom lip. "You may not believe this, but I've never had a vase. In fact, I've never needed one. I'll have to put them in a sink full of water for the time being, but I'll find something to put them in. I'm very resourceful."

"I'm disappointed you haven't ever had need of a vase."

She supposed he would be surprised at that. There were a lot of things Kara never had need for—a doll of her own, brand-new clothing, a bicycle, a car. Years ago, she'd learned to make do, to be satisfied with what she had and not yearn for things she didn't. Now, each item she purchased for herself, whether a necessity or a simple extravagance like her soaps and lotions, had been provided by her own earnings. She treasured the feeling of self-reliance. "People don't need much in life. Friends, family, a home."

He studied her for what seemed a long time. She wondered if he believed her or whether he thought she was crazy. She might never know, because he didn't respond.

"I appreciate the flowers," she added. "Would you like to come inside?"

"No, I should make some phone calls. Check on things back home."

She nodded, although thoughts of him leaving for another home and another life saddened her. "Have you decided when you'll leave?"

"Maybe in a week."

She would miss him. Friends were hard to find, and he'd been a good one—having her for dinner, taking her and Ashley to the ER, helping her out of the tree, standing up to Jason at the Pacifica, then taking her home.

And kissing her senseless—more than once. Her cheeks warmed at the memory of his touch, of the swirling heat that had pooled in her stomach. As powerful and enticing as each of those kisses had been, she and Michael had both felt awkward later. It hadn't meant anything. Not really.

He'd apologized for his part in that last breathless encounter, but she'd been equally to blame, and they'd vowed not to let that happen again. He really was a gentleman. And a friend.

But what had she offered him in return for the kindness he'd shown her? She didn't have anything to give him and couldn't imagine what she'd buy if she had money to spare. Maybe she could do something for him, at least return the dinner invitation. "Would you let me cook you a meal before you go?"

"Sure," he said, giving her a lazy smile that suggested he no longer felt uncomfortable giving her the flowers. "I have the fixings for spaghetti. I can bring them over, and we can cook together."

"Tonight?"

"Why not?" he asked. "Unless you're working or already have plans."

"No. I'm off tonight. And my only plans were to eat light."

He raised a brow. "Not because you're dieting, I hope." His eyes swept the length of her, and she noted approval, appreciation. Something more. Something that shot through her, causing her to brush at the greasy smudge on her shirt, then try to straighten the lopsided topknot that held her messy hair.

He flashed her a warm smile, placed a hand on her shoulder and gave her a gentle squeeze. "You look pretty."

"Don't tease me," she said.

"I meant what I said, Kara. Even with a smudge on your face, you have a natural beauty."

It touched her to think he might find her attractive, even with her hair in disarray and wearing an oversize dirty work shirt.

Of course, that didn't matter. She and Michael were friends. That was all they'd ever be. She tossed him a playful grin. "No, I'm not dieting. I just don't fix a big meal when I'm eating alone."

"So," he asked. "Do you want me to bring over the pasta and the ingredients for my killer spaghetti sauce?"

Why not? she asked herself. Why eat alone when she could share dinner with a friend? "Sure, but remember, I help Lizzie with the kids at bedtime, so I won't be ready to cook until after eight o'clock."

"No problem," he said. "I'll come over before you leave, then work on the sauce while you're gone."

"You're making the sauce from scratch?" she asked.

He put a hand on his chest and took a step back. "Surely you didn't think I would try to slip canned spaghetti sauce by you?"

She laughed. "I leave for Lizzie's at seven o'clock."

"I'll see you then, and when you get back, I'll have dinner ready."

She watched him walk away, tall, determined, the sun rays catching the gold highlights in his hair. He was gorgeous. Too gorgeous for a male friend. But they both had separate lives. A temporary friendship was all they could hope for.

It was all Kara would allow.

Michael strode to his cottage, his mind rehashing his conversation with Kara. Her innocence stirred him, as did the pleasure she found with the simple things in life. It saddened him to know that she lacked the resources for things he considered necessities—a house, a car, a healthy bank account.

When he left Harbor Haven, he'd see what he could do to secure each item she deserved. It would be simple for him. He could write a personal check and never even miss the funds.

And he'd be returning to Los Angeles soon. He certainly couldn't stay away forever. Bertha was a whiz when it came to running his office and screening his calls. Since he hadn't talked to her in two days, she'd probably have a stack of messages. Knowing the competent woman, she'd have everything under control. Funny, but the matronly, good-natured employee was like family to him—more like a mother than the one he had.

He sat on the rattan chair next to the telephone, picked up the receiver and dialed his office.

"Pacific Coast Cardiovascular. Can I help you?"

"Bertha, it's me. How are things going?"

"Well, you've had a slew of phone calls—most of which I fielded. Dr. Crane asked if you're going to donate a trip on the jet again for this year's benefit auction for MMI. The program is being printed tomorrow morning, and he needs to know. I thought you would but didn't want to commit until I spoke to you."

"Sure." Michael had done whatever he could for Mercy Medical Intervention, in addition to traveling to Third World countries and providing his skills to critically ill children. "Tell him I'll also donate a two-week stay at the chalet in Vail."

"All right," Bertha said. "And Dr. Margaret Templeton called. She said you attended med school together. She left her private number and said she'd be home, since she's not on call."

Maggie? He hadn't talked to her in a year or more, but they'd developed a great respect for each other, professionally speaking, and they'd become good friends, even though they practiced across the country from each other. "Her private number, huh? I wonder what that's about?"

"She didn't say."

They briefly discussed several other messages, then after agreeing to check back with Bertha on Monday, Michael said goodbye and hung up the phone.

He sat back in the chair and stretched out his feet.

Maggie Templeton. He'd call her, of course, but he couldn't help wondering why she wanted to talk to him.

To offer her condolences about the breakup of his marriage? No, she'd sent him a note, knowing he wasn't one to discuss his personal life. She'd told him to call if he needed someone to talk to, someone to offer support. But he hadn't taken her up on it. He hadn't needed to because he'd handled the distasteful mess on his own.

Maybe she was referring another patient or wanting to discuss a compelling case. Either way, thoughts of pretty Maggie drew a slow, easy smile.

Tall and leggy, blond with stunning brown eyes, she'd had to struggle to gain respect in school. Most of the male medical students had tried to hit on her, but she'd made it clear that her priority was graduating at the top of the class. And she'd done so, right below Michael.

From what he'd heard, she'd begun dating only after establishing a successful pediatric practice back East. Like Michael, she'd married someone not affiliated with the medical field. A stockbroker, if he remembered correctly.

He picked up the phone and dialed the number Bertha had provided. Maggie answered on the third ring.

The familiar sound of her voice caused him to smile. "Maggie, it's Michael."

"Hi." She sighed, and he detected weariness in her voice. "I'm glad you called."

He knew better than to quiz her. She'd get to the point soon enough, but his curiosity was significantly piqued.

"I'm contemplating a relocation of my practice," she said.

The comment struck him as odd. Doctors didn't relocate thriving practices without a great deal of thought and a compelling reason. He, of all people, knew that. "Why are you considering a move?"

She sighed, showing evidence of a heavy dilemma. "Tom and I separated a couple of months ago."

So her decision was on a personal level. "I'm sorry."

"Well, I don't need to cry on your shoulder, although I'm sure you understand at least part of what I'm going through."

"I suppose it's never easy," he said.

"Tom found someone else. I think it would have been easier to deal with if she'd been another stockbroker or someone from the secretarial pool in his office. But no, he had to choose another pediatrician in my office."

"I'm sorry," he said.

"Me, too." She sniffled, and he suspected she was wiping the tears from her eyes. God, how he hated a woman's tears. He thought of Kara, and his heart twisted. Two in one day. What were the odds of that?

"And what's worse, they're expecting a baby next month."

Michael ran a hand through his hair. His heart went out to his old friend and classmate. She didn't deserve a blow like that. "I'm sorry, Maggie. What can I do to help?"

"Not much, I'm afraid, but I think relocating across the country might help. Can you give me the name of a top-notch pediatric group that could use a new doctor?"

"A brilliant, compassionate, new doctor," Michael corrected. "Give me a week or so. I haven't been practicing much since Denise's trial, but I'll make a few phone calls and see what I can do."

"Don't tell me *you're* cutting back on your patient load. Sounds like you need a friend."

A friend? He needed more than that, although he wasn't sure who or what. He thought of Kara, her friendly smile, her loving heart. The way her kisses fired his soul.

No, not Kara. Someone from the medical field, someone who would understand him and his passionate dedication to his career. Someone like a brilliant, compassionate pediatrician planning to relocate her practice.

Having Maggie move out to Los Angeles suddenly seemed like a very good idea. Something that would benefit them both. "Yeah, I can use a friend, and it sounds as though you can, too. I've missed you."

"Well, find me a place to practice, and I'll be packed before you know it."

"Take care, Maggie. You're a survivor. I'll call you next week."

"It was good just hearing your voice, Michael. Thanks."

After the call ended, Michael continued to stare at the telephone. He couldn't help but think that his life had taken an interesting turn.

Kara took two of the many small candles that decorated her bathroom and placed them on the table next to the peach-colored roses displayed in a mason jar. Certainly not fancy, but she liked the effect.

She glanced at the clock. Nearly seven. Michael would be coming soon, before she left for Lizzie's. He said he'd bring the fixings for dinner, which was a good thing. Had he not come up with the idea to share his spaghetti dinner, she would have invited him later in the week, after she'd gone grocery shopping.

The house was clean and tidy. She'd showered and, after trying five different outfits, scolded herself for being silly. She settled on a pair of jeans and a cream-colored sweatshirt. This wasn't a date, and she certainly didn't intend to entice her neighbor into thinking it was something more. She caught her reflection in the mirror that adorned the small dining area of a home that was little more than a studio apartment in size.

Definitely not the apparel of a vamp. Still, she'd taken

a great deal of time on her hair, pulling the sides away from her face and into two gold barrettes. Heart barrettes, she realized with a gasp. Would he think she…

Get a grip, Kara, she reprimanded herself. *Friends don't walk on eggshells around each other. And men don't read meaning into the hair clips women wear.* This was a laid back evening. Jeans and sweatshirts. Spaghetti and garlic bread. Friends and neighbors.

She strode toward the built-in teakwood buffet and turned on the portable radio that served as her entertainment center. Playing with the dial, she finally located a station that played soft hits.

A knock sounded at the door, and she jumped. What in the world had her so edgy? she wondered, as the romantic words of a love song registered. Too romantic. She quickly flipped the switch, turning off the radio and the inappropriate mood music, and went to the door.

She expected to see Michael, so his presence on her front porch didn't surprise her. But her reaction, a flutter in her tummy and a pulse that kicked into overdrive, caused her a great deal of alarm.

Surely it was just the aftershave he wore, a musky woodland blend. Or the fact that he looked endearingly awkward as he juggled two paper bags and a bottle of wine.

''Are you going to let me come in before I drop something?'' he asked, brown eyes glimmering and lips curling in a boyish grin.

''Of course.'' She stepped to the side, hoping he hadn't thought she was gawking at him. Because that's what she'd been doing. And her heart was still zipping around in her chest.

He wore a pair of worn Levi's and a chambray shirt with the cuffs rolled up to reveal well-developed forearms. His jeans fit as though he'd been born to wear them. His mere presence filled her small home, giving it an added vitality. He sauntered into the kitchen and un-packed his brown bags as though he made spaghetti every day.

She couldn't help but smile.

He glanced up as he held the bottle of red wine. "What's so funny?"

"Nothing really. You just seem so…" *At home.*

She bit her lip and tried to come up with an alternative observation. The only thing she could think of was how handsome he looked, how different her home felt with him inside, but she couldn't share that, either.

"I seem so what?" he asked, placing the bottle on the countertop.

"You seem so…competent."

He raised a brow. "And what's funny about that?"

"Nothing." She joined him in the kitchen and began to open cupboards. "Do you need me to show you where anything is?"

"I'll find whatever I need. Don't you have kids to kiss good-night?"

"Yes," she said, gathering her wits for the first time since he entered the house. "If you'll be all right without me, I'll go now."

He placed the bags and the wine on the countertop, then pulled out a loaf of French bread. "I'll be fine," he said, crossing those well-defined forearms and giving her a lazy smile. "Take your time. The spaghetti sauce will take at least an hour."

Eager to slip away, Kara nodded.

Each evening she gave Eric and Ashley her undivided attention. The effort had always been easy, but tonight she wasn't so sure. She feared her thoughts would drift to the handsome man she'd left in her kitchen.

Long after Kara had closed the front door, Michael stared at the empty living room. He had closets in the guest bedrooms of his house that were bigger than the living area of this cottage. He didn't remember ever being inside a room so humble yet so warm. Each piece of mismatched furniture, each throw pillow and picture frame was placed with care. An ambience filled the room. Like Kara, her home bore a beautiful simplicity that touched his heart.

The entry to his and Denise's home had boasted a marbled foyer and a crystal chandelier. The house, like his marriage, had been cold. Uninviting.

After his wife's arrest, he'd hired a Beverly Hills decorator to make changes. It had cost what he guessed might be an EZ Suds fortune to rid himself of reminders of Denise, yet warmth was still lacking.

He glanced at the table where his roses sat in a glass jar surrounded by candles. Humble, yet beautiful. He shook his head, amazed at what Kara had done with so little, then prodded himself to get busy. She'd be back before he knew it, and he wanted the spaghetti sauce simmering, the red wine uncorked and ready.

Suddenly, he wanted the meal to be special. As special as Kara and her modest little house.

By the time she returned, the scent of spaghetti sauce filled the air. Michael stood in the tiny kitchen, preparing a salad of romaine lettuce, cherry tomatoes and cucumbers.

"It smells delicious," she said, closing the front door.

"Thanks." He watched her move through the house as though she were the guest and not him. He noted a wariness in her eyes and a timidity in her step, like a doe easing her way into a meadow. Alert and cautious. Gentle and beautiful. As she passed the worn, floral printed sofa, she ran a hand along the overstuffed cushions that lined the back.

"Did you get the kids tucked in?" he asked, hoping to dispel her uneasiness.

She smiled, and the shyness left her face. "It's my favorite part of the evening, the time of day when everything is put into perspective. Do you have any idea how comforting it is to rock a baby to sleep, to hear a child's prayers and feel two small arms wrapped around your neck?"

He didn't, he supposed, although holding Ashley in the ER had come close. He recalled the softness of her small body in his arms, the tap of her little foot against his thigh, the milk-laced smile she'd flashed him before drifting to sleep. "You make it sound as though I'm missing something," he said, wondering for the first time in his thirty-six years if he actually was. It didn't seem possible.

She gazed at him in that impish way, head tilted to the side, sea-blue eyes twinkling, small hands on denim-clad hips. "You haven't been around kids much, have you?"

Although he wasn't a pediatric cardiovascular surgeon, he was called in on some of the more critical cases. But the children he was familiar with were seriously ill, severely injured or in recovery. It wasn't the same.

"Not really," he admitted.

She looked at him as though he'd been remiss. "Don't you plan on having kids of your own?"

He shrugged, a bit surprised by the question. He and Denise had never talked of having children. Quite frankly, he hadn't given it much thought. He'd been too busy building his practice. And Denise, he supposed, had been too selfish to want a baby.

Or maybe she just hadn't wanted his baby. He didn't really know. The idea was a bit foreign, he had to admit, but the thought of his kid toddling around had an interesting appeal. "I suppose having a child warrants consideration."

"Boy or girl?" she asked, apparently intent upon probing and pushing him to exercise his imagination in a direction it had never wandered.

"I don't know—one of each might be nice." As the words hovered in the air around him, he had to admit the thought had some merit. Of course, he'd need a wife— one who would be loyal to him, with strong maternal instincts. Because if he did choose to have kids, they wouldn't be shipped off to exclusive boarding schools. And they wouldn't have an army of ever-changing nannies to watch over them, like he had. He'd never do that to a child of his own.

"I want five or six," she said, her expression lighting up with something wistful yet vital. "Of course, I'll settle for two—Eric and Ashley."

Kara would be a wonderful mother. He envisioned her driving a minivan and cheering on the sidelines at soccer games. She'd rock her babies and sing them lullabies. The image brought a wistful smile. "Those kids would be lucky to have you for a mom."

"Thanks," she said, hope dancing in her eyes. Then she made her way to the kitchen and neared the pot simmering on the stove. "Can I help?"

He caught the scent of melon, of something faintly tropical. As she tiptoed to peek into the pot, he struggled with an inane urge to lift her. Or was it an urge to get his hands on her, to pull her close? The intimacy of the small kitchen stirred something domestic, something strangely romantic in his soul. Whose idea had this been, anyway? Domestic intimacy with Kara was the last thing he needed.

She elbowed him in the ribs, playfully, he supposed, but it jolted his attention to the simmering pot of tomatoes, garlic and basil. "I asked if I could help."

"Yeah," he said, his voice a bit sappy. "Why don't you butter the bread?"

"Sure." She reached for the loaf of French bread that rested on the counter and went to work.

Michael managed to get the pasta boiled to perfection,

the table set and the garlic bread toasted just right, although he wasn't sure how. Each time he stole a glance at Kara, he battled an increasing attraction, in spite of the oversize sweatshirt that couldn't begin to conceal her femininity. Somehow, he managed to get the meal on the table.

The soft glow of candlelight danced in the gold highlights of her hair, reminding him of fire and precious metal. As they sat across from each other, an odd sense of contentment swept over him. He lifted a water glass half full of an expensive Merlot. ''To the serendipity of friendship,'' he said, toasting the interesting twist of fate that had sent a special young lady into his life.

She lifted her glass, one that didn't match the one he held, and instigated the perfunctory clink. The dull sound of everyday glass instead of the resonant tinkle of crystal didn't dim the brightness of her smile or lessen the elegance of the gesture. He would remember this meal as simple but special. And definitely one of the best he'd ever had.

As they feasted on spaghetti and marinara, Kara drew Michael's attention, captivating him with the lilt of her voice, the sparkle of her eyes, the warmth of her smile. He hadn't wanted the meal to come to an end.

''How about some music as we clean up,'' Kara suggested. She pushed her chair from the table and strode to the teakwood buffet, where a portable radio rested.

She fumbled with the dial until she found a jazz station, then paused in reflection. She flashed him a fey smile before changing the channel. ''I better find something else. I've always had a whistle-while-you-work attitude.''

But Michael didn't give a hoot about whistling. Or working. Or cleaning up.

All he could think of was the beauty of the woman

standing before him in a sweatshirt that bore a sprinkle of spaghetti sauce. He stood, but not to clear the table.

Instead, he joined her by the old radio that had probably provided music for two decades or more. He reached for the yellow plastic knob and found the jazz station she'd passed.

"Dance with me." He lifted his arms and watched her eyes widen, her teeth nibble her bottom lip. It seemed like forever before she offered him that impish smile and stepped into his embrace.

They swayed to the seductive sounds of a sax, hearts beating in time and breaths mingling. He stood nearly a foot taller than her, yet their bodies fit together in an interesting way—soft and hard, gentle and strong.

When the music ended and the deejay began to play another soulful tune, Michael knew he should let go, step away. Clear the table, do something to get his thoughts back on track, but all he wanted to do was hold her close, nuzzle into her hair and lift her mouth to his.

Despite reason, and in spite of his resolve to maintain a platonic, neighborly relationship, desire for this vibrant young woman shot to his core. If he didn't kiss her senseless, the reason would be hers alone, because at this moment all he could do was lose himself in her.

He brushed her hair aside and caught her cheek in his hand. Lifting her face, he searched her eyes for reluctance or disapproval.

Instead, he found passion in those teal-blue pools. When she slipped her arms around his neck and raised parted lips to his, he was lost in a mindless, emotional rush that threatened to carry him away.

And for some completely irrational reason, he didn't care to save himself.

Chapter Nine

Kara knew kissing Michael was the wrong thing to do. But when he held her in his arms, when they swayed to the sensual strains of a lazy saxophone, she found herself overwhelmed by his musky, male scent. All she wanted was to kiss him, taste him and experience the strength of arousal, the power of sexual need.

Until their first kiss, she'd only read about passion in the romance novels she occasionally found time to read. It would be a long time before she could allow herself the luxury of a romantic relationship. What would it hurt to experience a bit of what she'd only imagined?

When his lips touched hers, she melded into him in a move so unlike her, she felt possessed by someone else, someone desirable and wanton, someone who hadn't held onto her virginity because it was all she possessed and controlled.

He thrust his tongue into her mouth, but instead of a shy, tentative response, her tongue boldly sought his. The other kisses they'd shared had begun softly and gently before growing into something deep and sexually charged; this one was different. It began with raw need, with hands touching, stroking, grasping for more.

Michael's hand slipped under her sweatshirt. His fingers, splayed on her skin, sent ripples of heat to her heart and soul. She'd never had anyone touch her so intimately, yet instead of pulling away, calling a halt to the mind-tingling exploration, she lifted an arm and turned just enough to allow him freedom to touch, tease, tantalize her further. Never had she imagined a man's caress could release such desire, such heat. His fingers nimbly searched for the snap that held her lacy bra together, and as it opened, freeing her breasts to his touch, her nipples hardened in response.

Stop him, reason whispered.

Not yet, passion countered.

His mouth released its hungry hold of hers, and he trailed kisses along her jaw to a sensitive spot below her ear. All the while his hands explored her breasts. His thumbs circled her nipples until they hardened and ached with need.

In an instant, her sweatshirt was slipped over her head, and she stood before him, bare except for the dangling lace bra that hung from her shoulders.

Cover yourself.

Not until you learn what happens next.

He knelt before her and took a nipple into his mouth. His tongue circled the pebbled knob. Her knees buckled, and she whimpered softly.

''Kara,'' he whispered in near reverence, his voice husky.

She relished the sound of her name upon his lips, lips that promised to unlock precious, primal secrets she had yet to learn. Secrets she hadn't allowed herself to dream of, let alone explore.

What had gotten into her? How had she let things progress this far? She wanted to kneel before him, lower them both to the floor, beg him to show her the things lovers knew.

Lovers.

She and Michael.

As glorious as that might be, for this moment, for this evening, she couldn't allow it to go on. She wasn't Michael's lover, nor could she allow herself to be. Not until she had secured custody of Eric and Ashley.

She placed her hands upon his shoulders and pushed herself free of his tantalizing mouth, his expert touch. "I'm sorry. I can't... I shouldn't have..."

Michael released her and blew out a long, weathered breath. "I'm the one who's sorry. I don't usually lose control like that."

"Neither do I," she said, trying to cover her tingling breasts with a bra that suddenly seemed too small. Her fingers trembled, and she fumbled with the snap.

Before she could stoop to pick up her discarded sweatshirt from the floor, she realized he held the garment in his hands. Their eyes locked, and he handed it to her.

She clutched the sweatshirt to her heart. "We came close to making love, didn't we?"

He nodded. "Yeah. Right here on the living room floor. You deserve better."

Better than the floor? Or better than him? She had her doubts about the latter.

Still on his knees, he furrowed his brow. "That was an odd question you asked. You knew how close we were, didn't you?"

"I guess so." She slipped the sweatshirt over her head, yet she still felt vulnerable, naked before him.

He took her hand in his, his gaze steady and piercing. "Kara, have you ever made love before?"

She nibbled her lip and shook her head. "No."

He plowed a hand through his hair, then studied her in a bewildered manner.

"What's the matter?" She couldn't see how her virginity should be an issue, especially since she had no intention of having a sexual relationship with him anyway—not that her recent behavior was a clue. She certainly hadn't acted like a woman determined to keep her distance.

He sat on his heels and studied her for a moment, then slowly got to his feet. "I've never made love to a virgin before."

"Well, I guess you still haven't," she said, trying to garner a smile and make light of an awkward situation that left her stunned and surprisingly aware of both her femininity and her sexuality. Her uncharacteristically sensual response was, she suspected, due to curiosity more than anything—well, that and the devastating rush she experienced at his touch. His kiss was heady, that was for sure. She hoped he didn't think she was a tease. "I apologize for leading you on. I don't suppose it was virginal behavior, but there's something about the way you kiss me that makes me lose track of good sense."

Flattered that he had the same mindless effect on Kara that she had on him, Michael wanted to pound his chest in some egocentric, primeval act, but remained civilized—at least on the outside. "I'm glad I'm not the only one swept away by the heat of the moment."

"In spite of what just happened, I meant what I said about a relationship. The kids are my priority."

As they should be. God knew Michael wanted nothing more than to wrap Kara in his arms, carry her to bed and introduce her to passion and desire. But morning would come, and he couldn't promise her forever, which was something a woman like Kara needed. What she more than deserved.

The image of a sex-crazed young intern crept into his conscience, and he didn't like it. She'd just admitted to being a virgin, for God's sake. A pure and innocent woman. "When the time comes for you to have that relationship, I hope you find someone special to share yourself with." *Someone who can offer you more than I can give.*

She smiled, granting him a brief glimpse of a magic he'd never experienced before and didn't think he merited. "If I didn't have Ashley and Eric to think about—"

He cupped her face with both hands, interrupting her words. He didn't know what she was going to say, going to suggest, but he wouldn't allow her to lose her virginity on the living room floor to a man who wouldn't—couldn't—be more than a brief affair or a passing fancy. The reality of their situation slapped over him like a wet blanket. "Kara, the man who makes love to you will be a very lucky man."

"I wish it could be you and now," she said, her voice soft, her eyes sincere and hopeful.

Thoughts of making love to Kara stole into his conscience and clobbered his senses. *It's only sexual desire, simple biology,* he tried to tell himself, but something mushy and sappy happened to him whenever he was near Kara. It made him uneasy.

Since childhood, he'd learned to shove emotions back into the far recesses of his mind. It was the only way he could manage to live far from home, from his family. It was how he detached himself from his patients in order to give them the best medical care he could.

"I wish it could be me, too, sweetheart, but that's not going to happen." He gave her a brief kiss on the cheek meant to diffuse the sexually charged ions bouncing in the atmosphere. Instead, it did something strange to his racing heart. "I've got to go home."

She nodded. "I understand."

Did she? How could she when he didn't understand a damn thing himself? He gave her a quick hug, then strode for the door. It was only when he reached the privacy of his cottage that he realized he'd left her to clean up the mess.

But he had a hell of a mess to clean up himself, and it didn't have anything to do with dirty pots, pans and dishes.

He reprimanded himself for wallowing in his thoughts. He just needed to get laid, and as much as he wanted a physical relationship with Kara, it wouldn't do either of them any good. Kara needed a guy who could promise forever. And Michael needed a hot, no-strings-attached relationship with someone like him.

Someone like Maggie.

But thoughts of pretty Kara danced in his head and kept him tossing and turning until dawn.

Michael decided it was best to avoid Kara, a decision that lasted all morning and well into the afternoon.

He'd taken a long, early morning walk along the shore, where he'd come to the conclusion that his days in Harbor Haven were over. He would return to Los Angeles this afternoon.

He still dreaded facing the press that had hounded him, but maybe with the support of a respected pediatrician, the reporters and cameramen would finally realize his life was no longer interesting, his past just that—behind him. When he returned to the cottage, he placed several calls, the last of which struck gold.

Dr. Henry Rayburn, an acclaimed pediatrician, planned to retire in three months, and the Pacific Pediatric Medical Group was looking for a top-notch doctor to replace him. With Michael's recommendation and Maggie's qualifications, her search was over. He called her in Boston to give her the news.

"I can't wait to get out of town," she said, and he knew exactly what she meant. Her husband's affair with another doctor in her practice hadn't been easy to deal with, and the sooner she could leave her troubles in Boston, the better. Who, more than Michael, understood that?

He told Maggie he'd send his jet for her, but she refused. She did, however, agree to stay at his house until she'd acclimated to Southern California and found a place to live.

Maggie, with her friendly smile and bright blue eyes, was sure to liven his surroundings. Maybe he'd actually look forward to going home after work again.

After he and Denise had married, she'd grown increasingly resentful of his dedication to his medical practice, and quite frankly, he'd gotten tired of listening to her complaints. He found excuses to stay at the hospital instead of going home.

As Michael packed what few clothes he had purchased in Harbor Haven into a shopping bag, he grinned wryly. He had a closet full of Louis Vuitton luggage at his house in Los Angeles.

Paper bags, mason jar vases, a secret tree house and a pretty redhead who relished the simple things in life—this visit to Harbor Haven had given him a glimpse of reality. As much as he enjoyed the respite, he had a practice to return to. And Kara had her own game plan.

He'd miss her and figured she'd probably miss him, too, but the sooner he left, the better for both of them. She had every intention of creating a family of her own—one that certainly didn't include Michael.

A flying soccer ball interrupted his solitude. It bounced onto the porch and slammed against the living room window; the glass didn't break, but the entire cottage shuddered.

He left the brown bag on the bed and went to the front door. Stepping onto the porch, he spotted a wide-eyed Eric climbing the steps to retrieve the ball.

"Sorry, Michael," the boy said. "I don't kick so good with my bad leg, so I was using the other one. And Kara said maybe we should practice more, and the ball wasn't s'pose to go near your house, and…"

"Kara's right, sport." Michael retrieved the ball and handed it to Eric. "Your aim will get much better with practice."

The boy seemed relieved that he met with understanding rather than a scolding, then he smiled happily. "Hey, why don't you play with us? I don't want Kara to feel bad, but she's a girl. And even though some girls, like Christy Colwell, can kick better than any boy in my class, Kara never played soccer before. We're learning together, and I thought maybe you could—"

Eric paused, shuffled his feet, then looked at Michael with such hopeful eyes he couldn't bear to tell the boy no. Michael glanced at Kara, who waited patiently near a makeshift goal that was marked by two rocks.

She wore blue jeans and a long-sleeve flannel shirt. Her hair, tousled by the wind, gave her a wild, playful appearance. As much as he'd like to ignore her, he couldn't help wanting to join in the fun. But did she want him to join her soccer class?

Even from the porch, he could see a pink tint to her cheeks. From exertion or embarrassment, he couldn't be sure. The passion they'd experienced last night had left them both awkward and apologetic, but he doubted either one of them wanted to end their special friendship.

He just needed to put some physical distance between them, which was going to happen this afternoon. What would it hurt to be near her—one last time?

Michael glanced at the bright-eyed child standing before him. "You don't suppose the girl will mind if you bring in a ringer, do you?"

Eric cocked his head. "What's a ringer?"

"It's like a pinch hitter in baseball," he explained. Michael had played both rugby and soccer at the elite boarding school he'd attended, but once he went to college, a serious and professional attitude toward his medical career afforded him little time for sports. Or for recreation of any kind, for that matter.

"Kara's really cool, for a girl. She's nice to cats and stray dogs and everything. She won't mind if you play." Eric turned to Kara. "Guess what? Michael's going to play, too. Now I'll really get better at kicking, and I won't be the last kid chosen when they pick teams at recess."

Kara, cheeks still rosy, brushed a strand of copper-colored hair from her face, then smiled. "I don't suppose you could coach us? It's important for us to improve our skill."

Michael was struck by Kara's enthusiastic support of the boy. He doubted the court could find a better mother for the kids than her. And at that moment, he decided to do whatever he could to support her efforts to become their guardian—money, legal representation, a letter on her behalf. Those kids would be Kara's forever, if that's what she wanted.

As Michael began showing Kara and Eric the drills he'd learned years ago, he noticed Eric's uneven gait. A limp, once slight, became more pronounced as the practice progressed, but the boy never once complained. Michael refrained from asking Kara more about the injury, but studied the boy while they played. One of Eric's legs was shorter than the other.

He wondered what kind of orthopedic problems they'd encountered, what treatments they'd used, what follow-up they intended. Before he left Harbor Haven, he'd talk to Dr. Weldon—possibly offer his help in locating a specialist who might give a second opinion.

Michael called a halt to the practice, realizing the boy's determination to master the sport wouldn't allow him to ask for rest.

"Gosh, Michael," Eric said, his breath coming in short spurts. "You sure know a lot about soccer. Thanks for helping me. I can't wait to show the kids at school how good I'm getting."

Within the last forty-five minutes, Eric's aim had dramatically improved, and Michael felt an odd sense of satisfaction he hadn't expected. He smiled and gently ruffled the top of Eric's sandy-blond hair. "You'll be playing like a champ in no time, if you keep practicing those drills I taught you."

"We will, won't we, Kara?"

She gave the boy a hug, then smiled warmly at Michael. "I don't know how to thank you."

Interestingly, Kara's skill had improved, too. She listened avidly to everything Michael suggested, and although she wasn't athletic in the classic sense of the word, she had gumption—as his favorite nanny used to say. Admiration for Kara wasn't the only thing that continued to grow. So did attraction, which was something he damn well better put aside.

"Eric," Kara said, glancing at her wristwatch. "It's nearly dinnertime. You better go wash up."

"All right." The boy turned to Michael. "Thanks again for helping me. Can you play again tomorrow?"

Something tugged at Michael's heart. He didn't want to disappoint the kid, but this was the last day he'd be in town. "I'm going home this afternoon."

Eric, visibly saddened, bit his bottom lip. "Gee, just when we were getting to be best friends."

Michael smiled. "Hey, sport, we can still be friends. I'll give you my telephone number."

"That's not the same," the boy said, kicking at the ground with his good leg.

No, it wasn't, Michael realized. He recalled another boy not much older than Eric, complaining to his father over the telephone when the other kids had gone home from boarding school for turkey dinner.

Why did I have to stay here? It's Thanksgiving.

Son, I have business in Paris. Your mother and I won't be home until December first. That's why I called—to wish you a happy Thanksgiving.

It's not the same.

The boy was right, and Michael glanced at Kara for help.

Kara could see Michael was struggling to explain why he wouldn't be able to cultivate a friendship with Eric. It was the same reason, or at least one of the same reasons, she and Michael couldn't pursue a relationship with each other. They had separate lives.

Last night, she'd lain awake for a long time, thinking about the magic she'd felt in Michael's arms, imagining what it would be like to make love to him. She wished she hadn't had such a compelling reason for telling him no. And when sleep finally came, she'd dreamed that they'd actually made love, first on the floor, then in her bed. Morning had found her hugging her pillow. And feeling very much alone.

"Why do you have to go?" Eric asked.

"I have responsibilities in Los Angeles," Michael said, his gaze catching hers and asking for assistance in explaining to Eric.

As much as she knew how difficult goodbyes were for adults, she realized it was even more of a blow to a child who had already lost his two most vital relationships. She garnered a smile and pulled Eric close. "You knew Michael was only visiting Harbor Haven. Maybe he'll come back for his next vacation.''

''Sure,'' Michael said, but his expression told Kara he hadn't intended to return.

''Eric, why don't you go on inside before Lizzie has to call you. By the time dinner's ready, you'll be all washed and ready.''

''Okay,'' the boy said, then he turned and limped toward his house.

Kara blew out the breath she hadn't realized she'd been holding, then turned to Michael and offered a grateful smile. ''We both appreciate your help.''

Michael only nodded, his eyes on Eric's progress toward the house. When the door closed behind the boy, he faced Kara. ''Tell me about his injury.''

''I told you about the car accident. He cracked his pelvis and suffered some severe lacerations to his left leg. It's amazing how he managed to get his sister out of the car seat and to the side of the road. That's the part that amazed the doctors and the public.''

''Who was the attending physician?''

She tilted her head, surprised by his serious questions until she remembered that he worked at a hospital. He obviously had a medical background and would be interested in the details of the case. ''Dr. Weldon was the attending doctor, and he called in an orthopedic surgeon. We were told Eric would gradually regain the full use of his leg, but things were up in the air for a while.''

Michael, more serious than Kara had ever seen him, nodded slowly and pensively. ''And the limp?''

''Well, he was in a wheelchair for a while, then crutches. His limp progressively got better, or so it seemed. I haven't seen much improvement lately, and in fact, it might be worse. I'll talk to Dr. Weldon about it, but it may be that Eric is more active now, and so it just seems to be worse.''

Michael stroked his chin, the furrow of his brow still prominent. "I'd like to have a friend of mine examine him."

"A friend?"

"Dr. David Cunningham. He's a renowned pediatric orthopedic surgeon based in Boston and top in his field."

"Wow," Kara said. "How do you know him?"

"We went to school together."

High school? College? She realized how little she knew of this man. "Which school?"

"Harvard Medical School."

Harvard? Medical school? Kara swallowed hard. Was Michael a doctor? He'd said he worked at a hospital. She glanced at the blue sedan in the parking lot. Maybe he hadn't graduated. It seemed to her that a doctor should drive a better car than that, although she supposed he could be rather eccentric. Or maybe his practice was floundering.

"You're a doctor?" she asked.

"Yes."

His response provided more questions than answers. Who was this man who had stolen her heart?

Her heart? Kara crossed her arms. He hadn't stolen her heart, not really. She was just enamored by his touch, by the kisses that drove her wild. Surely what she felt for Michael was more physical attraction than anything.

Kara would really need to know a man in order to fall in love, and she certainly didn't know Michael very well at all. He had plenty of secrets. Too many of them, and the fact he'd kept them from her hurt something fierce.

Did he think she couldn't be trusted? Or did he consider her so transient in his life that he didn't bother saying anything? Her eyes sought his. "Why didn't you tell me?"

"Tell you what?" he asked, as though he really didn't have a clue about what information he'd withheld.

"Why didn't you tell me you were a doctor?" she asked, then suddenly felt odd for questioning him. What difference did it make what this visitor did for a living? He was only a temporary neighbor—something she'd known all along. "I'm sorry. I suppose it doesn't matter."

"I didn't mean to be deceitful, but I wanted some time alone, some time to think. So, for that reason, I haven't been entirely honest." He sighed, then glanced toward the sea, as though calling upon some nautical force to bolster him before explaining. "I'm Dr. Michael Harper, although I'm surprised you don't recognize me."

Kara furrowed her brow and studied the man before her. Was she supposed to recognize him? As her mind spun into overdrive, trying to pin a name to the face, recognition struck like an unexpected wave that nearly knocked her to her knees. "The doctor whose wife laundered illegal campaign funds through his medical office?"

His jaw tensed. "One and the same."

He'd mentioned an ex-wife but hadn't gone into detail. Now Kara knew why. The woman, who was also his office manager, had been having an affair with a candidate for the United States Senate. Kara didn't suppose that was something he liked to remember. "I don't watch television or have much time to read the newspaper, but I've heard about you. I guess I just didn't expect someone famous to show up in Harbor Haven."

A glimpse of anger crossed his face, but pain lingered in his gaze. "That wasn't the kind of fame I wanted. For some reason, the press has dogged me and made it next to impossible for me to practice medicine. I hoped to disappear long enough for someone else to catch the public eye."

From what she understood, Michael's fame had been well deserved due to his surgical skill and medical missions of mercy to Third World countries, but that wasn't the focus of the tabloids. Handsome Wealthy Heir Couldn't Keep His Wife Happy was one of the recent headlines she remembered reading in the checkout line at the grocery store.

As for not satisfying his wife, Kara wouldn't believe that claim for a minute. If the kisses she'd shared with him were any indication of his sexual ability, his wife was a fool for more reasons than one.

Kara hadn't taken the time to study the photograph or read the article, but she could imagine how the publicity had hurt him. Her heart went out to him. She touched his cheek, the bristles lightly scratching her fingers. He hadn't shaved this morning, and she wondered why. Had he been as distracted by memories of their intimacy last night as she had?

She quickly dismissed the frivolous thought. "I hope you can get back to work soon and that your visit to Harbor Haven gave you the break you needed."

He placed a hand on hers, clasping it against his cheek. "Thanks, Kara."

"Well," she said, breaking eye contact and pulling her hand away. "When will you be leaving?"

He crossed his arms. "First, I'm going to call David Cunningham and set up an appointment for Eric."

"But you said he practiced in Boston," Kara said. "How—"

"I'm having my pilot bring my jet to Palomar Airport. I'm taking you all to Boston."

Boston? On his jet? A flood of emotions swept over Kara, gratitude competing with a growing sense of turmoil.

Chapter Ten

Kara sat on Lizzie's couch and listened while Michael told the older woman who he was. He hadn't yet announced his plan to secure a second opinion for Eric when a look of disbelief crossed the older woman's face, and she fumbled for the glasses that hung from a gold cord she wore around her neck.

Lizzie slipped them on, then carefully got to her feet and, her steps slowed by the arthritis that plagued her, walked closer to the overstuffed chair on which Michael sat. Bending close, in a movement Kara would have normally found comical, the older woman examined Michael carefully, then slapped her hands upon her thighs. "Well, I'll be darned. You're really him."

Michael smiled, as though not offended by her scrutiny. "I've made an appointment with David Cunningham, one of the leading pediatric orthopedic surgeons in the country. David is on vacation in Europe, but he agreed to see Eric as soon as he returns to Boston."

"Boston?" Lizzie asked.

Michael nodded. "I asked him whether he could come out here, but his schedule will be unusually heavy when he gets home, so Eric will have to go back East."

Lizzie shook her head, and her shoulders slumped. "Michael, that's very nice of you to go to the trouble of calling your friend, but even if we had the money to pay the specialist, we can't afford to travel across the country."

"There won't be any cost," Michael said. "I'll fly you all to Boston in my jet. And David wouldn't think of charging you a dime."

Lizzie placed a hand upon her chest. "This is too good to be true." Then she turned to Kara. "Isn't it, honey?"

Kara took a deep breath, suddenly finding it difficult to breathe in the small room. As much as she wanted Eric to have the finest medical care available, talk of flying across the country in Michael's private plane made her uneasy. And she didn't have the slightest idea why. "It's wonderful, Lizzie."

As Lizzie made her way to the sofa, she paused in midstep. "Oh, dear. I don't think Dr. Weldon will let me fly."

"Let me talk to Weldon," Michael said. "I'll see what he has to say. Maybe he won't mind, since I'll be traveling with you."

Tears formed in Lizzie's tired blue eyes, and she wiped them with the back of her hands. "Bless you, Doctor. You're an answer to prayer."

"If you give me Dr. Weldon's number, I'll let him know what we've been discussing."

While Lizzie searched for her address book, Kara studied the man seated across from her, a man she'd kissed intimately, a man she thought she knew. Admiration for him grew steadily, but so did apprehension.

Sure, she was thrilled to know Eric would be examined

by a prominent surgeon Lizzie couldn't afford and state aid didn't provide, but she was also racked by other emotions. She had nearly lost her head, not to mention her heart and virginity, over a man who was way above her in financial means and social status.

Like smoke snaking through a keyhole, the cruel words of Jason Baker's mother came back to taunt her, reminding Kara of the indigent background she'd never tried to hide and of the false accusations the wealthy matron had hurled at her.

Dating my son is quite an opportunity for you, isn't it?

Kara's stomach twisted. Thank goodness she hadn't allowed herself to fall in love with Michael. She had a feeling Michael's wealth made the EZ Suds fortune seem like a cash-filled coffee can buried in the backyard.

Michael smiled, warm and steady, and she tried to return it. Her friendship with Michael, stronger than any she had ever experienced, was plagued by insecurity and self-doubt. The only thing that kept her from running out the door was the knowledge that she'd refused an intimate relationship with him. Now, more than ever, she needed to keep her distance.

No one would ever be able to say she was after Michael for his money.

Michael had returned home to place his phone call to Dr. Weldon. He wanted the freedom to discuss both Eric's and Lizzie's cases openly.

Weldon said Eric's recovery was not progressing as they had hoped. He had intended to suggest a return visit to the orthopedic surgeon who had done the original surgery. Weldon apparently kept up with the medical journals, because he was aware of some of David's successes.

"Do you have a problem with Lizzie making the

trip?'' Michael asked. "I'll stay close and keep an eye on her."

"I'd rather she use the time to relax," Weldon said. "Her health is more tenuous than Kara knows or Lizzie will admit—hypertension, diabetes, asthma, heart disease."

"Either one is serious within itself."

"It's only a matter of time before she has to give up custody of those kids—either because of hospitalization or death. Another doctor who wasn't so personally involved would probably be more insistent. But Eric, in particular, needs the emotional stability Lizzie represents. That's what his therapist tells me, and I tend to agree. The accident was an awful blow for the boy. He saved his sister's life but was unable to help either of the parents. For some reason, the boy carries a load of guilt."

"What about Kara?" Michael asked. He figured she'd offer the kids stability when Lizzie could no longer assume full responsibility.

"Kara's a godsend. You'll never meet a nicer young woman. Good with the kids and loyal to Lizzie. They've become a family of sorts, and it's only because of Kara's active involvement with the child care that I've not forced the issue of Lizzie taking a much needed break."

"Then I'll take the kids and Kara to Boston."

"Sounds like a good plan to me," Weldon said. "I'll drop by daily to check on Lizzie while you're gone."

Again, Michael was struck by the older man's concern for his patients. "Not many physicians make house calls anymore. I admire you for it."

"Well, I'm from the old school, I guess. My father was a doctor, and his father before him. I practice medicine the way in which I've seen it work best."

Michael supposed so. And it appeared there were a few things he could learn from the old-school family physician. "Thanks, Doctor. I'll keep you updated on what we learn in Boston."

"By the way," Weldon said. "Those kids are lucky to have Kara. She's devoted to them."

"I've noticed," Michael said. Kara would be the kind of mom who'd be home when her kids came in from school, who'd find time to talk to them about their day, about their hopes and dreams. She'd be the kind who would make cookies on rainy days and allow friends to come over and play. Things like that were important to kids. They sure would have been to Michael when he was Eric's age. "Kara will be a great mother to those kids."

"A man would be lucky to have her, too."

Michael didn't speak for a moment, his thoughts perilously close to those Weldon had just uttered. Kara deserved a man who came home from work at the same time each day, a man who would help her tuck the kids into bed each night, who'd coach soccer on Saturdays while she cheered on the sidelines. "A man would be damn lucky to have Kara for a wife, Weldon, but I'm not that man, if that's what you're suggesting."

Weldon laughed. "I'm not suggesting anything of the kind."

Wasn't he? Michael wasn't so sure, but the fact that his own thoughts had easily wandered in that direction didn't sit well with him. He'd make a lousy husband for a young woman who deserved the best.

"Of course, now that you mention it, you ought to give Kara some thought."

Some thought? Hell, that's all he'd been thinking about lately—how she turned him inside out with her smile, how her sweet kisses made him want to be the guy who came riding up to her door on a white stallion. Good grief, his imagination had run away with him ever since he'd kissed her in that tree house. Michael shook his head. "A doctor needs a special kind of woman."

"Kara, as you may find out in Boston, is a special kind of woman. I married one just like her nearly fifty years ago."

"Kara deserves better than a doctor who's rarely home."

"Maybe so," Weldon said with a chuckle. "Give me a call from Boston."

"I will." Michael hung up the phone and tried to conjure some sense of reality. What could he offer a wife and kids, other than more money than they knew what to do with?

The trade-off, it seemed, would be his interminable absences, the pages that called him away from the dinner table. Teary-eyed kids who had to suck up the disappointment when they searched the crowd for a father's face while they performed in a school play, a dance recital or a ball game. And a wife who slept too many nights alone.

Kara and the children deserved to be happy and to have a full-time husband and father.

In spite of Michael's resolve to distance himself, he still envisioned coming home to find Kara in the kitchen, Ashley munching on a graham cracker in the high chair and Eric coloring a picture at the table.

He raked a hand through his hair. He was a fool to even consider being a part of something like that.

Besides, he had his own worries. He would head back to Los Angeles tonight and take care of a few things Bertha couldn't do for him. Then he'd take Kara and the kids to Boston. He snatched the telephone to call his pilot and schedule the trip.

Back to Boston.

Did he dare go home without visiting his parents?

Some old habits and formalities were hard to break.

* * *

Three days later, Michael drove his Jag south on Interstate 5 toward Harbor Haven. His mind should have been on the road. Instead his thoughts drifted to Kara and the day he'd told her and Lizzie about his offer to snag a consult with David Cunningham in Boston.

She'd withdrawn from him the moment she'd learned who he really was—something quite opposite to what he was used to. Frankly, it had him perplexed.

Maybe she'd only meant to distance herself from him, something on which they'd both agreed. Those kids needed stability. And a mother. What, other than money, could he offer them?

He'd left Harbor Haven that afternoon, but rather than go home, he'd driven straight to the office, where Bertha, bless her heart, had kept everything running smoothly without him. Still, he had a list of telephone calls to return and a few questions only he could answer. Fortunately, his absence, as Bertha had suggested, seemed to diffuse the media's attention on his every move. It felt good to be home, with life back to normal.

As far as Eric's consultation with David Cunningham, everything was set—the appointment made, the flight plans in order.

Michael could have driven to the Santa Monica Airport, then flown to Carlsbad in the Citation with his pilot and copilot. Instead, he'd packed a suitcase and thrown it in the back seat of his Jag. He needed time to think, even though he'd had plenty of time to contemplate—at night, while he should have been sleeping.

He'd gone home with the intention of forgetting her, or at least the mushy weakness he felt whenever she was near. Out of sight, out of mind, the old adage said, but it had been absolutely impossible to keep Kara out of his thoughts.

Her memory haunted him—her dimpled smile, the way

she playfully cocked her head to the side, the lilt of her laughter. He'd hoped to exorcise her from his conscious thoughts, but God help him, the taste of her kiss, the heat of her touch had not only driven his senses wild, but had melded themselves in his mind.

He made the trip to Harbor Haven in less than two hours, and as he pulled into the gravel drive, Eric hurried to greet him. "Hey, Michael! You're back!"

An odd sense of warmth settled in his chest. When was the last time someone had greeted him like that, with unabashed enthusiasm? Michael smiled and waved.

The boy dropped the soccer ball he'd held and crept closer to the driver's door. "Did you get a new car?"

"No, it's mine. I'd borrowed the other one." Michael scanned the cottages, hoping to catch a glimpse of the smiling young woman whose memory had plagued him. "Where's Kara?"

"At the tree house," Eric said matter-of-factly. "I was going to go with her, you know, just to talk and stuff like we always do, but she said I should stay here and help Grandma. I don't know why, though. We're already packed."

Kara was at the tree house? Alone? For a moment he wondered whether she'd found herself stuck, but he quickly brushed the idea aside.

Maybe she just needed time alone, as he had. He wasn't sure whether she'd appreciate him interrupting her thoughts, but he didn't like her out in the wooded lot by herself.

"Why don't you meet me inside your grandma's house," Michael said. "I think I'll go tell Kara it's time to go."

"Okay." The boy took one last look at the Jag, and Michael smiled.

"You like my car?"

Eric shrugged. "I guess so. When I grow up, I'm

gonna have a truck with great big tires and a loud engine. But your car is okay—for a car.''

Michael smiled, pleased by the boy's honest appraisal. ''Thanks.''

As Eric made his way home, Michael walked the path toward the secret tree house, hoping he'd meet her returning to the cottage. There was something about Kara and tree houses that set his imagination soaring.

Kara sat upon the roof of her favorite treetop sanctuary, her cheek resting on a branch. She was going to miss the solitude of Harbor Haven. The sense of dread she'd felt when Michael first told her who he was and what he intended to do for Eric had only increased, and she wasn't sure why.

Granted, she was thrilled to know Eric would be examined by one of the best orthopedic surgeons in the country, but her uneasiness centered around Michael. Around his identity, his fame and, she supposed, his fortune. She'd never been comfortable around people who had money, even less so after that debacle of the dinner party at Jason Baker's house.

Once she and Michael had been equals. Now, she realized how much actually separated them—wealth, education, social status. Old feelings of insecurity welled up, feelings she'd fought hard to overcome since childhood.

Kara, as much as she disliked the idea, was still on the receiving end, so it seemed. Had it been her who needed the specialist, who needed the medical second opinion, she would have turned Michael's offer down. But she could never deny Eric the same opportunity.

A branch snapped, alerting her to someone's approach, and she quickly swiped the back of her hand against her cheek, just to make sure the moisture building in her eyes hadn't become tears. She glanced to see who dared to trespass upon her solitude.

Michael.

He stood along the pathway, wearing a pair of khaki slacks and a white, long-sleeve shirt, casual apparel that reminded her of a *GQ* cover model come to life. Dappled sunlight highlighted the gold in his hair. Had he ever looked so handsome? Her heart nearly burst from her chest, and it almost hurt to look at him.

In fact, it did hurt. This was a man who was very much out of her league—like a movie star. Or a god.

Dr. Michael Harper was a respected surgeon and wealthy as sin—a man most women would give an arm to claim as their lover. And she, Kara Westin, a nobody, had known him. Had kissed him, had nearly become his lover.

He flashed her a somewhat sheepish smile that caught her off guard. "Do you come out here alone very often?" he asked, making his way closer to the tree.

She shook her head. "Only when I need time to think."

"Are you worried about Eric?"

"No," she said, not wanting to discuss her selfish fears. "I'm actually excited for him."

He slowed his steps, but his gaze never left hers. He studied her intently, as though he sensed her turmoil, as though he knew the heaviness weighing on her heart had nothing to do with Eric and everything to do with him.

"Are you afraid of flying?" he asked.

"I've never flown before. I guess I'm a little apprehensive." She offered him a smile and hoped his questions would stop. There was far more to her pensive mood than that, but she didn't want to discuss it.

"I can fix you a drink once you're on board, and we've taken off. That might help settle your nerves."

Would it settle her discomfort with hobnobbing with the rich and famous? Knowing she'd shared intimacies with a man whose social status she had no intention of broaching? She'd have to drink herself into a state of drunkenness, and she still doubted that would ease her mind.

"I'll be okay, once we're off the ground," she lied.

He ventured closer. "It's nearly time to leave. Why don't you let me help you."

She nodded, then braced herself on the branch to start the slow climb down. Why did her heart race when she saw him? When she imagined him touching her, assisting her descent?

It's just a trip to the doctor's office, she reminded herself. One flight to Boston, and another flight back. Just a couple of days. Surely, there'd be no need to meet his friends, to socialize with people who would patronize her, make her feel less than worthy.

Oh, for goodness sake. You're being silly, she told herself. *Michael is a friend who happens to be rich and famous. He's a doctor with connections that may improve the quality of Eric's life. He never treated you in a condescending manner before, why would he now?*

As she made her way down the wooden steps nailed to the trunk of the tree, Michael touched her calf. In an attempt to steady her, she assumed, but the heat of his touch reminded her of how much they'd shared, how her body responded to his kiss—of the rebellious way it responded now.

"Careful," he admonished, as she descended the last three steps.

"I'm all right. Really. I've done this a hundred times." She turned slowly from the tree and faced him.

He flashed her a lopsided grin. "I remember one time when you were stuck and needed my assistance."

"I'm glad you didn't call the fire department," she said, recalling the day vividly—she and the cat stuck high in the branches. Michael helping her down. The mesmerizing gaze they'd shared on top of the rustic tree house. The kiss that weakened her knees and darn near caused her to spin out of control.

"So am I," he said, his gaze catching hers once again.

Michael didn't know why he did it, why he pulled her into his arms. For God's sake, he hadn't meant to. Why did his sense of reason fail him whenever Kara was near? The scent of springtime and flowers snaked around him, taunting him to kiss her again, to see if she tasted as good as she smelled.

Her memory had haunted him for the past three days, and it seemed his body had a mind of its own. But a doelike apprehension in her eyes held him at bay. Was she afraid of him?

"What's the matter?" he asked, dropping his arms and stepping back when he really wanted to pull her closer and chase away her fears.

She swallowed softly before speaking. "I was worried that you were going to kiss me again."

"Would that have been so bad?" he asked.

If they intended to follow through on their decision to go their separate ways, it wouldn't have been good. But he had to ask, had to know whether she'd come to resent his touch, his kiss. That would be a tough blow. He didn't mind maintaining his distance—he knew they wanted each other more than was prudent. But it would kill him to think she no longer desired him.

"Yes, it would have been bad. I'm not experienced in this kind of stuff."

He assumed she meant passion and desire, but he'd never considered himself much of an expert at the female thought process, at least on an emotional level. "What kind of stuff?"

She worried her bottom lip, then sighed heavily and looked him right in the eye. "Sex, I suppose."

He tilted his head, not quite sure what she meant. "It

would only have been a kiss, and to be truthful, I'd meant to refrain, but…''

She shook her head. ''No, it wouldn't only have been a kiss, not to me.''

Women were a confusing lot. Still unsure what she was getting at, he crossed his arms. ''I'm not following what you mean.''

''I may not have much experience with men, but I've been kissed a few times. And the kisses you and I share aren't the same. They make me crazy with desires I've never felt before.'' She crossed her arms, as though in a face-off of some kind. ''And each one leaves me wanting you more, wanting you in a way I've never experienced.''

Michael blew out a sigh. She was right, of course. Her kisses left him wanting more, too. More than was wise, especially if he meant to walk out of her life as soon as they returned from Boston.

''You're right about one thing, Kara. What we feel for each other, at least in a physical sense, is strong. Too strong, if neither of us is ready for that type of commitment. You're not the kind of girl I'd make love to, then leave.''

''Thank you,'' she said. ''I think.''

He bent to give her an affectionate kiss, one to seal their friendship. He hadn't meant for the kiss to progress, but strange things happened when Kara was in his arms. And apparently, those strange forces were at work for her, too, because she rose up on tiptoe and wrapped her arms around his neck.

They came together like lost lovers, mouths locked, hips grinding, hands caressing. The passion they'd shared before came rushing to the forefront, completely bypassing any thought of gentleness.

And she'd been right. It was more than a kiss. Much more. He'd never experienced such sexual intimacy with his clothes on. And something told him he might never experience the like again.

"Hey, are you guys kissing?" Eric's voice called from the pathway.

Kara and Michael jumped apart as though someone had sprayed them with a garden hose.

Michael shifted his weight to one foot, then crossed his arms. "I just helped her climb down, and she offered me a kiss in appreciation."

"I don't know," Eric said, his head tilted to one side. "My mom and dad used to kiss like that."

Michael and Kara glanced at each other, as though each was hoping the other would know what to say to the boy.

"Do you guys love each other?" Eric asked.

The question hung in the air until Kara spoke. "There's all kinds of love, Eric. Love for your family, love for your friends, love between a man and a woman. Michael and I are good friends."

"Oh," the boy said, scratching his head. Then he brightened. "Oops, I almost forgot. Lizzie wants you to come to the house. Some guys with cameras and stuff are there. They want to talk to all of us. I think we're going to be on TV."

Damn. Michael dragged a hand through his hair. Reporters.

He hadn't expected them to find him, not now. Not here. He gritted his teeth and clenched his hands. He had half a notion to hide in the tree house until they left.

"The press loves human interest stories," Kara said. "I guess word got out about Eric's good fortune and your kindness."

Or maybe those reporters who'd been stalking him had followed him to Harbor Haven. But what did it matter? He'd only managed to slip the press for a few days. Now they'd come back like gangbusters.

He'd meant his assistance in securing medical treatment for Eric to be an anonymous gesture, something between him, Kara and the kids—not something to garner more attention for himself, for his past.

Kara placed a hand on his shoulder. "What's the matter?"

"Nothing," he answered. "Nothing at all."

"I suppose we should go back to the house. They'll have a ton of questions to ask."

Yeah, they would, Michael conceded. And he'd been asked most of them a million times already. And this time they'd drag Kara and the kids into the sordid mess he'd tried hard to escape.

He cursed himself for allowing his emotions to get in the way of his reason. He should have been more careful.

Now he was going to suffer the consequences.

He took one last look at the tree house, then followed Kara and Eric to the waiting horde.

She didn't have any idea what was in store for her. But he did. And he didn't want any part of it.

Chapter Eleven

Eric swept through the front door of Lizzie's cottage, eager, it seemed, to return to the excitement. The screen slammed shut before Kara could admonish the child to be careful.

She hadn't ever felt totally comfortable around the reporters who occasionally stopped by to check on Eric's progress, but she'd respected the public's concern for Eric and Ashley. She usually tried to keep a low profile, and it appeared Michael had the same thoughts. His steps had slowed, and Kara wondered whether he would join them at all.

"Here they are now," Lizzie said to a tall, lanky cameraman as she pointed toward the front door. "Isn't it wonderful what Dr. Harper has offered to do for my grandson?"

"It is," a shapely female reporter said. She strode past Eric and Kara to meet Michael on the porch.

"Dr. Harper, I'm Ellen Dickinson with the *San Diego Gazette.*"

The brunette, dressed in a pink silk blouse, black slacks and blazer, extended her hand to him. Michael paused for what seemed like forever. And for a moment, Kara wondered whether he would accept the cordial gesture.

Kara found his rudeness surprising, especially since he'd always behaved as a gentleman.

"Doctor," the reporter began. "Eric is considered a hero around here. The people in the community will be pleased to hear of your generosity."

Michael nodded, yet didn't speak.

Lizzie smiled proudly. "He's offered to fly Kara and the children back to Boston for the appointment, and it won't cost us a thing. As far as I'm concerned, Michael Harper is a hero."

Kara expected a smile or some word to downplay what he'd offered. Instead, she watched tension settle in his stance and saw no sign of it easing. She elbowed him in the side. "Aren't you going to say something?"

His gaze settled on hers, and she caught a glimmer of pain, of anger, of darkness brewing—things she'd never seen in him before. She wished she hadn't prodded him, but it was too late.

"What do you want me to say, Kara?"

She didn't like his tone, the absence of a smile when he spoke to her. "They just want to write an article about your kindness to Eric."

"My life has been front page news for too long. I hadn't intended for any of this to leak out." He shot a glare at the reporter that suggested he held her responsible for all the problems he'd had with the media, not just today but in months past.

"Oh, dear me," Lizzie said. She pressed a liver-spotted hand to her chest and fingered the small pearl-shaped buttons on her sweater. "I'm sorry if my happiness caused you additional grief."

Michael's expression softened, but only slightly. "My problems aren't your fault. My ex-wife created a major public scandal, and the press won't let it die. It's affected my practice, my privacy. My life." He turned to the reporter and sighed heavily. "I don't suppose you'd keep this quiet?"

"Dr. Harper," the reporter began. "I can imagine your life has been disrupted more than seems fair, but we don't need to mention your recent past. Eric is a celebrity around here, and the people who have prayed for his recovery, those who have donated their money to a trust fund and written letters in support of Mrs. Campbell's custody, all share a deep concern for his well-being."

"I understand, Ms.—"

"Dickinson." The attractive woman supplied her name. "But call me Ellen."

"Ellen," Michael began, "if you'll allow me to take Eric to Boston, I'm sure Mrs. Campbell and Kara will give you an exclusive—after the fact."

The reporter looked to Kara and Lizzie.

"Certainly," Lizzie said. "If it's all right with Michael, I mean."

"That's my preference," he said.

"I suppose we could wait," the reporter said. "I always like an exclusive."

Kara watched the tension ease from Michael's face. She hadn't realized how much the press had hurt him, hadn't imagined the disruption of his life. The embarrassment. She wanted to go to him, hold his hand, tell him how sorry she was that his ex-wife had done such despicable things. Instead, she stuck her hands into the pockets of her jeans.

Before anyone could comment further, Lizzie staggered and took several steps back. Her face grew pale.

Michael was beside her in an instant. "What's the matter?"

"My head," she said, before her knees gave way. Michael scooped her frail body into his arms and carried her to the sofa.

"Call 911," he ordered Kara.

The reporter eased closer. "What's the matter?"

Michael didn't answer the woman.

Kara fumbled with the telephone, trying to punch the numbers. *Oh, dear God. Don't let his happen, not to Lizzie. Not to the kids.* She muffled a sob but couldn't quell the stab of fear in her heart. She wasn't ready to lose her dear friend.

"Grandma," Eric whispered, stepping closer. "What's wrong with Grandma?"

Michael, his eyes assessing Lizzie, his hands checking her pulse, glanced quickly at Eric before resuming his work. "She's going to be fine, sport."

Kara gave the details and address to the dispatcher on the telephone, surprised at how concisely she responded in spite of her fear for Lizzie. What would Eric and Ashley do if something happened to her? What would Kara do without the woman who was more of a mother to her than her own had been, than any of the five foster mothers had been?

"They're on their way," Kara said. Her heart raced, and her stomach knotted. She ran clammy hands down the sides of her denim-clad hips, wishing there was something she could do to help.

"Now call Dr. Weldon," Michael said.

Glad for some guidance, Kara quickly did as she was told. What if this had happened yesterday? When Michael hadn't yet arrived? As she dialed Dr. Weldon's office, she glanced at Ms. Dickinson, who was writing furiously.

A series of flashes caused her to look at the cameraman

who was busy recording Lizzie's crisis. Suddenly as angry as Michael, she wanted to scream at them, to ask them to leave, but Dr. Weldon's receptionist answered the phone, and Kara had to stay calm and rational. "I'm calling for Lizzie Campbell."

"Tell Weldon to meet us at the hospital," Michael interjected. "I think she's having a stroke."

Kara, responding like a robot, repeated Michael's words. Fear swirled in her chest, but she fought it by focusing on Michael, reminding herself he would do his best to care for Lizzie.

A siren sounded in the distance, and Kara sighed in relief. Let them arrive in time, she prayed.

"Dr. Weldon," the woman on the telephone said in a quiet, muffled tone. "Lizzie Campbell is being transported to the hospital with a possible stroke."

The doctor must have snatched the telephone from the receptionist, because his voice sounded over the line. "This is Dr. Weldon. Who am I speaking to?"

"It's Kara. Michael's with us."

"Thank goodness for that. She's in good hands, but I'll be happy when she gets to the ER."

"The paramedics have just arrived," Kara said, as the ambulance screeched to a stop.

"Listen, Kara. I should have spoken sooner, but Lizzie can't care for those kids any longer. If you want custody of them, you'll have to start the process. Even with your help, Lizzie's health won't allow her to take on the day-to-day responsibility of two small children."

"I understand," Kara said, although she wasn't ready to admit Lizzie's vulnerability. The kids still needed their grandma, and Kara still needed her friend.

"Good. I'll meet you at the hospital."

Kara nodded, then realized the doctor couldn't see her response over the telephone. "Okay. Goodbye."

She hung up the receiver, wishing she had as much

confidence in the system as Dr. Weldon. Why did this have to happen now?

Ashley, the sirens and excitement disturbing her nap, let out a wail, and Kara hurried to her crib.

"I'm here, sweetie," Kara said to the sleepy-eyed infant who'd already pulled herself to a stand and let go of the railing to reach for Kara.

"Ma," Ashley said, a word she used interchangeably for Lizzie and Kara.

"Mama's got you," Kara whispered, pulling the little girl near. Her eyes welled with tears, and her heart nearly ached with love. "And I won't ever let you go."

Kara, with Ashley on her lap, sat between Michael and Dr. Weldon in the waiting room at Oceana Hospital while Eric played quietly on the floor. The small boy appeared to be engrossed in a colorful structure he'd built with Lego blocks and completely unaware of the seriousness of his and Ashley's dilemma.

"I expect Lizzie to recover," Dr. Weldon said. "But we'll have to keep a close eye on her for the next seventy-two hours."

Kara looked at Michael. For confirmation, she supposed. Or maybe for assurance. She wasn't sure what she would have done if he hadn't been here with her. His presence was comforting.

He caught her hand in his. "I've called David Cunningham and rescheduled Eric's appointment. I knew you wouldn't want to go now."

He was right. She couldn't leave Lizzie. They were a family, and families stuck together. She nodded at Michael and squeezed his hand. "Thank you. I couldn't possibly leave her until she's out of the hospital."

"You're also going to need to request custody," Michael said. "Taking care of the kids is too much for her."

Kara glanced at Dr. Weldon, who nodded sagely. "It's

time for Lizzie to let them go. In fact, running the cottages is too much for her. She's going to have to slow her pace.''

Kara couldn't believe this was happening. Sure, she knew someday Lizzie would be too sick, too old to take care of the kids, but she wasn't ready to lose Lizzie's daily presence or her loving influence. And the kids weren't ready, either. They still needed her.

Maybe Kara could move into Lizzie's cottage, take over the office and manage the rentals. ''I'll do whatever I can to help. What if I lived with her and took more of the burden?''

Dr. Weldon shook his head. ''That little house has only two bedrooms. You'd be bumping into each other in the hallway. I'm afraid it's still too much. Besides, you can't take care of Lizzie during her recovery, run the cottages and take care of the kids. As much as it bothers me to suggest it, Lizzie needs to move into an intermediate care facility.''

Kara shook her head. ''No. I won't allow it. I'll think of something else—''

Michael released the hand she'd forgotten he held, then slipped his arm around her. ''I'll help. We'll find you a larger home, hire a nurse and—''

Kara jerked her gaze from Dr. Weldon to Michael. ''No. I won't take your money.''

He furrowed his brow, as though shocked by her independence. ''Be reasonable, Kara. Your options are limited.''

They certainly were, she had to admit. But her mind wasn't limited. And she'd learned long ago the importance of having options. In the past few years, she'd made it a point to not only have a game plan, but an alternate or two. She'd think of something, come up with an idea that would work while maintaining her integrity, her sense of self-reliance. She'd—

A sob caught in her throat, and she pulled her hand from Michael's. "I appreciate your offer, but I don't want anyone taking care of me."

"You need to show the courts you have a home, a means of providing for the kids," Michael said. "You need my help."

"I need some time to think," Kara said, getting to her feet and shifting Ashley to her hip. She looked to the corner where Eric was still busy building. Another time, she might have made a fuss over his achievement, clapped her hands at his clever engineering skill. But not today. She felt like a wet washrag, one full of water that needed to be wrung out. "Eric, it's time to go. Please put the toys away."

"I'll drive you," Michael said.

"No," she said. "We'll take the bus. It stops on the corner by our house."

"Kara," Michael began. "Would you please listen to reason?"

She lifted her chin. "I appreciate your help, not to mention your concern for Lizzie and the children. And I'm pedaling as fast as I can, trying to keep up with all that's happening to me. But, Michael, for years I was tossed around like a piece of driftwood in the ocean. I'm charting my own course now."

As Eric tossed the last Lego into a blue plastic container, Kara stooped to pick up Ashley's diaper bag. "Come on, Eric." She held out her hand, and the little boy took it.

"I don't mind riding the bus," he told Michael. "It's kind of fun."

Kara winced, unsure how much of their conversation the child had overheard. He appeared so content, so engrossed in his play, that she'd forgotten he was in the room.

"Are we going to tell Grandma goodbye?" Eric asked

as their tennis shoes squeaked along the shiny white tile of the hospital corridor.

"We'll stop by her room and say good-night, not goodbye. And we'll come back to see her tomorrow. Hey, who knows?" Kara asked, her voice straining to sound upbeat and bright. "Maybe they'll let us take her home."

"Cool," Eric said. "I wouldn't want to leave her here forever."

"We won't." Kara gave his small hand a gentle squeeze. "Families stick together."

Kara and the children didn't stay long at Lizzie's bedside, since the nursing staff had insisted she rest, but they left assured that the dearly loved woman was in good hands.

They made their way through the hospital lobby, then paused before the glass door. A swarm of reporters stood outside. Kara recognized Ellen Dickinson, the reporter from the *Gazette*, who had stopped by Lizzie's for an interview. Obviously, she'd followed them to the hospital where she now waited with a group of journalists and a television crew.

The attractive brunette offered Kara a smile and a shrug, as though assuming Kara would understand why she couldn't let the others beat her out of a story, why the terms of the bargain she'd struck with Michael no longer applied.

So much for Michael's offer of an exclusive.

She supposed there was little the woman could do, seeing how eager the others were to get the story. Harbor Haven was a small town, and news traveled fast. Prior to learning about Michael's reluctance to have public attention, Lizzie had shared her good news with her friends at the EZ Suds. And who could blame her? How many people had the good fortune of a famous surgeon befriending their small family and making as generous an offer as Michael had?

Kara sighed. She could understand Michael's reasons for anonymity, but his situation was very different from Eric's. People cared deeply about the heroic little boy and the baby sister he'd carried from the burning car. From that day on, Eric and Ashley had been adopted into the hearts of the community.

Kara understood the attention and curiosity. She would answer the reporters' questions as truthfully and quickly as possible, then head for the bus stop.

"Why are we waiting here?" Eric asked, glancing around the empty lobby in which they stood.

Gathering my courage, Kara wanted to say. Instead, she gave his small hand a squeeze. "I'm sorry for dawdling."

As she and the children exited the hospital, cameras flashed, and a television reporter thrust a microphone under her nose. "Miss Westin, we hear Mrs. Campbell was rushed to Oceana Hospital this afternoon. Will you tell us what happened?"

"She suffered a minor stroke," Kara said. "Dr. Weldon believes she'll recover, but they'll keep her a few days for observation."

"Miss Westin," another man said, a pen and paper in his hand. "Is it true that Dr. Michael Harper, the renowned heart surgeon, has taken an interest in Eric?"

Kara felt as though she'd been surrounded, and she scanned the crowd, hoping for a way out. She wanted to be understanding of their professional concern, to answer their questions, but she really wasn't prepared for this onslaught. "Dr. Harper has been a good friend."

"It's been rumored that Dr. Harper volunteered to fly Eric to Boston for a second opinion—all at his own expense."

"Yes," she answered, spotting an opening in the

throng of reporters. ''Dr. Harper has been very generous. If you'll excuse me, I need to get the kids home. They're hungry and tired.''

''How did you meet Dr. Harper?'' another reporter asked.

Kara had the urge to scream, ''No comment,'' but she continued to push her way through the crowd. ''Excuse us,'' she said to a cameraman blocking her way.

When the man stepped aside, Jason Baker slipped into the hole, blocking her escape. Her mouth dropped when he stuck a bouquet of flowers in her face. ''I heard Lizzie was in the hospital and thought I'd stop by and say hello.''

Kara glanced behind her, and a flashbulb went off in her face. ''That's nice, Jason. But Lizzie can't have any more visitors today. You can leave the flowers for her at the nurses' desk, though.''

His bulky form eased closer. ''Where are you going?''

Ashley began to fuss, and Kara swayed from one side to the other in an effort to soothe her. ''We're going home. It's been a long day.''

''Let me give you a ride.''

Kara wanted to remind him of the restraining order she'd filed against him, but she didn't care to discuss something like that in front of a group of reporters. Under normal circumstances, she would have flatly refused Jason's offer. She glanced at her wristwatch. In less than five minutes, the express would come by on its way to Harbor Haven. She certainly didn't want to start anything with him, but at this rate she would never make the bus. ''You can walk us to the bus stop.''

Kara expected him to give her that cocky, I'm-better-than-anyone smile, and she wasn't disappointed. ''You'd be riding in style everyday if you didn't play hard to get.''

What had ever made her think he was anything but a

jerk? "On second thought, Jason, why don't you take a scenic drive down the interstate during rush hour?" She stepped around him and, clutching Eric's hand, made her way down the sidewalk.

Undaunted by her anger, Jason tagged along behind her. "You don't have to get all huffy and puffy, Kara. I was just trying to help."

"Please, Jason," Kara said. "I don't want your help."

Another reporter, followed by the television cameraman, stepped in front of her. "One more question before you go, Miss Westin. When do you expect the doctors to allow Mrs. Campbell to fly to Boston with Eric?"

"I'm traveling to Boston with Dr. Harper and the children. Mrs. Campbell wasn't going to accompany us. As soon as the doctor assures us of her recovery, we'll reschedule the trip."

"Oh," Jason said, his voice escalating in discovery. "Now I get it."

Kara wanted to kick him, but she doubted it would shut him up. What crazy thing did he think he had figured out?

"You've decided the recently divorced doctor has more money than me, so you've had a change of heart."

Kara's jaw dropped, and as cameras continued to flash, she quickly locked her lips, but not before biting her tongue.

Tears welled in her eyes. She wasn't sure whether it was from mortification at what Jason had just implied in front of every newspaper and television newscaster in the area or because her tongue was throbbing in pain. Damn him.

"Two kids with a hefty trust fund and a rich doctor to pay your way. My mother was right. Things have sure begun to look up for you, haven't they, Kara? Cocktail waitress one day—socialite the next."

Kara wanted to defend herself, but who was she to

challenge the word of Jason Baker? What could she say to counter the claims of a man who had his picture in the society pages more often than Miss Harbor Haven?

Instead of arguing or allowing him the chance to say more, she pulled Eric a little too roughly through the crowd and strode toward the bus stop as fast as the poor boy's legs would carry him.

The reporters hadn't chosen to follow her. Which, she realized as she reached the covered shelter of the bus stop, was really too bad.

Because as they began asking questions and searching for information, it was Jason's story they would hear.

Chapter Twelve

Michael left Oceana Hospital after dark, but instead of heading north on Interstate 5, he drove west on the side streets until he reached Pacific Coast Highway. He could have returned to Los Angeles that evening. In fact, he probably should have gone home rather than hang around the hospital to offer his advice.

Lizzie would require monitoring, but the stroke had been minor. Weldon had everything under control. So why had Michael stayed at the hospital and offered his opinion on a case that wasn't his?

Probably for the same reason he'd joined MMI and donated countless hours to sick kids in underdeveloped countries. Michael Harper had a heart, in spite of his ex-wife's arguments to the contrary.

He cared deeply—about his patients, about underprivileged kids.

And, as much as he hated to admit it, he cared about the little family Kara had adopted. He'd grown fond of

Kara, too. Her playful spirit and loving heart touched a place in his soul he'd buried long ago.

Still, a clinical voice whispered to him, prodding him to back away, to disassociate himself from a situation that was sure to throw him back in the headlines and into the media limelight he'd shunned.

If he had any sense at all, he'd turn around and head north for the evening. Maybe send Bertha with Kara and the kids to Boston. The details could easily be handled over the telephone; he'd orchestrated similar medical consultations scores of times. He could keep his distance and, in fact, he *should* keep it.

But he wouldn't.

Michael had made a personal commitment. He'd offered his assistance, like he had to many other people in need. But he knew this was more than a charitable donation. He actually *wanted* to help.

He wanted to help Kara.

If there was ever a person who needed him, it was the proud young woman who had refused his financial assistance. There had to be something he could say to convince her, something he could do—anonymously, of course—that would change her mind.

Without a home, a live-in nurse, a steady, secure income, Kara would never receive custody of those kids. He admired her stubborn determination, but her vow of self-reliance was bound to be her downfall.

Michael turned down Harbor Drive and headed toward Campbell's Cottages, where he intended to spend the night. In the morning, he'd approach Kara one more time, after she'd had time to think about the reality of her situation. He'd convince her that his monetary offer had no strings attached. If she would accept his gift, from one friend to another, it would enable her to keep the kids.

And Kara needed Ashley and Eric every bit as much as they needed her. Of that, he was certain.

Michael pulled into the darkened parking lot and climbed from the car. He slipped his hand into his pocket only to realize he no longer had a key to the cottage he'd once rented.

The vacancy light still shined in Lizzie's window, even though the house was nearly dark. The porch light burned in silent welcome. He had no choice but to bother Kara this evening.

Crickets chirped, and the scent of night-blooming jasmine filled the evening air. As he strode toward the front door, the leather soles of his Italian loafers crunched on the gravel walkway. He paused on the porch, then knocked lightly. It seemed like a very long time before Kara answered, but he doubted it was more than a minute or two.

Teal-blue eyes widened in recognition. "Michael."

She stood before him, wrapped in an old, oversize bathrobe and wearing a towel around her hair. He didn't see signs of pajamas or a nightgown and couldn't help wondering what, if anything, she wore underneath.

She touched the lapel of the robe she'd belted at the waist. Her small fingers fidgeted with the neckline and drew his gaze to a V-shaped expanse of throat and a hint of cleavage. The robe gaped with each breath she drew, teasing him with a more intimate view.

"Is something wrong?" she asked.

"With Lizzie? No," he said, unable to tear his gaze away from her. His heart rumbled in his chest, and he couldn't understand why. Her appearance was anything but sexy. The darn robe looked like something a grandma would wear, but the sight of Kara, fresh from the shower and wrapped in chenille, did more to stir him than if she'd been draped in silk and satin. "I gave up my key, and I'd like to stay over, if that's all right."

"Oh, sure." She backed away from the door and let him inside.

Michael glanced around the darkened room, realizing Eric and Ashley had probably been put to bed. The little family had an evening ritual, he reminded himself, almost sorry he'd missed it.

"Are the kids okay?" He knew the day had been trying and probably frightening for them.

"I had to have a long talk with Eric, but I think he's all right now. I guess he overheard more than he should have."

"He's a smart boy."

She nodded while making her way to the scarred oak desk in which Lizzie kept the keys to the rental cottages. "I assured him she'd be okay." She withdrew the key to the cottage Michael had rented, then, as she placed it in his hand, her eyes locked on his. "She will recover, won't she?"

Michael smiled, then nodded. "Yes, Kara. I think she's going to be fine, at least this time."

She managed a timid smile while nibbling her bottom lip.

To see her like this, hurting but trying to be strong, clawed at his gut in a way he wasn't used to, in a way he didn't know how to hide. He cupped her cheek and lifted her gaze to his. "Lizzie may live to be a hundred, but she needs some time to recuperate."

A tear slipped from Kara's eye and trickled down her cheek. She brushed it away with the back of her hand, but another took its place. Michael caught it with his thumb.

"I love Lizzie," Kara said. "She's been a good friend and the only mother figure I've ever really known."

"I know," Michael said. "She'll be all right."

Kara nodded. "I've been alone for so long, you'd think I'd be used to it."

No one ever got used to being alone. Of that, Michael was sure. He'd suffered loneliness at a young age, but had learned to compensate. As an adult, he immersed himself in work, involved himself in critical medical discussions, surrounded by professionals yet always alone. He didn't allow it to bother him anymore, but it tore at his heart to think of Kara not having someone to love, someone to listen to her worries and fears, share her joy and laughter.

He took her in his arms, even though it was probably a stupid thing to do. But instead of pulling away, she slipped into his embrace—as though she belonged there.

Michael rested his cheek against the damp towel on her head. The scent of peach shampoo swirled around him. So fresh, so clean. He closed his eyes and allowed himself the luxury of her touch. Kara *did* belong here, he realized, in his arms, next to his heart.

The thought struck him like a shot in the dark.

What a complicated mess. He could easily grow to love Kara, if he'd ever lay his feelings on the line. She had the ability to make him whole, to fill the gaps in his life, to provide a simple happiness that had always evaded him. But other than his money, what could he offer her? Even if she cared for him the same way he cared for her, his devotion to his patients and his practice would rob her of the smile he'd grown to love. Michael couldn't commit himself totally to a relationship, not like Denise had demanded and not like Kara deserved.

So what was he going to do about it?

Nothing. He had no way of knowing how Kara really felt about him. And that, more than his vulnerability, bothered him more than he dared to admit. For the time being, he would hold her close, relish her scent and imagine claiming her as his.

Kara could have held Michael forever. This embrace, more than the others they'd shared, provided her with comfort and a strength she'd never had before.

How good it felt to cling to him, to accept the warmth of his touch, the stability of his presence. Lord knew she could use a friend, someone with whom she could share her broken heart.

From the time she'd put the kids to bed, she'd wandered Lizzie's house, alone and afraid. She was going to lose the kids. The reality cut like a knife.

Her friend and confidante was in the hospital. But now she had Michael.

Kara closed her eyes and inhaled his musky scent. A woman could fall in love with a man like him. And perhaps Kara had already fallen—before she knew who he really was.

Dr. Michael Harper. Wealthy beyond belief. Skilled surgeon. A man she could never allow herself to want. A relationship with a man of that caliber was simply out of the question. Impossible.

Had he been the other Michael, the one she'd first met, the handsome stranger who'd come to Harbor Haven, things might have been different. She could have leaned upon him and, had the timing been right, the distance not so far, she might have allowed herself to fall in love with him.

She didn't doubt there were things about Michael Harper that she did love—his gentleness, his kindness to her and the kids. But there was so much more to him than she could comprehend. More to him than she could ever bring herself to love or to be a part of. Kara didn't belong in his world, and she sure as heck wouldn't allow herself to visit.

But tonight, only tonight, she needed a friend. Someone to confide in, a shoulder to cry on.

"I'm going to lose the kids," she said.

He pulled her closer. "Not if I can help it."

Kara took a deep breath and stepped away from his embrace. The towel, once wrapped tightly on her wet head, skewed to the side, and she shoved it in place. "I appreciate your offer. Really, I do. But I don't think you understand my reluctance."

"I admire your pride," he said.

She shook her head. "It's not just pride. Everyone I ever cared about was taken from me. I lost my father in an accident when I was only five. And according to the people at Child Protective Services, my mother's drowning her problems in alcohol jeopardized my welfare."

"I'm sorry."

Kara took another deep breath, then blew it out slowly. "My father's half sister took me in for a while, but every time I turned around, she pointed out how expensive everything was. How the cost of feeding and clothing me put a big dent in the family budget." The memory still hurt, like hunger gnawing in her tummy. "I was a skinny kid, afraid to eat for fear I'd end up in an orphanage."

"It must have been tough. I can't imagine anyone placing a burden like that on a child."

Kara wrapped her arms around her middle. "I guess I should have eaten my fill. By the time I was seven, a woman from the state came to pick me up. She'd found a new family for me, she said. But I knew better. I'd become too much of a burden to be a part of a real family."

Compassion settled deep in his eyes. "I take it things didn't get much better."

She shrugged. "I guess they didn't get worse. No one else mentioned how much it cost to raise me, but I never forgot. The check they received for me came on the first, and I always hoped it would last until the end of the month."

"Kara, this is not the same."

"I know," she said, thinking of Eric and Ashley. She'd scrub floors and take in ironing in order to provide for them. "I want to give those kids everything a parent is supposed to give, no matter what it costs me."

"It might cost your pride," Michael said. "You may have to accept help in spite of your self-reliance."

Her lips quivered, and as she tried to suck back the sadness, the tears began to fall.

Michael swept her into his arms. She wanted to push him away, to stand tall on her own, but she couldn't back away from his strength, from his gentle touch. From his compassion.

She felt as though she'd sold out.

Michael held her for what seemed to be forever, yet it wasn't nearly long enough to quell the strange sensations that swept over him—the yearning to make things right, the compassion, the desire to make her his. Now, wasn't that a fine complication to an impossible dilemma?

He could marry her and solve all her financial problems in a heartbeat.

But when reality struck, when he returned to his practice with the dedication his patients deserved, he'd break Kara's heart for sure. Michael would never hurt her.

"What am I going to do?" she asked. The earnest question stirred his soul.

"You're going to request custody of the kids."

She sniffled, and he realized she was still crying. "The courts won't give me custody. I don't have any way of providing for them, other than the trust fund set up on their behalf. I wouldn't dream of touching their money. It's for their future."

He held her close, stroked her back. "Let me help."

She shook her turbaned head. "I can't."

"Would you give them up before accepting help?" Michael asked. "If so, I think you've got your priorities out of whack."

She stepped from his embrace, the towel tilted to one

side. He stifled the urge to right it, as well as the desire to remove it from her head entirely, freeing those fiery red curls.

"Those kids are my priority," she said, crossing her arms. "My only priority."

"Then accept my help."

A tear trickled down her cheek, and she bit her bottom lip. It hurt him to see her struggle over something that seemed like such a simple solution.

"For the kids," she whispered. "Only for the kids."

Michael wrapped her in his arms again, wanting her pain to ease, her conscience to clear. A part of him wished she had that same devotion to him, that she'd make *him* a priority in her life. But he'd given up wishing a long time ago.

"You'll have a house within the month," he told her. "Five bedrooms."

"Five bedrooms?" She pulled away again, eyes wide with disbelief. "I can't live in a five-bedroom house. That's entirely too expensive. Why, the rent alone—"

"You're not renting a house," Michael said. "I'm paying cash for it. And five bedrooms isn't too many. There will be one for each of you, with a room for Lizzie's nurse."

"It's too much," she said again, taking another step back.

"I'm setting up a bank account for you. You won't need to work unless it's something you want to do."

"Why?" she asked. "Why are you doing this?"

Because I love you, he wanted to say, but the thought scared him. Michael Harper didn't fall crazy in love. He wasn't the emotional type.

"Because I can afford to do it," he said instead. "And I can't think of anyone more deserving than you, Lizzie and the kids."

She nibbled her bottom lip, as though reason and pride

still battled inside her. "I'd offer to repay you, but I don't think I'll ever be able to do that."

"You don't owe me a dime." And she didn't because, if truth be told, he was the one indebted to her. She'd etched a rainbow onto the drab canvas of his life—tree house shades of green and brown, highlights of autumn on auburn curls, teal-blue eyes that reflected the sea, heartwarming colors that touched his soul.

He was glad she'd agreed to his help, but for some reason, he felt less than victorious. Instead of relief, awkwardness settled over him. He didn't have the foggiest idea why.

"I guess I'd better take that key to the cottage. I'm tired and ready to turn in." It wasn't the truth, but it was the best he could come up with. "Do you need a ride to the hospital in the morning? I assume you'll want to visit Lizzie."

"I intended to take the bus."

"I'll give you a ride. What time do you want to leave?"

She appeared to struggle with his offer of transportation, which seemed silly to him, since she'd just acquiesced to him buying a house, setting up a trust fund and hiring a nurse. She'd need a car, too, he realized. And driving lessons.

He enjoyed a rare sense of satisfaction in being able to provide all the things she lacked, all the things she deserved. His heart warmed, and he couldn't help but smile.

"Okay," she said, although he figured she'd rather cart those kids across town by public transit. "Can we go first thing? I promised Eric we'd leave right after breakfast."

"Is eight o'clock too early?"

She shook her head. "No, we'll be ready."

Michael fingered the key she'd given him. "I'll see

you in the morning.'' Then he turned and let himself outside.

After Kara closed the door behind him, he stood on the porch for much longer than was necessary, feeling very much alone. His heart, still warmed by her acceptance of what he could provide for her, remained empty.

He made his way to the small cottage that had once been his home. Lizzie might not be released from the hospital for days. Did he want to stay in Harbor Haven?

Here, he felt as though he were a kid with his nose pressed up against the window of a pet store—outside looking in.

Yet thoughts of returning to Los Angeles left him feeling lonelier than ever.

Kara, with Ashley on her hip and holding Eric's hand, entered Lizzie's hospital room. They approached the bed slowly, not wanting to disturb her, but the woman heard them come in.

"What are you doing here?" Lizzie asked. "You're supposed to be in Boston."

"We couldn't leave town," Kara said. "Not while you were in the hospital."

Lizzie kissed Eric, then Ashley, before focusing her attention on Kara. "That trip to Boston was planned, and there's no reason for it to be postponed."

Kara knew how important Eric's consultation with Dr. Cunningham was to Lizzie. It was important to her, too, but not if she had to worry about Lizzie's health. "As soon as Dr. Weldon releases you, we can reschedule."

Lizzie crossed her frail arms over her chest. "I want Eric to meet with that orthopedic surgeon, and I'm not about to wait until Doc Weldon gets it in his fool head to release me."

"But you're in the hospital," Kara reiterated.

"This is the perfect time to go," Lizzie countered. "Good heavens, I couldn't be in better hands."

Actually, her old friend appeared as feisty as ever. Kara certainly didn't want to raise her blood pressure by arguing. "Are you sure you'll be all right?"

Lizzie arched a gray brow and pointed a finger at Kara. "Stop fussing about me, young lady." Then she smiled at Eric. "You have your heart set on flying in an airplane, don't you, honey?"

Eric nodded eagerly.

At the brisk sound of footsteps on the tile floor, Kara turned to find Michael in the doorway.

"How are you feeling this morning?" he asked Lizzie.

"I'm about ready to jump out of this bed and check myself out if you two don't take that boy to Boston." She shook her head. "Dr. Weldon said I'm going to be all right. And you, Dr. Harper, agreed with him."

"Yes, I did," Michael told Lizzie. Then he strode closer to Kara, his gaze catching hers. "She'll be fine, but it's your call."

"What about Dr. Cunningham?" Kara asked. She knew specialists had busy schedules. It wasn't easy to get in to see them. "You canceled the appointment, didn't you?"

"He'll see us tomorrow or the next day. It's not a problem."

Wasn't it? Packing the kids and flying to Boston in Michael's plane felt like a big problem to her. Shoot, Kara hadn't ever been out of Southern California. But if Lizzie was going to throw a fit and cause herself complications, and if Michael could change the appointment...

Kara sighed in resignation for the second time in less than twelve hours. "Okay. The kids and I will be ready whenever you are."

Michael checked his watch, which by now Kara realized wasn't a fake Rolex, as he had indicated to her before, but the real McCoy. It irritated her that he'd lied about it. Maybe she'd bring it up later, when they were alone.

But she didn't want to be alone with him. As long as she kept the kids between them and continued to view Michael as her benefactor and no more, she'd be all right.

"I can have the plane ready in an hour," Michael said. "And you're already packed, right?"

Kara thought of the worn leather suitcase she'd borrowed from Lizzie. "Yes, we're packed."

"Good," he said. "I'll call my pilot, then we'll head home for your luggage."

Lizzie was going to be all right, Eric had an appointment with one of the top orthopedic surgeons in the country, and Michael had promised to provide for all of her needs.

Life was perfect, or so it seemed.

So why did Kara feel as though she were bobbing in a sea of sadness?

Chapter Thirteen

Michael waited in the hospital lobby for Kara and the kids to finish their visit with Lizzie. He glanced at his watch. Ten minutes ago, he'd told his pilot of the latest schedule change and was assured they could take off in less than an hour. He'd prefer to get the trip under way before word of his involvement with the kids leaked out.

"Would you like a paper, sir?" A blond candy striper stood before him, hugging the local newspaper to her chest. She smiled, flashing him a glimpse of metallic braces.

He usually read the paper in the morning over a cup of coffee, but today he hadn't taken time for coffee or reading. He reached for the issue the teenage volunteer handed him. "Thanks."

"Hey, Michael," Eric called as he entered the lobby ahead of Kara and the baby. "Are we going to fly on the airplane today?" The boy held his hands to his side, fingers crossed.

"You bet, sport. And I'll have the pilot give you a tour of the cockpit." Michael folded the newspaper and tucked it under his arm.

"Wow," Eric said. "I can't wait to tell the kids at school."

Kara, with Ashley riding on her hip and a pink diaper bag slung over her shoulder, joined them near the entrance. She offered a smile, but one clearly meant for Eric. Her eyes, devoid of the vitality Michael had grown to expect, caught his for only a moment before she broke the gaze by placing a kiss upon the baby's chubby cheek.

Michael surmised she still felt uneasy about accepting his help. He wished he could say something to make her smile again. Her withdrawal and the growing distance between them bothered him more than he cared to admit.

"Come on," he said, more to Eric than to Kara. "We'll stop by your house and pick up your luggage, then we'll head for the airport."

"Cool." Eric looked over his shoulder at Kara. "Isn't this the neatest day of your whole life?"

"It sure is," she said. Her voice sounded sincere, but Michael could sense a lack of excitement, an absence of warmth in her smile.

Throughout the drive to the cottage and on to the small, coastal airport, Eric chattered, obviously thrilled with the entire experience. It pleased Michael to share it with him. If only Kara reacted with the enthusiasm she usually had for new discoveries—a Frisbee, a tree house, a soccer game.

At that moment, Michael realized he'd do almost anything to put a smile back on her face. Anything except renege on his offer of help.

He parked the car, then handed Kara the folded newspaper. "Here, would you take this for me?"

She nodded, tucked the *Gazette* into the diaper bag,

then spoke to Eric. "Why don't you be in charge of your backpack."

"I'll help Michael with the suitcases, too," the boy said.

Michael ruffled Eric's hair. "That's all right, sport. If Kara and Ashley take the diaper bag and you carry your backpack, I'll get the rest."

Duke Dunn, the pilot, must have seen them pull into the private parking lot reserved for noncommercial flights, because he met them at the car. "Need some help, Doctor?"

"Sure," Michael said. After the introductions, he pulled two suitcases from the trunk. "Duke, can you get the car seat out of the back of the car?"

That particular model had been heralded on television commercials as the easiest to use and the safest on the market, but Michael had his doubts about both claims. He couldn't get the darn thing not to wobble.

Duke, a father of three boys, quickly unhooked the infant's seat and carried it to the plane, with Eric on his heels.

The boy could scarcely contain his excitement, and the pilot chuckled several times as they walked toward the plane.

Michael carried two suitcases while Kara walked beside him with Ashley in her arms. The baby oohed and aahed as though she knew she was about to experience something special, but Kara remained pensive.

Did it bother her that much to accept his help? So much that it would adversely affect their friendship? Or was she nervous about flying?

As they stepped into the cabin, she scanned the leather upholstery, the built-in bar, the television and VCR, taking in every convenience. Instead of warming up or making a comment about the plush accommodations, something almost everyone did upon entering the jet for the first time, she seemed to withdraw more, as though the reflection of his wealth bothered her. He suspected it probably did. She'd let him know in no uncertain terms how proud she was to provide for herself.

He raked his hand through his hair. Most people were impressed by his plane, by his generosity. But Kara, as he'd realized early on, was unlike anyone he'd ever met.

While Eric got a tour of the cockpit, Michael secured Ashley's car seat in one of the cabin seats. The fool thing still gave him trouble, but he managed to make it reasonably immobile.

Eric, having learned just about everything a six-year-old boy needed to know about aeronautical science, chose the "very bestest" seat, one with a window view and near the cockpit where his two new friends would fly the plane.

"We're going to stop in Kansas City," Eric reported. "It takes a lot of fuel to fly clear to Boston, since it's so far away."

"Is that so?" Michael asked the boy, even though he knew they'd need to take on fuel. That was one of the reasons he'd contemplated purchasing a larger jet. For reasons of convenience and expedience, he supposed. But then again, how many times did he take time to travel? In the past, only when Denise prodded him. He supposed a larger jet wasn't really necessary.

Kara took a seat next to Ashley, who whimpered at being restrained in the car seat. She handed the baby a couple of toys from the diaper bag, then adjusted the seat belt. Her demeanor was stiff, formal, not at all like the bubbly young woman Michael had grown to admire. Surely she'd relax and be herself again once they took off. Once they neared Boston.

"Would you like a drink?" he asked her. "A Bloody Mary, a glass of wine?" He hoped she'd agree, on the outside chance that her nerves were more at play than anything.

"No, thank you." She settled into the seat and crossed her arms. "Maybe later."

"I'm kind of thirsty," Eric said, his eyes taking on the enthusiastic light Kara's had been lacking.

"How about a soda?" Michael asked.

Eric nibbled his bottom lip as though worried he'd be denied. "Is it okay, Kara?"

She smiled lovingly at the boy, and Michael couldn't help wishing that sparkle of warmth had been directed at him. He missed Kara's effervescence more than was reasonable, and he found the distance between them unsettling for reasons he couldn't understand.

"Sure, Eric. It's a special occasion, isn't it?"

Rather than wait until they were airborne, Michael took time to fix a lemon-lime soda. As he handed a glass to the boy, he wished he'd poured something for himself. Something strong. This was going to be a heck of a long trip.

As the plane taxied down the runway, he took a seat, then leaned toward Kara. "Would you mind handing me the paper?"

"Sure." She reached into the diaper bag and passed it to him. Her concentration returned to the small, oval window and the landscape passing by.

Michael unfolded the newspaper. He glanced at the headlines, then his gaze swept to the bottom of the page and he grimaced. Kara and the kids had become front page news.

And so, unfortunately, had he.

He must have grumbled or maybe rustled the paper in anger, because Kara leaned over his shoulder.

"What's the matter?" she asked.

He wanted to keep the words to himself, to protect her

from what she would read. Instead, he handed her the newspaper.

Yesterday afternoon, Elizabeth Campbell, the elderly caretaker of Eric and Ashley Campbell, the children orphaned in a fiery car crash last year, was rushed to Oceana Hospital, having suffered a minor stroke. A hospital spokesman reported her condition as good, yet questions regarding her health persist, as does public concern for the welfare of Eric and Ashley. Kara Westin, a friend of the family, is caring for the youngsters while Mrs. Campbell is in the hospital.

On a brighter note, Dr. Michael Harper, whose wife was recently sent to prison for laundering illegal campaign contributions to Senate candidate Daniel Walker, has taken a special interest in little Eric Campbell.

"Lizzie told people down at the EZ Suds that Dr. Harper had set up an appointment with an orthopedic surgeon in Boston," Jason Baker, a local businessman, reported. "And Dr. Harper is supposed to be taking them in his private plane to meet the specialist."

Baker shared his concern over the welfare of little Eric and his sister Ashley. "I hope the court pays special attention to the people wanting to take those poor kids," Baker said to reporters. "Otherwise, any two-bit cocktail waitress might apply for custody. And I'd worry that hefty trust fund might be more appealing than motherhood."

As of press time, no requests for custody had been filed with the court, but Eric and Ashley have gained a foothold in the heart of every citizen in this community, and speculation abounds.

Kara wanted to scream in her own defense. How dare Jason imply she had ulterior motives for wanting custody of Eric and Ashley? The money in that trust fund was for the children's future, not for her use.

But who would believe her?

Not Jason.

And certainly not most people who read the *Gazette*.

A tear trickled down her cheek, and she caught it with her finger.

"I have half a notion to sue Jason Baker for libel," Michael said. "He didn't come right out and accuse you of anything, but it was pretty clear who he meant by 'two-bit cocktail waitress.'"

She looked at Michael, hoping he'd reassure her but knowing he wouldn't be able to. "This could get ugly."

"You're right." He reached across the seat and took her hand. For a moment, she savored his touch, his compassion. "The tabloids will probably get wind of this. They've been hounding me for the past six months, so I'm sure my involvement will only increase their curiosity. And their unfounded speculation."

"I'm sorry. I know you didn't want to be dragged into our mess."

He gave her hand a squeeze, but she noticed the tension in his face, the pursed lips, the furrowed brow. "I'm used to it, Kara, but I don't like the idea of you facing the things I've had to endure—lies, accusations, not to mention a loss of privacy."

"I'll be fine."

He gazed at her, his golden-brown eyes intense, digging deep into her soul and seeing things she'd rather keep locked inside. "I'll do whatever I can to protect you, to make everything work out for you."

She shook her head. "You can't protect me from gossip. And even the money you've offered me won't be enough. Jason will insist I've snagged myself a rich benefactor, a Daddy Warbucks, and that won't really be a lie. Will it?''

Indecision, or something equally troubling, brewed in his eyes. His gaze never left hers. "Marry me," he said.

Her mouth dropped open, revealing her surprise. "What did you say?''

Marry me. The words resounded in Michael's head like a brass band. Had he said them? Kara couldn't possibly be any more surprised by his suggestion than he was. Michael went to great lengths to make decisions. Where had this one come from? His conscience?

Or his heart?

Although sucker punched by his own suggestion, he realized the idea had merit, at least on an altruistic level. The press could be intrusive, vicious at times. And he knew his financial support wouldn't be enough to secure a warm, happy future for those kids and Kara. Nor would it be enough to protect her from gossip and speculation.

"Yes," he said. "I want you to have those kids, legally and permanently. Marriage to me would secure custody.''

Her auburn brows furrowed. "Michael, I can't marry you just to secure custody of the children.''

"Why not?''

"Marriage should be based on love and respect.''

Still unsure of his feelings and unwilling to acknowledge them out loud, Michael offered a rational response. "I respect you. And like you a great deal. Love could definitely grow.''

"You'd marry me just so I could get custody of the kids?'' She shook her head slowly. "It doesn't seem right. What would you get out of it?''

What would he get out of marriage to Kara? Plenty.

It was Kara who would get the short end of the stick, when it came down to it. But he had no trouble coming up with lots of reasons marriage to her and becoming part of the little family she loved would benefit him.

"You make me laugh. And you make me want to experience Christmas with a Charlie Brown tree decorated with strings of cranberries and popcorn." He gave her hand a squeeze, then stroked his thumb against the soft, silky skin on her palm. "And not to mention, your kisses curl my toes and cross my eyes."

A red splotch that matched the tint of her cheeks marked her throat and neck, places he'd love to bury his lips. "There's more to marriage than hot kisses."

"How much more?" he asked. His thoughts turned to something more intimate than Christmas trees and home-made ornaments. Something a heck of a lot more than her inexperience could imagine.

She ran the tip of her tongue across her lips, then glanced at Eric, who was pressing his nose against the window and occasionally brushing the fog away from the glass. This conversation wasn't one either of them wanted anyone to overhear, especially a small child, but Eric, a sublime, starry-eyed grin on his face, looked lost in adventurous, little-boy thoughts.

Michael returned his attention to the conversation at hand, to the idea of taking Kara to bed. Of kissing her senseless, of making love until the early morning hours, of waking in her arms. Seeing the new day dawn in her first morning smile. The sensuous image gave "happily ever after" a whole new twist.

If he were a man prone to romance and emotion, rather than reason and good sense, he might believe he could make her happy long after they said, "I do." But how many nights would he be there to hold her in his arms, to stroke the smooth, ivory-colored skin, to kiss her senseless, to bury himself in her softness? To wake with her in the morning?

Dreams like that didn't belong to either of them, because Michael could never promise or guarantee his time. It made him feel more than a little guilty to imply they'd have something special between them, something even remotely like forever after.

"Michael, I find you very attractive. And you're a good friend."

Ah, here it comes, he thought. The I-want-to-be-friends speech. He hadn't expected a declaration of love, yet the friendship lecture was a blow. He readied himself for the inevitable I-love-you-like-a-brother explanation. As he'd grown so adept at doing since early childhood, he shut down his attention.

It was, he supposed, a protective mechanism built into a little boy's heart and soul. Who wanted to listen to what was bound to come next?

"I do love you," she said. "More than you could ever love me."

Huh? What had she said? Did he miss the brother part? Normally, he concentrated on conversations, the words said, but not this time. And for the life of him, he wasn't entirely sure what she'd said. He could have sworn she said she loved him. At least, a little bit. And in the right way. "Excuse me?"

"I can't imagine marrying someone who could never love me in the way a husband should love a wife."

What about loving him the way a wife should love a husband? Had she mentioned loving him? He could have sworn she said something like that, but he didn't have the courage to ask again, the guts to tell her he hadn't been listening.

His heart pounded like a runaway freight train on a downhill track. He was feeling something pretty darn close to love for her, too.

There was some real potential here, not just for the sake of the kids, he realized. And even if the late-night calls, his sudden absences eventually hurt her, he suspected she might weather the pain for the sake of the kids. At least, some small, budding seed in his heart hoped she would.

He gave her hand another squeeze. "We can announce our plans in Boston."

"Our plans? Michael, are you listening to me?"

No, he wasn't, other than the part that sounded like she cared for him in the right way. Women hated it when men ignored them, at least that's what the author of that stupid book had said, the book his ex had insisted he read. And Michael hadn't meant to ignore Kara, he'd only meant to brace himself for a brush-off.

"Kara, we care for each other, we enjoy each other's company, we respect each other. And sex is bound to be off the charts."

What more could either of them want? Other than her eventually wanting more of his time. But he wouldn't consider that now. Not while he was helping her secure the happiness and well-being of the kids.

She again looked at Eric, as though worried he'd over-hear their conversation. The boy made engine noises, swiped a hand across the glass to clear his vision, then aimed a finger and, making bulletlike sputters with his lips, fired at an invisible enemy.

Kara glanced at Ashley, as though the sleepy-eyed baby understood every word they'd said.

"Marry me, Kara."

Had he actually said that again? Out loud? This whole conversation seemed unreal, like Eric's mock air raid. But Michael had not only said those words, he was actually trying to persuade her.

"I don't know." She worried her lip. "I need to think about it."

"Then let me help." He reached over, unbuttoned her seat belt, then drew her onto his lap.

She moved reluctantly at first, then, as his hand cupped

her cheek and guided her lips to his, she wrapped her arms around him and sighed.

This was crazy, absurd, Kara thought, yet she hungered for Michael's kiss, for the taste of him, for the feel of his arms around her. His tongue stroked her lips, and she opened her mouth to allow the kiss to deepen.

He'd been right about something. Their kisses were toe-curling, eye-crossing and out of this world. She lost all reason when she was in Michael's arms. And in spite of two strangers in the cockpit, of little Ashley wide awake in her car seat, of Eric sitting only two seats away, Kara relished the coiling heat in her tummy, the soar of her heart, the fire of his touch.

She could envision kissing him forever, holding him until everything made sense or until nothing mattered anymore but him.

And her.

And the sizzling passion they shared.

The kiss, which probably lasted a full three minutes, ended way too soon, and she fought the urge to drag his lips back to hers.

"See what I mean?" he asked.

She nodded, yet didn't speak. No question about it, she could kiss Michael like that forever. And as though he'd read her mind, he flashed her a cocky grin that she found endearing.

He shifted in his seat, and she realized the lap upon which she sat had grown harder, more defined than when he'd first pulled her into it. Apparently, he found their kisses moving, too. But she wanted a relationship built on more than financial security and the promise of physical pleasure.

"There's more to life than kissing," Kara managed to utter. She knew marriage to Michael would be her undoing. She'd have to meet his family. And his colleagues.

His friends. People who lived in a world very different from hers. Recollections of the Bakers' dinner party unfurled in her memory, and she removed herself from his lap. "I'm not from your world," she said, taking her seat and buckling the belt. "And I've never really wanted to visit, let alone live there."

"Then we'll make a world of our own."

Kara shook her head. "Michael, you're a respected surgeon. And you come from a wealthy family, one that makes owning a chain of EZ Suds seem like poverty. I would never fit in. I don't think you have any idea how humble my background is, how out of place I feel around people who have never lacked for anything."

"You'll fit in if you're my wife."

"Is that so?" The image of Mrs. Baker's condescending smile was still too strong for Kara to be persuaded.

"Just wait and see."

"All right," she said. She would think about his proposal, but she doubted she could allow herself to do something so wild and bold as to marry Michael and enter a society that wouldn't accept her or treat her with the respect his wife deserved. "I'm not sure anyone or anything in Boston will convince me to do anything except decline your offer."

As much as Michael hated to admit it, Kara had a valid point and a real concern. Meeting his parents had been tough on his ex-wife, a woman who was well-versed in the art of conversation. He wasn't sure how Kara would fare against the austere couple. He loved his parents, but growing up in a sprawling estate had plenty of down sides.

How his friends viewed his mother and father had never bothered him, but his heart constricted when he thought of what Kara might think. Or more important, how they might treat her. His mother had always been cool and withdrawn, not to mention demanding, which was one reason he chose to practice medicine across the country. In fact, having always distanced himself, detachment came easy for him. Still, he had an ace in the hole.

Michael was an only child. And his parents had better accept Kara with grace and charm or he would pull rank, the likes of which Beatrice Raleigh-Harper and her husband, Charles, had yet to experience. For a couple who hadn't had the time to spend with their son as he grew up, the tables had turned.

Now they were the ones unhappy with a relationship based on telephone calls and e-mails. That level of intimacy suited Michael just fine—as long as he was on the west coast. Relocating his practice would undoubtedly change life as they all knew it, because he couldn't avoid them if he was living in the same town.

Besides, he loved his parents, and they loved him. They were a family, even if their home and holidays hadn't been the kind depicted on television. And even if his childhood had been unbearably lonely at times, he had never doubted their love. He'd just yearned for more of their time.

As soon as the pilots prepared to touch down on Massachusetts soil, Michael would telephone his parents, announce his arrival and request a limousine to transport them from the airport to a five-star hotel.

His mother would undoubtedly suggest they stay in one of the many guest rooms at the family estate, but Michael wouldn't consider it. He needed time to explain his intent to marry Kara and adopt Ashley and Eric. Time to hear his parents vent. Time to prepare Kara and the children for a meeting.

It was a perfect plan, yet the closer they got to Boston, the more uncertainty settled over him like a foggy haze.

Chapter Fourteen

As the plane neared Boston, Kara closed her eyes and uttered what could only be considered a prayer for strength. She dreaded facing the unknown but resolved to keep her chin up and her back straight.

For the past hour, Michael had talked nonstop on his cell phone, placing calls all over the country. He spoke to a woman named Bertha, then placed a call to request a limousine to meet them at the airport. During one of the quick, nearly one-sided conversations, he reserved a hotel suite.

Private jets, limousines, penthouse suites. It seemed so surreal. Kara felt as though someone had thrown her into one of the maximum capacity washers at the EZ Suds and put her on the spin cycle.

The last call he made was to a Dr. Templeton. Kara had tried not to eavesdrop, since the doctors might need to discuss a patient or something equally confidential, but her heart dropped when she heard the friendly tone of

Michael's voice and realized Dr. Templeton was a woman named Maggie.

She quickly reprimanded herself for even a vague sense of jealousy. Since she had no intention of agreeing to Michael's offer of marriage, and he was only her benefactor, his affairs—geez, wrong choice of words—his associations were none of her business. As the plane began its descent, Michael ended his last call and turned off the phone.

Within minutes, the jet landed, then taxied to a private hangar.

"You'll have to change your watch. It's three hours later here," Michael told her.

She merely nodded, acknowledging the information. The stem on her watch no longer worked. She would have to mentally adjust by adding three hours whenever she checked the time.

Kara removed Ashley from the car seat, then carried her off the plane just as a sleek white limousine pulled curbside. The Massachusetts plates read HARPER. Undoubtedly, the limo belonged to either Michael or his parents.

She tried hard not to gush over the fancy car and to remain nonchalant, just as she had with the jet. The extravagant lifestyle was one to which Michael had been born, one in which he belonged. She couldn't have felt more out of place if she'd been invited to Buckingham Palace for tea. She'd try to keep her unease to herself; she had no intention of oohing and aahing like a child on her first visit to the zoo.

Eric, on the other hand, was delighted with the entire experience, as was Ashley. And for that reason, Kara managed a smile. She was grateful that Michael had provided the kids a once-in-a-lifetime field trip to the land of the rich and famous, even if it caused her a great deal of discomfort.

Eric especially loved the limousine ride through downtown Boston. Kara, in spite of her reluctance, could scarcely believe the view of the city provided through the sun-tinted windows of the snazziest car in which she'd ever ridden. Even Ashley, her car seat secured into a tufted leather bench seat, sucked her finger while admiring the plush interior of a vehicle that looked more like a living room than an automobile.

When they arrived at the entrance of the New England Garden Towers where Michael had booked a suite, Kara wanted to object. They certainly didn't need to stay in a place as elegant as this, but it seemed most of the decisions had been taken out of her hands.

"I'll carry Ashley," Michael said.

Since she wasn't sure how she'd balance the child and climb from the car, Kara nodded. There was, she supposed, a graceful way to exit these fancy vehicles, but she hadn't paid enough attention to the Academy Awards preshow to figure it out.

A tuxedo-clad valet opened the door for her, then she bent her head and climbed out. Eric followed, his eyes brighter than she'd ever seen them, his smile touching her heart. New experiences thrilled him, and she was reminded of his happiness the day he'd kicked his first soccer ball through a makeshift goal and the day he'd climbed to the top of the tree house. It wasn't the gold and grandeur that had excited him, she realized, it was merely the adventure. Of that, she was glad.

Michael took her arm and escorted her into the lobby, a spacious, glass-encased showcase that all but glistened.

"Our bags—" Kara turned to look for the luggage they'd brought.

"The bellman will bring them up."

"Oh," she said, as he took her hand. She wished she'd wiped her palms upon her denim-clad hips so he wouldn't notice how damp and clammy they'd become.

As he led the way, the worn leather soles of her shoes mocked the marbled foyer of the lobby. There was no way she could ever live like this. No way.

Kara had dreamed of falling in love one day, of getting married, but her dreams had always included a small home in the suburbs, a picket fence, a man who loved her as much as she loved him. She couldn't marry Michael and live in a world in which she'd always be a fake, a cubic zirconium in the midst of diamonds.

She'd have to pray Lizzie's endorsement and Eric's wishes for her guardianship would be enough to sway the judge to choose her over the others who might apply for custody of Eric and Ashley.

Yet the truth reared its head. Without Michael's financial help, and undoubtedly without his name on the court documents, Kara didn't have much chance of getting the kids she'd grown to love. And she couldn't bear losing them.

"All right, let's go to our room," Michael said, after he'd checked them into the hotel. "We're taking the elevator all the way to the top."

"We get to stay in the highest part?" Eric asked, the timbre of his voice showing his excitement.

"That's right. When we look out the window, we'll be able to see all of the city. You'll especially like the view at night."

"Wow," Eric said.

When the elevator opened, Michael ushered them down the hall to the only door with a number. "This is it."

He swiped the room key and opened the door.

Eric entered first. "Wow," he said again.

Kara couldn't think of a better word for the child to utter and had to bite her tongue to keep from repeating it. The sitting room of the suite was larger than the cottages back home.

"You can have your choice of bedrooms," Michael told her. "There's a room for the kids, and one for me, too."

Her first thought was that he'd spent entirely too much money. They certainly didn't need a room like this. But how could she complain? The cost of this suite wouldn't put a dent in Michael's weekly lunch money. She sighed, more in exasperation over their differences than anything.

"There are in-room video games," Michael told Eric. "Let's see if we can figure out how it works."

"Cool." The boy was beside him in a flash. And before long, they had found a nonviolent, age-appropriate game with bright colors and annoying squeaks, beeps and electronically created musical tones.

"A friend of mine knows a great baby-sitter," Michael told Eric. "Her name is Kathy, and she'll be here in an hour or two. Kara and I are going out for the evening."

"We're what?" Kara asked. No way was she leaving the kids alone with a stranger on their first night in town.

"We're going to have a late dinner with my parents."

Over my dead body, Kara thought. "I don't think it's a good idea to leave the kids with someone they don't know."

"Kathy is a premed student at Boston College."

"I'm sure she's perfectly capable, but I—"

Michael caught her by the arm and pulled her close. "I know you're not excited about meeting my parents, but it's the first step in what needs to be done."

"I'm not so sure—"

"I'll be with you, to hold your hand and lead the way."

Somehow, that didn't make Kara feel any better. He cupped her cheek, then kissed her brow, and she felt the need to pull him close, to latch onto his strength. To believe that everything would, indeed, be all right.

"I'm going out for a while," he said. "There's a room

service menu on the table by the phone. Why don't you order something for the kids to eat?''

A sense of panic hovered over her. "You're leaving us here?''

"I have an errand to run. I won't be gone long.''

She wanted to ask where he was going and why, but that really wasn't any of her business. Was it? It was not as though they had a real engagement or commitment to each other. Michael was little more than her benefactor. It would be best if Kara learned to keep her place.

Michael found an upscale women's clothing store not far from the hotel. With the help of a classy, well-dressed saleswoman, he purchased several new outfits for Kara. He guessed her to be a size three. If the clothes didn't fit, they'd be too large.

He didn't need the saleswoman's assistance for choosing appropriate undergarments. It was easy to imagine Kara in feminine whispers of silk, satin and lace, and he enjoyed the shopping process.

The shoes weren't as easy. Since he wasn't sure what size she wore, he purchased several pairs for her to try, which made him feel like Prince Charming bearing glass slippers for Cinderella. He shrugged off the storybook comparison. He was on a mission of practicality, not one of romantic benevolence.

Meeting his parents would be difficult enough for Kara to bear. He didn't want her to feel ill at ease because she wasn't properly dressed. Dinner at the Raleigh-Harper estate was always formal, and he wanted her to feel good about herself.

His parents could be formidable at times. And without a doubt, they'd peruse Kara from head to toe. But he meant to marry her, and they'd best keep that in mind. She was a special lady. A queen, as far as he was concerned. A lovely young woman his parents would eventually come to respect.

One of his purchases was a simple but elegant cream-colored St. John's knit that was destined to be one of several staples in her closet, at least for this season. He had no doubt it would accentuate that fiery shade of hair, her ivory complexion and those teal-blue eyes. He couldn't wait to see her in it, and he hoped to put a smile back on her face, the warmth back in her heart.

By the time he returned to the suite, a room service cart had been left outside the door. Good, she'd fed the kids.

When he let himself in, Eric looked up from the television screen. "Hey, you missed dinner. It was really cool. This guy brought it right into our room. He hung around for a long time, just trying to make sure everything was okay."

Probably waiting for a tip, Michael thought. He'd have to make sure the guy was taken care of. "I'm glad you got a chance to eat."

"Kara didn't eat much, though," Eric said, his eyes still glued to the television screen, his lips skewed in concentration, and his fingers working the remote.

Michael scanned the empty room. "Where is she?"

"She's giving Ashley a bath. You should see the tub, Michael. It's big enough for all of us. Just like a swimming pool."

Michael chuckled. "I'll bet it is."

He made his way to the bathroom, following the sounds of water splashing, the baby squealing and Kara laughing.

Would coming home be like this from now on? he wondered. It was a strange but oddly comfortable thought. And it surprised him how Kara and the kids had made a hotel room feel like home.

When he entered the master bathroom, Kara looked up

in surprise. She'd pinned her hair up, but several damp tendrils had escaped. Her lopsided grin caught him off guard. He'd missed her cheerful, playful side and hoped her brightness had returned permanently.

Ashley screeched a happy greeting and slapped her hands into the water, splashing Kara in the face. Michael couldn't help but laugh.

Kara swiped her arm across the dribbles on her forehead and smiled. "I hope you don't mind us using your tub."

"It's for us to share." The thought of him and Kara sharing the tub caused a silly grin of his own. He'd have to add this new fantasy to the one he had of making love in a tree house. For a man who had never exercised his imagination, thoughts of Kara were becoming powerful aphrodisiacs.

"What do you have?" she asked, noticing the boxes in his hands.

"I picked up some things for you."

He expected a smile, but her mouth dropped and her eyes furrowed in dismay. "You're ashamed of the way I dress."

"No," he said, defending his purchase. "I want you to feel good about yourself when you meet my parents."

Her eyes darkened, and she bit her lip. She didn't believe him.

He stepped closer and knelt beside her. Water on the cool, marbled floor dampened the knees of his slacks, but he didn't care. "Kara, you deserve the best of everything in this world, the best I have to offer. And the sooner you begin to carry yourself that way, the better."

"The better for what?" she asked.

"The better for Eric and Ashley," he said, pulling out an ace he held. For goodness sake, didn't she understand what he meant? What he wanted to do for her? If not for him, then she needed to do it for the kids.

She seemed to ponder his argument, then looked at him with luminous eyes. "All right," she said. "When are we leaving?"

He didn't feel quite as good about her acquiescence as he'd expected. He'd hoped she would be happy with his purchases, pleased to meet his parents. Thrilled to marry him.

"Kathy will be here in about twenty minutes. How long will it take you to get ready?"

"Not long," she said.

And she'd been right. In twenty minutes, Kara had bathed and dressed. She stood before the bathroom mirror, wearing an off-white knit dress that fit perfectly. She'd never owned something so nice, so classy. She raised her hands to her hair, only to notice the worn leather of her watch. She removed it from her wrist and laid it upon the countertop. No need to mar the dress with adornments.

There was no way she was going to fret and primp as though this were a once-in-a-lifetime evening and she had to impress royalty. Other than the dress she wore, Kara would be herself. Like it or leave it, the Harpers of Boston would meet the young woman who had pulled herself up by the straps of her secondhand boots.

She applied a light coat of lipstick, a quick brush of mascara, and other than the scented body lotion she wore, that was it.

It was pure Kara Westin inside that fancy knit dress.

Like it or leave it.

Fifteen minutes later, after meeting the competent young woman who would baby-sit the children and leaving a list of instructions about their care, Kara took Michael's arm and proceeded to the hotel lobby where the limousine awaited them.

"Have I told you how lovely you look?" he asked, as they walked through the revolving glass door.

He had. Several times since she'd walked out of her room and into the living area of the suite they shared. He'd taken her by the hand, his eyes caressing her. She detected sincerity in his voice, appreciation in his gaze, both of which warmed her and gave her more confidence than she'd ever had. She squeezed the crook of his arm where her hand rested. "Yes, you have. Thank you."

He brushed her lips with a velvety kiss that chased whisper-soft shivers from her head to her toes. "Thank you, Kara."

She cocked her head to the side. "Why are you thanking me?"

"For what you do to me, I suppose." He smiled a slow, sensuous smile that caused her heart to race.

"It's the dress," she said, although she didn't believe the expensive knit had made a difference. Maybe it was her attitude. She felt more confident, more in control than she had in a long time. And she wasn't entirely sure why. She'd expected to be a bundle of frayed nerves, but having a new attitude seemed to make all the difference in the world.

"It's not the dress," he said, his voice husky yet soft.

Before she could speak, the limousine driver climbed from the car. "Champagne is open and on ice, sir."

"Thank you," Michael said as the driver opened the passenger door. "I thought we'd toast our engagement before we get to my parents' house."

Meet his parents.

Dinner at their house.

Memories of Mrs. Baker came flooding back, and Kara felt her self-confidence slump. She had no intention of celebrating an engagement that shouldn't take place, but a glass of champagne might take the edge off her nervousness and waylay the dread that had crept into her soul.

It was important that she make it through this evening with her pride intact. It was important for the kids.

And for herself, she realized.

She didn't think she could handle another mortifying dinner party.

But it seemed she'd landed right in the midst of one.

Michael could scarcely keep his hands off Kara in the limousine ride to his parents' home. Her scent tantalized his senses, and each time he looked at her he was reminded of tree-ripe peaches and fresh cream. Her unadorned elegance made him want to keep her by his side forever.

Forever.

He blew out a slow breath. Kara made him think of storybook endings, dreams and fantasies he'd never had before. He poured champagne for them both and handed her a crystal flute. "To the most beautiful woman in the world."

She flushed and pulled back her glass, unwilling to toast. "Let's not get carried away. I feel well-dressed and looking my best, but I'm certainly not a beauty in the classical sense."

"You are to me—inside and out." As the sincerity of his words passed between them, their gazes locked.

"Thank you." She raised her champagne, albeit reluctantly, then allowed the flutes to clink and the toast to continue. "May this evening go moderately well and be over in no time at all."

Michael smiled. "I know how difficult this must be for you."

"Do you?" She took a sip of champagne, then studied him over the rim. He watched memory and pain swirl in her eyes. "I had gone to dinner at Jason's house as a friend, not a date. His mother had all but accused me of pursuing him for financial security. I couldn't wait for the evening to end. And I swore I'd never allow myself to get into a situation like that again.''

"This dinner won't be easy for you," Michael said. Why lie? His parents would assume the same thing Mrs. Baker had, most likely. "But I intend to marry you. Everything I have will be yours. And we're facing my parents as a team. You're not in this alone."

"I've never experienced the finer things in life. I'll be out of place this evening, like a backwoods cousin coming into the big city for the first time." She brushed and fidgeted with the knit hem that rested upon her knee.

Michael placed his hand on top of hers, stilling her nervousness, he hoped. Her skin felt cool to the touch, and he wrapped her small, tapered fingers in the warmth of his palm. "You'll do just fine."

"Will I?" She rolled her eyes and shook her head. "I won't even know which fork to use."

Maybe not, Michael realized, but it didn't matter. It was time his parents learned to accept people for who they were. Kara was the finest human being they'd ever come in contact with—and the Harpers had entertained royalty. He cupped Kara's cheek, his thumb slowly stroking the downy softness. "Honey, use any fork you like, and I'll follow your lead."

He hoped his support eased her mind, made her feel as competent as she truly was. But before they could discuss it further, the limousine pulled into the long, circular drive of the Harper estate.

When they exited the vehicle, Kara stood proud—and as tall as her petite stature would allow. Michael slipped an arm around her waist and pulled her close. "You look stunning. And they'll be swept off their feet by your honesty, your compassion, the brightness of your smile. Just as I've been."

She offered him a dimpled grin that held a hint of mirthful skepticism. "Your parents will meet the real Kara Westin. Whether they like her or not."

"They'll like her," he said, hoping he'd convinced her. His parents would accept her. Eventually. And once they realized they'd better welcome her into the family or risk alienating their only son, things would be easier for all of them.

Michael opened the front door, and he and Kara stepped inside. For a moment, she scanned the interior of the foyer, and her steps slowed. Then, with a slight toss of her head, she regained her pride.

Atta girl, he wanted to say. Instead, he took her hand.

"Michael?" his mother's voice called from the circular stairway. "Is that you?"

"Yes," he answered.

"Good. It's been entirely too long since you've been home."

It had, he supposed, as far as she and his father were concerned. He hadn't been home since Christmas, and he'd only stayed a day and a half then.

Beatrice Raleigh-Harper swept down the stairs, her silvery hair pulled into a neatly coifed twist. She wore forest green, a color she often chose to accentuate the golden highlights of her hazel eyes.

"Mother, I'd like you to meet Kara Westin." He released his hold of her hand to allow a conventional greeting. "Kara, this is my mother, Beatrice Harper."

Kara took her cue and reached for the older woman's hand. "How do you do, Mrs. Harper?"

"Quite well, thank you." Elegant, but as stodgy as ever, his mother accepted the greeting with as much warmth as formality would allow. "It's always nice to meet a friend of Michael's. With his practice in California, it's not often that we do."

Beatrice gave Kara a regal once-over, a habit of hers

that Michael had long ago grown used to. He hoped Kara wouldn't be unnerved by it, but she flashed the older woman a warm smile. It didn't thaw his mother in the least, but it made Michael proud. "Kara and I are more than friends."

A sterling silver brow lifted slightly.

Before Michael could answer, his father strode through the arched entry to the living room. "It's good to have you home, son."

Michael shook his father's hand. "Dad, may I present Kara Westin, the woman I intend to marry."

His mother gasped softly, then regained her composure.

"Well, this is a surprise." Charles Harper fingered the knot of a blue silk tie that was, as usual, impeccably straight. Yet he, too, complied with the dictates of custom and took Kara's hand. "How do you do?"

"I'm fine, thank you." Kara handled herself with the grace and ease of a woman familiar with social protocol.

"How about a cocktail?" Charles asked. "Let's go into the study."

"That's a good idea," Beatrice added.

Here it comes. The inquisition. Where did you meet? Who are your parents? Are you good enough for our boy? Well, Michael would put a stop to the questions before they began. He placed his arm around Kara's shoulder and, following his parents, guided her into the study.

"What can I get you?" Charles asked.

"I'll have a Scotch and water." Michael turned to Kara. "They have anything you could possibly want."

"A glass of white wine," Kara said. "Please."

"Is Chardonnay all right?" Charles asked. "I have an extensive wine cellar. If you have a favorite label, I'll be happy to locate it."

"I'm not much of a connoisseur," she said. "I'll have whatever is easiest."

Charles pulled a bottle of wine from a refrigerator with a wood-grained door that matched the mahogany bar. "I have a bottle already chilled. It's a California wine, which I suppose is apropos."

"So, Kara," Beatrice began with that staid but inquisitive tone she used when curious. "Where did you and Michael meet?"

"In Harbor Haven. It's a small town about two hours south of Los Angeles. Michael vacationed there."

"A vacation?" Beatrice asked. "That doesn't seem like a very long time to know each other before making a serious commitment like marriage."

Before Michael could interject, Kara spoke. "It isn't. Michael offered marriage as a means for me to acquire custody of two small children."

Charles glanced up while pouring Kara's drink, just long enough to overfill the glass and splatter wine over his hand. His eye caught Michael's, and he reached for a linen towel to clean the mess.

"Marriage should be given a great deal of thought," Beatrice said.

"Now, just a minute," Michael said. "There's more to it than that. I want to marry Kara and adopt Ashley and Eric. I want us to be a family."

Charles handed a fresh glass of wine to Kara. His steel-gray brows furrowed in thought.

"Thank you." Kara took the crystal goblet and freshly starched linen cocktail napkin.

"Adopting children is a big step," Beatrice said, her voice an octave higher than normal.

Kara responded with grace and honesty. "Eric is six, and Ashley is almost a year old. They're very special children. I'd love to be their mother."

"I see," Beatrice said, although Michael knew she

didn't see anything at all. His mother's gaze locked on him. "Son, you've been through a rather horrid year and a half. I'm sure your emotions are a bit skewed, to say the least. I suggest you take this slowly."

"I've never been so sure of a decision in my life. I intend to marry Kara, if she finds me worthy." Both sets of parental brows raised in silent harmony. When Michael glanced at Kara, he found her equally surprised by his statement. "Kara is the most loving, genuine person I've ever met, and I'd be honored if she would agree to be my wife."

"If I agree to marry you," Kara said, "I'd insist on a prenuptial agreement. I don't want anything of yours, and if the marriage doesn't last, I don't want you obligated to pay alimony or child support."

"Don't be ridiculous," Michael said, ignoring the startled expressions of his parents. "I refuse to sign a prenuptial. And this marriage *will* last, unless you ask for a divorce."

Charles handed Beatrice a Manhattan, her usual evening cocktail, then took a drink of the vodka martini he'd made for himself.

"Kara's right about the prenuptial," Beatrice said. "Thank goodness you and Denise had one."

"Yes, you and Dad insisted upon one," Michael admitted. "And in hindsight, it proved to be an excellent idea. Denise made a mess of my life, not to mention my privacy, and she nearly landed me in prison. Maybe, on a subconscious level, I knew she was capable of dishonesty and deceit. But Kara is different. Her heart is pure."

"Thank you for the vote of confidence," Kara said. "But if we marry, I'll insist upon signing an agreement."

Beatrice and Charles looked at each other. Befuddled, Michael supposed, by the strange argument they were witnessing. A smile tugged at the corner of his mouth. Proud, sweet Kara was inadvertently giving the Raleigh-

Harpers a stunning example of her integrity. He hoped it was enough, at least for this evening.

A knock sounded at the study door, and Charles answered.

"Excuse me, sir," the butler said. "There's a phone call for the doctor."

"Who is it?" Michael asked, hoping it wasn't the sitter.

"She said her name was Maggie Templeton."

Kara looked at him, surprise etched on her face. Maggie's call had caught him by surprise, too.

"Excuse me," Michael said. "I'll take it in the other room."

Kara nodded, although the expression she wore, one of stunned apprehension, made him feel as though he'd abandoned her completely. Still, he knew Maggie wouldn't have called unless it was important, and although there was a phone in the study with the ringer turned off, he chose to speak to her in private.

Michael picked up the telephone in the living room. "Hello, Maggie."

"I'm sorry to bother you," she said, "but a drunk driver caused a major pileup on the freeway, and I've got a ten-year-old girl en route with a blunt force trauma and possible cardiac tamponade."

Compression of the heart, Michael realized, probably due to a penetrating injury to the chest. If blood clots were present, they'd need to open the chest wall and remove them. "How can I help?"

"I need a second opinion or, better yet, the most skillful cardiovascular surgeon I can find. The girl won't live without surgery, and her chances of survival are questionable with it." Maggie took a deep breath and exhaled slowly. "This is personal, Michael. This little girl's younger brother died last year due to a genetic liver disorder. We weren't able to get a donor organ in time. I've grown close to the family, and Jillian is the only child the parents have left. I can't let her die without knowing I did everything in my power to get her the best treatment available.''

''Where is she headed?''

''Boston General.''

''I'll leave now.''

''Thank you, Michael.''

''It's not a problem,'' Michael told Maggie. But it was going to be a big problem for Kara. Could he leave her with his parents? Without the benefit of his support?

It was either that or tell Maggie no. But he wouldn't let Maggie down, nor would he refuse to help the child facing surgery.

Memories of the arguments he'd had with Denise pounced on him. Denise had grown resentful, and he suspected Kara would, too. But he didn't have time to contemplate the repercussions.

This was it, he realized. The first of many disappointments his future wife would face. Guilt clawed at his chest, but he had to go. He was about to drop a bomb on Kara, then desert her when she needed him most. But it couldn't be helped.

She'd be angry and hurt, feelings Denise had struggled with many times. Yet leaving Kara with his parents bothered him more than she would ever know.

When he returned to the study, his parents and Kara watched him intently.

''I have to go to Boston General,'' he said. ''A ten-year-old girl was in a traffic accident. She's in critical condition and needs surgery.''

''Don't they have another surgeon available?'' his mother asked. ''You just arrived, and dinner is nearly ready.''

''Yes, but the child's not expected to live through surgery, and Maggie wants to assure the parents that the little girl has the best surgeon available." He reached for Kara's hand and pulled her to a stand. "Honey, I feel like a heel leaving you here, but I can't tell Maggie no."

"Of course you can't," Kara whispered. "I understand."

Her eyes bore evidence of her sincerity, but also her apprehension. God, how could he do this to her, especially when she'd told him of the dinner party she'd faced in the past. He checked his watch. He didn't have time to chat, to contemplate. His decision had been made. A child's life depended upon him.

"We'll see to it that Kara is taken back to the hotel," his father said. "That will give us a chance to get to know her."

That's what he was afraid of—an inquisition. "Maybe it would be best if Kara went with me. The limousine driver can drop her off at the hotel after he takes me to the hospital."

"But she hasn't eaten yet," his mother said. "You go on. We'll have dinner without you."

Michael looked at Kara, expecting tears and controlled anger. What he found was pride glistening in her eyes.

"Go," she whispered. "I'll be fine."

Michael swept her into his arms and kissed her. He expected Kara to withdraw, to pull away in embarrassment, but she leaned into him and returned the embrace and deepened the kiss—not so much in a sensual, sexual manner, but in a deeper sense. This kiss was laced with emotion and commitment.

It was a public display of affection he'd never witnessed between his parents, and one they'd never seen him exhibit, but he didn't care.

Let them see how much he appreciated this young woman who would face the wolves without a defender in sight.

Chapter Fifteen

"So," Mrs. Harper began. "Are you in the medical field, too?"

For a moment, Kara hesitated. The woman hadn't asked anything inappropriate, but Kara wondered whether that was a subtle, classy way of asking what line of work a person was in, a way of placing someone on a particular rung of the social ladder.

The old feelings of insecurity began to flex their muscles, but she fought them off with pride and honesty. "No. I'm working as a waitress at the Pacifica Bar and Grill, but just until I have enough money set aside to attend graduate school. I intend to be a schoolteacher."

"How nice," the older woman said, yet she didn't smile. Not really. And Kara realized Mrs. Harper didn't like the idea of having a daughter-in-law who worked at all, let alone at a bar and grill.

"I imagine you will be able to quit work once you and our son marry," Mr. Harper said.

Kara didn't think he was making a statement, but rather, as his wife had done, was quizzing her about motives and plans. Well, they certainly didn't need to pry. She'd make it easy on them, because all she had to offer was the truth.

"I'll continue to work so that I can afford tuition."

Mr. Harper placed his drink on the side table. "But as Michael's wife, you won't have any worries about money. You won't need to work."

"On the contrary," Kara said. "I have no intention of allowing Michael to support me."

"Isn't that a bit out of the ordinary?" Mrs. Harper asked, a silvery brow arched, blue eyes probing.

Kara fingered the stem of her wineglass, then caught the older woman's gaze. "I imagine it's unusual, but being self-reliant is very important to me."

"I suppose that's admirable," Mr. Harper said. "But certainly not necessary."

She decided to lay her cards on the table, humble as they were, then brace herself for snooty or patronizing responses from Michael's parents. "I love your son, but if the fate of Ashley and Eric weren't in the balance, I would never agree to marry him."

They both looked stunned.

Mrs. Harper recovered first. "Why not?"

"I come from a poor background, and as I'm sure you both know, my social status is worlds away from his. I'd never feel comfortable. And I couldn't bear to have people whispering behind our backs. Michael deserves so much more than that." She placed her wineglass on the small linen napkin and set it on the table. "And quite frankly, Mr. and Mrs. Harper, I deserve better, too."

Kara expected raised brows or at least some subtle agreement. What she received instead was a couple of slow smiles and something akin to cautious respect.

A knock sounded at the door again, and this time when

Mr. Harper answered, the butler announced that dinner was ready.

"Ladies," Mr. Harper said, pointing toward the door. "Let's continue this conversation in the dining room."

The dinner progressed without Michael and, so it seemed, without a hitch. Kara answered his parents' questions and made a few comments of her own.

They thanked her for coming and said they were glad to have met her. Kara wasn't entirely sure they meant it, but she appreciated hearing the words, just the same.

Joseph, the elderly limousine driver, took her back to the hotel, then waited to take the young medical student who had watched Eric and Ashley home.

Michael had given Kara money to pay the baby-sitter before he left for the hospital. The amount had surprised Kara, since she knew how long it took to earn that kind of money. Kathy was on financial aid, Michael had explained, but still worked to put herself through school. Paying her well not only assisted the young med student's plight, but assured them of her services next time they needed a competent sitter.

"It's too much," Kathy said, when Kara handed her the hundred-dollar bill.

"Michael thinks you deserve it."

"Thank you. And please thank him, too. I sure appreciate it."

Kara smiled, pleased to be a part of Michael's generosity. "How were the kids?"

"Perfect." Kathy reached for her backpack and slung it over her shoulder. "For the most part, Eric took care of Ashley. They sure love each other. It was heartwarming to see."

Kara knew what she meant. Those kids were easy to love. "Did you have any trouble getting them to bed?"

"Not at all. I read them a story like you suggested, and they went right to sleep. You know, I've done a lot of baby-sitting in the past, and I've never had an easier job. Those kids were a pleasure to watch.''

Kara couldn't have been any prouder or happier if she'd given birth to Ashley and Eric herself. ''Thank you for helping us out.''

''Anytime,'' Kathy said. ''Well, I guess I'd better go.''

Kara led the way to the door. ''The limousine is waiting outside for you.''

Kathy paused before leaving and chuckled. ''This has been a real experience for me. I've never been shuttled to work in a limousine before. And I've never been paid so well.''

The whole Harper lifestyle was a new experience for Kara, too, but she didn't mention it.

''Thanks again,'' Kara said, as Kathy stepped out the door. ''Good night.''

After looking in on the sleeping children, Kara kicked off her shoes, settled into an easy chair and took the television remote in hand. She stretched out her feet and clicked on the power. An old black and white movie was on, and although it was a classic romantic comedy, she dozed off before it was over and didn't wake until someone nudged her shoulder.

Michael stood over Kara and watched her eyes open. She caught sight of him, then scanned the living room, as though momentarily unaware of her surroundings.

''I was going to wait up for you, but I guess I fell asleep. How is the little girl?''

''All right,'' Michael said. ''So far.''

He hadn't really wanted to leave the hospital so soon. It wasn't his habit to leave until after the patient was out of recovery. But he'd been so concerned about Kara he'd wanted to see her, make sure she'd survived the evening with his parents.

He supposed he could have called to check on her, but

it was nearly three by the time he'd finished surgery and spoke to Jillian's parents, and he was afraid he'd wake the kids.

She yawned, then stood and gave him a hug. "I'm so glad you could help."

"Me, too." He wrapped her in his arms, unwilling to let a quick hug suffice. "I'm sorry about leaving you last night. How did the rest of the evening go?"

"It was all right," Kara said.

"My mother can be blunt at times. I hope she didn't upset you."

Kara gave him a lopsided grin, and he detected a hint of humor in her eyes. "I've met worse."

"I suppose that's good," Michael said, wishing she'd open up even more, grant him the lilt of her laughter, let him see the fun-loving twinkle in her eyes. "If I hadn't been called away—"

Kara cupped his face with both hands. "I'm so proud of you, Michael. You have a skill that can save lives."

Proud of him? No one had ever been proud of him. Not Denise, and certainly not his parents, who couldn't understand his desire to go to medical school instead of joining the investment firm with his father. He'd never explained his reasons for veering from the family business, but a lot of his drive was based on a desire to achieve something on his own, to be recognized as an individual and not part of a golden conglomerate. He'd earned a great deal of admiration and respect as a surgeon among his peers and his patients. But no one had ever voiced their pride in him. No one but Kara.

Her eyes glistened with sincerity, and suddenly, Michael realized he'd found the elusive gold ring, the award he'd been seeking all his life. She dropped her hands from his cheeks to his chest.

He wondered if she knew how those few words had

touched his soul, had stirred feelings of gratitude and appreciation.

All he could think of was making her his wife, of keeping her near, of seeing her happy—forever.

He tilted her chin with the tip of his finger, and for a moment lost himself in her eyes.

"Thank you," he said, his words a breath against her lips.

"For what?"

"Being proud of me." He doubted she'd understand what that meant to him. He'd yet to hear either of his parents say anything vaguely similar. Although, he suspected, they probably assumed things like love and pride were so apparent that they didn't need to be voiced.

She slipped her arms around his neck. "I admire your skill and your dedication to your patients. And I think you're a wonderful human being."

His heart swelled, and emotions swirled in his chest, but he wasn't about to contemplate them, analyze them. Instead, he kissed her, first with a slow brush of his lips, then with feeling.

And she kissed him back, equally caught up in the heady desire. He relished each heated touch, each soft whimper. No woman had ever moved him like this.

Kara turned him inside out. He wanted her. Badly. And he knew, without a doubt, that she wanted him, too. Her kiss drove him wild, and her touch sent heat coursing through his blood. He pulled his lips from hers and rested his forehead against the crown of her hair. When he spoke, his ragged breath gave his words a husky tone. "Kara, let me take you to bed. My bed."

His eyes searched hers for an answer, and she gave him a shy but determined smile. "I'd like that. Very much."

"I can't imagine anything sweeter than loving you." He lifted her in his arms and carried her into the master bedroom, enclosing them in privacy, then set her on her feet beside the bed.

She wore a plain white cotton gown and looked so virginal, so precious, that he couldn't help but stare. "You're beautiful."

"When you say that, I almost believe you."

"It's not a lie, Kara." As far as he was concerned, she was the most breathtaking woman in the world, her beauty etched as clearly on the inside as it was on the surface.

Her heated gaze locked with his, and she lifted the nightgown from her head and let it drop onto the floor. Wearing only a pair of white lace panties, she stood before him, her bare breasts and dusky nipples taunting him unmercifully.

Michael balanced over an abyss of raw emotions more powerful than any he had ever felt before. "I've never wanted anyone like I want you."

"Make love to me, Michael. Please." She pulled his shirttails from his pants and slowly undid each button.

Her fingers skimmed his skin, heating his blood and driving him wild. After removing his shirt, she ran her hands over his chest, relishing, it seemed, each corded muscle.

He slipped off his shoes and removed his clothes, then, taking her cheeks in both hands, he kissed her with reverent passion. He wanted her with a desire that went beyond reason and hoped he could control himself long enough to be gentle.

Her first time should be special, yet all he could think of was losing himself in her. He felt like a teenage boy about to embark on his first sexual encounter, while at the same time he felt like an experienced lover who had found his kindred spirit.

She cupped his cheek. "You'll have to show me what to do."

She pulled his mouth to hers, and he was lost in her taste, in her arms, in her soul. When the kiss had left them both breathless, he laid her on the bed and joined her.

He would take his time, make it good for her. Make it good for both of them.

Never had he felt so crazed with need, so vulnerable, yet so powerful.

And never had Kara felt so special.

Michael held her as though she was as fragile as a whisper. In his embrace, she felt safer than she'd ever felt in her life. And she was determined to give him all she had to offer.

Michael loved her with his eyes, his hands and his mouth. He stroked her in places she'd never been touched and stirred a passion so powerful, she didn't know if she'd ever be the same again.

She was drowning in love and desire. "Michael, please. I want you now."

He hovered over her with an expression of such longing that she wondered if it might be love. Not necessarily, she supposed. But no doubt he felt some of the same things she was feeling.

"It will hurt," he said, voice soft yet husky, "but I'll try to be gentle."

She didn't care about pain, all she wanted was to feel him in the place he needed to be, in the place she wanted him to be. She opened for him and placed a hand upon his bare hip, guiding him, it seemed.

He entered her slowly at first, as though trying to be careful. But she knew what she wanted and arched forward, drawing him deeper. The initial pain was surpassed by fulfillment as he moved inside of her.

The loving rhythm built to a powerful crescendo, making them one, taking them to paradise and somewhere beyond. As they peaked together, pleasure, like a million tiny stars, burst through Kara, touching her heart and soul.

Kara loved Michael and had willingly given herself to him, even though she hadn't decided whether she would marry him or not. But she would never regret making love to him. Never.

They lay there, in each other's arms, quiet and spent. Kara wished they could stay this way forever. Lost in love.

Well, at least on her part, she decided. Michael hadn't said anything about love.

Would his fondness for her and the kids be enough?

In the long run, she didn't think it would. She closed her eyes, and while relishing their closeness, wondered what Michael was thinking.

Had he enjoyed their lovemaking?

Did he have any regrets?

Michael held Kara close, but with each beat of his slowing heart rate, he felt more and more guilty.

He, of all people, had forgotten to use protection. How could he have been so foolish, so swept up in emotion that he'd completely lost his head?

There weren't any health issues to be concerned about, since he'd taken a precautionary blood test after he and his ex had split. But what about pregnancy? How could he have let that possibility slide by without notice, without forethought?

What if they had conceived a child?

A baby.

His and Kara's.

Instead of near panic, a warm smile tugged at his lips. Kara, her belly swollen with his child. Their child.

What would it look like? He tried to imagine an infant with her red hair and bright blue eyes, but what he envisioned instead was Kara in a rocking chair with a small bundle at her breast, a blessed smile on her face.

He glanced at Kara, hoping to see a smile now. One that would absolve him of guilt. Brushing a strand of hair from her cheek, he kissed her lightly.

And she smiled. Not a smile like he'd seen in the Madonnalike image of her and their child, but one of contentment.

That was okay, he supposed. He looked forward to sharing the afterglow, to letting her know how good it had been, how special she was. He pulled her close, wishing they could stay this way forever. And they might have, he suspected, if the telephone hadn't rung.

Michael rolled to the side of the bed and somehow managed to snag the phone on the first ring. "Hello."

It was the hospital.

Unexpected complications.

"I'll be right there." He sat up and began reaching for discarded clothing before he had even hung up the telephone.

Damn. Michael had never experienced such professional guilt. He should never have left the hospital before Jillian came out of recovery. Sure, other doctors did it all the time, but *he* never had.

Guilt attacked him from all sides.

It had been his guilt at leaving Kara alone with his parents that had made him rush home to see her, to make sure she had survived the experience without him. And now he was leaving her again, when he should be holding her and sharing the wonder of what they'd just done.

"What's the matter?" Kara asked.

"I've got to go back to the hospital. There are some complications."

"I understand." She placed her hand on his back.

Did she? He picked up the telephone and called for a cab.

"I'm sorry about leaving you like this." What kind of guy took a woman's virginity, then left her to lie alone? Denise had often complained when he had to leave, but he'd never felt as remorseful as he did today.

Maybe that's because Denise had wanted to be a doctor's wife, had wanted to enjoy all of the benefits without the downside. He supposed she'd deserved to suffer the consequences of his profession.

But Kara didn't. She hadn't signed up for any of this, hadn't deserved any of it.

"Take good care of that little girl," she said, sitting up on the bed and pulling the sheet up to her breasts. Hiding herself, it seemed. Withdrawing from the intimacy.

Guilt shot through him, but he couldn't take time to deal with it now.

"I'll try and make it up to you," he said. But he knew he could never make up for leaving her like this.

"Don't worry about it," she said. "I'm fine."

Fine, she'd said. But he didn't believe it for a minute. She should be lying in his arms, hearing him whisper sweet words to her. Instead, she was watching him slip on his shoes. When he reached the bedroom door, he paused. "Eric's appointment is at two o'clock this afternoon. I'll try to be back, but if I can't—"

"I'll take the bus," she said.

"The hell you will," he said, then suddenly felt sorry for his sharp reply. It wasn't her fault that he felt so guilty, so keyed up. In the past, he'd often left feeling defensive and angry.

But never guilty. Not like this.

He raked his fingers through his hair. "I'm sorry for snapping at you. You're not going to ride the bus, and that's final. I'll have the limo out front at one-thirty."

He offered her a sorry smile, one that conveyed how badly he felt about leaving her alone, about not being able to provide her with the emotional support she needed. But she'd already turned away. It was just as well, he supposed. How could he apologize for being a surgeon?

Then, feeling like a king-size jerk, he slipped out the door and hurried to take care of the little girl he should never have left.

Chapter Sixteen

Kara lay in the bed, breathing in the scent of Michael and their lovemaking. It would have been nice to have laid her head on his shoulder for a while longer, to have talked about the wonder of what they'd shared, but she understood why he'd rushed to the hospital. Michael was a hero, as far as she was concerned.

The poor girl's parents must be worried sick, but it must be some comfort to know a talented surgeon would try to save their daughter's life. She whispered a prayer for the child's recovery. It was a good thing Michael was in town and able to help. Kara again felt a surge of pride and respect.

She might be mistaken, but Michael had seemed to be surprised to hear how proud she was of him. He was a wonderful person as well as a remarkable surgeon. A woman would be lucky to be his wife.

And not because of his wealth and status, she reminded herself.

Still, she was unsure whether she should accept his offer of marriage or not. If she had only her own interests to consider, the answer would be no. But there didn't seem to be any other way to ensure her custody of Eric and Ashley; she'd do anything for the kids.

Closing her eyes, she tried to picture being Michael's wife, but for the life of her, she couldn't imagine all it would entail. Social functions and charity benefits. Formal cocktail parties and dinners. Hobnobbing with the rich and famous. She cringed and wondered how she could possibly handle the social aspect of their relationship, the reality of it.

She hugged a pillow that still carried his scent, held it close and inhaled slowly. At least their physical relationship promised to be incredibly good, even if the other aspects were worrisome.

Her mind was full of what-ifs, and her body still tingled from his touch. Unable to sleep, she lay amidst the tangled sheets and memories of what she and Michael had shared.

At the break of dawn, Ashley cried out. Kara slipped on her robe and went to the room where the children slept.

Ashley stood in the crib the bellman had provided, fussing and looking about the room. When she recognized Kara, she reached out her little hands.

"I'm here, sweetheart." Kara picked her up and held her close. "It's okay, Ashley, I'm here."

"Ma," the baby cried. "Ma."

The maternal endearment touched Kara's heart, and she soothed the baby while walking into the living room so they wouldn't wake Eric. He needed his sleep. The small desk clock read six o'clock, but it was still three in the morning back home.

"Ba ba," Ashley said.

"Good idea. I'll fix you a bottle, then we can sit in the chair and watch television."

Ashley had emptied the bottle and gone back to sleep when the news came on.

The weatherman wrapped up his report with the forecast of an early snow in northern Minnesota. When the camera returned to the news studio, a well-dressed newscaster told of a five-car pileup on the interstate last night.

Kara wondered if the little girl who was now Michael's patient had been injured in that accident. She whispered another prayer that the child would survive, all the while feeling proud of Michael, of his skill, of his reputation as a surgeon.

When Jason Baker's face flashed on the screen, she sat up straight. What in the world was he doing on national television?

She recognized the scenery and realized he was in California. Due to the daylight, she assumed the interview had been taped.

"It seems renowned surgeon Michael Harper has taken a couple of orphaned children under his wing," a female reporter said. "If you recall, Dr. Harper was exonerated of any wrongdoing in the recent arrest and conviction of his ex-wife and her lover, Senate candidate Daniel Walker. Mrs. Harper laundered illegal campaign contributions through the doctor's office. Since then, the doctor has maintained a low profile.

"I'm in Harbor Haven, California," the woman continued, a breeze blowing dark strands of hair across her face. "And this is Jason Baker, an area businessman who is a friend of the children's family. Mr. Baker, would you please tell us about the orphans Dr. Harper has befriended?"

"Sure," Jason said, flashing his cosmetically enhanced pearly whites at the camera. "About a year ago, their parents died in a car crash, but Eric, the little kid, got his baby sister out of the car seat and carried her to safety. Cute little tyke. Brave, too, I guess. Anyway, the community pitched in and donated a bunch of money to a fund for the orphans. I've got friends down at Coastal Savings and Loan, and they said there's about a hundred thousand dollars in the account already.''

''That's wonderful,'' the woman said. ''And how does Dr. Harper fit into all of this?''

''Eric, the little boy, was hurt pretty bad in the wreck. From what everyone in Harbor Haven is saying, his leg hasn't healed right. I guess Dr. Harper is flying him to Boston to see some top-notch specialist.'' Jason crossed his arms, displaying the biceps he was so proud of.

''That's wonderful news for little Eric,'' the woman said.

''Yeah,'' Jason interjected. ''But I hope someone watches out for the kids and all that money.''

Kara rolled her eyes. She didn't believe Jason gave a rat's hind end about the trust fund or the well-being of Eric and Ashley. He'd never shown the least bit of concern in the past, but the comments he'd made yesterday had earned him a quote on the front page of the local newspaper. Since his only other claim to journalistic fame was a mention in the society column as ''also attending,'' a television interview was undoubtedly a dramatic move up for him.

''You know,'' Jason added, ''Kara Westin, a cocktail waitress down at the Pacifica Bar and Grill, has set her sights on adopting those kids. And I wouldn't be surprised if she made a play for that divorced surgeon, too. But hey,'' Jason said, lifting his chin and flashing another smile at the camera, ''I guess you can't blame people for trying to better themselves.''

''Thank you, Mr. Baker,'' the reporter said. The camera followed her as she moved away from Jason. ''We'll have more on this story tomorrow. This is Joanna Haw-thorne, reporting from California.''

More tomorrow? How could Jason do that—make her look money-hungry and conniving?

If Kara ever got her hands on him, she'd punch him in the weak chin he'd had enhanced by a plastic surgeon in Palm Springs.

How dare he do that to her?

Tears welled in her eyes, and her shoulders slumped. What would the high-society folks of Boston think of her after hearing that?

Not much, she surmised. And there wasn't anything she could do to defend herself.

For a few hours, she had seriously considered Mi-chael's offer of marriage, but there was no way she could accept now. Not even with a prenuptial agreement. Her pride wouldn't let her.

She had lost Michael. And now she would lose the kids.

Then hard reality struck her like a two-by-four upside the head.

How could she lose what had never been hers?

It was nearly noon when Michael finally left the hos-pital and returned to the hotel. Ten-year-old Jillian Don-ahue had not only pulled through the surgery, but had shown enough improvement in her vital signs to be up-graded from critical to serious condition. This time, he had waited at the hospital until he was sure she was stable.

The sun had risen high in the gray autumn sky by the time the cab dropped him off at the New England Garden Towers. He wondered if Kara and the children were in the room.

He'd called the hotel earlier, but didn't get an answer. She'd probably taken them downstairs for breakfast, but now that he was away from the hospital, away from the medical crisis at hand, he began to worry.

Leaving Kara without taking time to enjoy the afterglow of their lovemaking had been more difficult than leaving her with his parents. He hoped it hadn't taken a toll on her. Or on the relationship he hoped to build.

He paid the cabby, but before he could slip through the lobby doors, a small, familiar voice called from the walkway that led to the street.

"Hey, Michael, you're back!" Eric hurried along the sidewalk, while Kara and Ashley followed several steps behind. "We're going to have lunch. Do you want to eat with us? They got a really cool restaurant here. That's where we ate breakfast. And do you know what? It's free. All you gotta do is sign your name and room number."

Michael smiled at the warmth of the greeting and the child's innocent understanding of the hotel charging system. He glanced toward Kara, hoping to share a smile, to see the glow he'd come to appreciate. Her smile seemed empty and lacking. He tried to hide his disappointment. "Sure, Eric. I'll join you for lunch."

Then he took Kara by the hand. "I'm sorry that I ran out like that."

"I understand," she said softly. "How is the little girl?"

"She's going to pull through."

"That's great news," Kara said, but her voice didn't match her words. Something was definitely wrong, and Michael knew what it was.

Just like he feared, he'd disappointed her, proved that he couldn't be a considerate lover or a good husband, that he wouldn't be a dependable father.

But it was only because of his job, his responsibility to his patients, he wanted to say in his own defense, but the words wouldn't come out.

In the past, any line of defense he'd used with Denise

hadn't worked. He doubted there was much he could say to Kara to make her feel better, so he just said the obvious. "I made it in time to go to the appointment with Dr. Cunningham."

He didn't think it was enough consolation, but it was the best he could come up with.

On the drive to Dr. Cunningham's office, Kara could scarcely believe the beauty of autumn in New England. She'd seen the colorful pictures of fall foliage in travel books, but never in person.

"Can I open a window?" she asked Michael.

"Sure."

Orange, gold and red leaves waved in the breeze and occasionally fluttered to the ground. "Look at the trees, Eric. Aren't they gorgeous?"

The boy edged closer to the open window and peered outside. "Wow. Our trees don't look like that. These look like they're on fire."

Kara laughed. "We don't get to experience the seasons like people in some parts of the country, that's for sure."

"Can we take some leaves home to show Grandma?"

"That's a wonderful idea," Kara said. She knew that Lizzie would be pleased. The older woman cherished everything Eric brought her and would probably give the gift a place of honor. "Your grandma will enjoy seeing the pretty colors. And since intersession is nearly over, school will start again in a few days. You can take some to show-and-tell."

"That would be so cool. I'll bet none of the kids have ever seen leaves like these before."

"Probably not," Kara said.

Ten minutes later, the limousine pulled up in front of a large, redbrick building that housed several different medical offices. While they exited the car, the driver pulled Ashley's stroller from the trunk.

"You're not comfortable riding in the limousine, are you?" Michael asked.

There was a lot more to Kara's discomfort than riding in a luxury vehicle, but she'd let it go at that. "No. I'd rather take the bus."

"Once we get back to California, you won't have to ride in a limo again. Not if you don't want to. I'll get you a car."

She started to interrupt, to tell him that things had changed, but it didn't seem like the right time to bring up the discussion, not with the kids present. She wouldn't postpone the inevitable for long.

Later today, after they'd seen the specialist, there would be plenty of time to talk. Plenty of time for her to tell him she couldn't marry him or accept his financial assistance.

"Which door is it?" Eric asked.

"The last one on the right." Michael set up the stroller so Kara could place Ashley in the seat.

"Can I walk ahead?" Eric asked. "I want to start collecting leaves for Grandma. And there's a bunch of leaves on the grass right by the office."

"Sure," Michael said.

When they reached the corner of the building, a door opened and a tall, graceful blonde exited the first office. She wore a colorful lab coat and carried a large gray envelope. Kara wondered whether she was a doctor or a nurse.

"Michael," she said, eyes lighting up.

He smiled back. Warmly. "Is this where your office is located?"

"It's on the back side of the building. I just came by to ask a colleague for a second opinion on this X ray."

For a moment, Kara felt as unimportant as a spot on the wall. She wondered whether Michael would ever get around to introducing her.

"Maggie, this is Kara Westin. A good friend of mine."

A good friend? Is that all she was to him? Why hadn't he introduced her as his fiancée? She really wasn't, not anymore, but he didn't know that yet.

"And Kara, this is Dr. Margaret Templeton."

While the women shook hands in greeting, Kara studied the tall, shapely physician. Golden blond hair lay upon her shoulders in an attractive but sophisticated cut. Caramel-colored eyes boasted intelligence and sincerity. She was striking. And obviously one of Michael's peers.

"How do you do, Dr. Templeton?" Kara asked.

"Please, call me Maggie," the attractive woman said.

"Maggie and I attended medical school together," Michael added, as though reading the curiosity in Kara's mind.

But could he read her apprehension? The gentle prod of jealousy? The old feelings of insecurity? This woman, Kara realized, was far more suited to be Michael's wife.

"Med school seems like such a long time ago," Maggie said, her voice a bit wistful.

Had they been lovers? Kara wondered. The image clawed at her heart, and she had to bite her lip not to wince or react.

"It will be good to have you in Los Angeles," Michael said. Then he looked at Kara. "Maggie's relocating her practice, and I helped her find a place."

"That's great." Kara feigned a smile. For goodness sake, what was the matter with her? If she was so dead set against marrying Michael, she certainly couldn't insist he remain single and celibate. Still, she didn't like the idea of him and this woman together. Of him with any woman, for that matter. But there was nothing she could do about it. Nothing at all, except hide her pain with a smile.

"There's a hospital benefit coming up next Friday. I

don't suppose you'd like to attend with me?'' Maggie asked Michael.

Kara's jaw dropped, but she quickly recovered. Was Maggie asking Michael out on a date? Right in front of her as though she was nothing more than a nanny to the kids?

Well, why not? she asked herself. That's exactly what she was, a well-loved baby-sitter. Besides, Michael hadn't given Maggie any indication he and Kara were anything other than friends.

She had half a notion to stomp on his foot or kick him in the shins, but she refrained from doing anything other than squeeze the stroller handle until her knuckles ached.

''I know how tough it must be for you to go to that particular function alone,'' Michael said. ''But our intention is to be back in California tomorrow or the next day.''

''I'm a survivor,'' Maggie said. ''I'll hold my head up and paste on a happy face.''

Kara wondered what she meant by that. She appeared confident and in control.

Michael gave Maggie a kiss on the forehead. ''You're strong. You'll make it.''

She nodded. ''I know.''

''Well,'' Michael said. ''We have an appointment in about five minutes, so I guess we'd better head for David's office.''

''I'll walk with you,'' Maggie said. ''It's on my way.''

As they reached the shady spot where Eric had stopped to look for leaves, Michael slowed his steps. ''Come on, sport. It's time to meet Dr. Cunningham.''

Maggie knelt and offered the boy her hand. ''You must be Eric Campbell.''

''Yes. How did you know?'' the boy asked while shaking the doctor's hand.

"I heard about you on television," Maggie said. "They say you're a hero."

Eric bit his lip. "Yeah, I know that. But I'm not a very good hero 'cause I didn't save my mom and dad."

Maggie glanced at Michael and Kara before answering the boy. Her compassionate eyes spoke volumes. "You know, Eric, I like to think of myself as a hero, too, but I can't save everyone. It's a very hard lesson for us heroes to learn."

Eric nodded. "Grandma said that God needs a lot of angels in Heaven."

Maggie placed a gentle hand upon his cheek. "Your grandmother is right."

In spite of the irrational waves of jealousy, Kara found herself liking Maggie. But something bothered her.

Maggie had heard about Eric's heroism on television.

What had she heard about Kara?

And what did she believe?

When they reached the door to Dr. Cunningham's office, Michael paused and spoke to Maggie. "I'll talk to you before we head back to Los Angeles."

"Thank you."

"Your ex-husband was a fool," Michael said.

Maggie smiled, her eyes locking on his. "So was your ex-wife."

Kara felt like a pair of old sneakers in the shoe section of a fancy department store. She glanced at her feet, then reached into the diaper bag and grabbed a bottle of apple juice, even though Ashley was contented, then bent to offer it to the baby.

"It was a pleasure meeting you," Maggie said.

Kara glanced up from an awkward, stooped position in front of the stroller and smiled. "Thanks. It was nice meeting you, too." She hoped the words sounded as though she actually meant them.

She did, of course, in a bittersweet sort of way.

When Maggie strode around the corner, Michael opened the door to Dr. Cunningham's office. "Come on. We'd better go inside."

They barely had time to fill out the paperwork and take a seat in the waiting room before Eric's name was called.

"Let's leave the stroller here," Michael said, taking Eric's hand. "Kara, why don't you just carry the baby?"

As they followed the nurse to an exam room, Michael felt oddly like a husband and father. It was an interesting feeling. A good feeling.

Within minutes, David Cunningham joined them. Introductions were made, and as was his custom, David got right to the point.

"I've studied the X rays, and it appears as though the growth plate is out of place. Not a lot, but certainly enough to be problematic. The postoperative films didn't detect an irregularity, but it's there now. I'd like to go in and correct it."

Michael glanced at Kara, who had been looking at him for confirmation of the diagnosis. He smiled and nodded slowly, then addressed David. "It's correctable, then."

"Yes, I believe so. I won't know for sure until I get in there and take a look, but the films don't indicate any damage."

"I don't want another surgery," Eric said, big tears welling in his eyes.

Compassion and understanding swept across Kara's face. "I know, honey. But it's important that we fix this problem before it gets worse."

"No," Eric said. "It's scary, and it hurts."

Michael had heard many kids say the same thing, display the same concerns. But this time, he wasn't just an observer or a detached surgeon. This wasn't a patient, this little boy was Eric. His son.

"Would it make you feel any better if I went into

surgery with you?'' he asked. "I'll stay the entire time, from the moment you close your eyes until you wake up.''

"Yeah," Eric said. "But they won't let anyone in the room. I asked if they'd let my grandma come in last time, but they said no.''

"Your grandma isn't a doctor or nurse," Michael said. Then he looked at David. "Do you mind?''

"Not at all.''

"When do you want to operate?" Michael asked.

"I'll have to check scheduling, but I assume you want this done as soon as possible.''

Michael nodded, then realizing it wasn't only his decision, turned to Kara. "What do you think?''

"I'm sure that would be best. But we'd better run it past Lizzie. She's the legal guardian.''

"Of course," Michael said.

And within minutes everything was settled. Or so it seemed.

David's office staff was competent and quick. In no time at all, the surgery had been scheduled for the day after tomorrow. Lizzie had been notified and agreed to sign and fax all the necessary forms granting permission for treatment. Eric, although reluctant to face one more operation, was resigned.

But Kara remained unusually solemn and introspective.

After they'd left the office and Eric had climbed into the limousine, Michael caught her hand in his. "What's the matter? Are you worried about the procedure?''

"No. I know he's in good hands. And I'm especially glad to know you've agreed to be there with him. It's comforting to him, and it certainly eases my mind.''

Her mind might be at ease about the surgery, but something else bothered her.

Something serious, he surmised.

Whenever Denise had gotten angry with him, he'd resorted to buying her gifts—a diamond bracelet, an emerald necklace.

But gifts weren't going to placate Kara. And God knew he wasn't very good at apologies or at talking things through. Emotional intimacy had never been his strong suit, which, up until now, had been a good thing. As a doctor, he couldn't allow himself to become emotionally involved with his patients.

But Kara deserved a husband who was sensitive. A man who wasn't at all like him.

He would try, of course, to get in touch with his feelings, assuming he had some lying dormant somewhere. Even if he did, he wasn't sure he knew how to access them.

For the first time in his life, Michael feared his best wouldn't be good enough.

And that scared the hell out of him.

Chapter Seventeen

The ride to the hotel was interminably long. Ashley had fallen asleep in the car seat, and Eric seemed lost in thought.

Although Kara stared out the window, Michael knew she wasn't looking at autumn leaves.

"When we get back to the hotel, I'm going to call Kathy and have her come play with you guys," he told Eric.

"That would be way cool," Eric said. "She's a lot of fun."

Kara turned to face him. Her eyes bore the weight of grief unspoken. "Why do you want to call a sitter?"

"Because you and I have to talk."

She nodded, then returned her gaze to the passing scenery.

Two hours later, Michael and Kara took the limousine to the coast. He hoped by providing the ocean, sand and salt air, he could replicate the ambience of the west coast.

And possibly the happiness they'd shared in Harbor Haven.

It was a quiet ride, much quieter than Michael had intended. The limousine pulled to a stop along the edge of a beautiful and, at this time of year, secluded stretch of shoreline.

"Come with me," he said, taking her hand in his. He helped her from the car, and they walked down a narrow, sandy path to the beach. There was a crisp chill to the air, but the scent of the sea was invigorating.

"It's beautiful," Kara whispered.

He was glad he'd chosen this place to bring her, glad he could tell her the words that begged to be said. He loved her. It was as simple as that. "I knew you'd like it. Let's take off our shoes."

She smiled at him, in that playful manner he adored. "You're loosening up, Doctor."

"You've been a good influence on me. Thank you." He dropped her hand long enough for them to remove their shoes.

The sand squished between his toes, and he had the urge to run down the beach, to chase waves like he'd done as a child. Some things in life couldn't be bought, he realized. The beauty of nature, good health and the love of a woman like Kara.

A seagull swooped overhead, and the water lapped gently on the sand. They walked for a while, both deep in thought, so it seemed, and relishing the beauty of the world around them.

Michael slowed his steps and pulled Kara to a halt. When she turned to see why he'd stopped, he caught her chin with his finger and tilted her gaze to his. "I don't like seeing you so sad. What's the matter?"

She blinked, and her eyes filled with tears. "A marriage between us will never work. I don't even know why I let you talk me into considering it."

Her words sucker punched him. "I'm sorry about leaving you alone after we made love."

"Don't be sorry. I understood why you left."

Did she? He wasn't so sure. But if that wasn't the cause of her sadness, he wasn't sure what was. He raked his hand through his hair. He wasn't any good at talking about feelings. Not his, anyway. But he wanted to know what was on her mind. In her heart.

"You know," she said. "We'll be in town for that hospital benefit Maggie was talking about. Maybe you should tell her you can go with her, after all."

So that's what it was. Kara was jealous of Maggie. Well, he'd just have to set her straight about that. "She wanted us both to attend with her. She hadn't meant for it to be a date."

"She's a pretty woman."

"Yes," Michael said, knowing where Kara's thoughts were headed. "And she and I are very good friends."

"So are we. Isn't that what you said to her?"

Michael blew out a sigh. He'd introduced Kara as his friend, but it hadn't been an attempt to minimize their relationship. "Actually, I'd already told Maggie that I intended to marry you. And until we got a chance to—" he paused, hoping he could explain his reason in a way she could understand "—until we discussed the new level of intimacy our relationship has reached—"

"Don't worry about it," Kara said.

But he did worry about it. He'd dashed off before they could bask in the newness of what they'd shared or talk about how she was feeling about things. He'd hurt her, and he didn't know how to make things better between them.

"Why didn't Maggie want to go to the benefit alone?" Her question, as well as the compassionate tone, surprised him.

"Maggie's husband was having an affair with one of

the other pediatricians in her office, and now he and his lover are expecting a baby. It was the talk of the office, as well as the entire hospital. And Maggie isn't happy about attending the same social functions, particularly this event, with them.''

Kara winced. ''That would be tough. Does she have to go?''

Michael found her sympathy for his friend and colleague surprising. ''Maggie served on a steering committee that helped get a new pediatric ICU built. She was instrumental in getting the grants and funding. The benefit is to help provide money for equipment. She really needs to be there.'' Michael dropped Kara's hand and slipped his arm around her waist, wanting more intimacy, needing it more than he was willing to admit.

''So,'' Kara said. ''Maggie has to pretend as though the affair and resulting pregnancy don't bother her.''

''That's about it. She's a bit insecure about some things, although she's always been professional and hidden her worries.'' Like he had, too, he supposed.

''Maybe you should go with her.''

Michael stopped walking. ''Listen, Kara. I'm not attending any social functions without you on my arm. I don't want any reporters coming up with wild ideas about who I'm dating.''

''It might take the focus off you and me,'' Kara said, her eyes reaching into his soul. ''And that wouldn't be a bad thing at all.''

''What are you talking about?''

She brushed a windswept strand of hair from her eyes. ''People think I'm after you for your money.''

''I don't care what people say.''

''I do,'' she said, her voice a mere whisper in the breeze. ''That's why I'm not going to marry you.''

''Don't say that.''

"I've already said it. I'm not going to marry you, Michael."

"But you may not get custody of the kids," he said, although that seemed to be the least of his worries. What was the matter with her? Didn't she care enough about him to ignore what other people said?

He pulled her close, held her against his chest, breathed the scent of citrus shampoo. "Say you'll marry me."

"I can't."

Time seemed to freeze, and he stepped away from her embrace. He took her hands in his and tried to read an explanation in her eyes. "You said you loved me."

"More than you'll ever know," she said. "And in spite of your money and status. But no one would ever believe that."

"I believe it."

She pulled her hands away. "It's not enough that you believe it. There will be a world full of people who'll think I seduced a rich husband. That would destroy me." Then she turned in the direction they had come, toward the parked limousine, and walked away.

He wanted to argue, but what she'd said was true. The majority of the world wouldn't believe she'd married him for love. Snickers and snide comments would destroy the light in her eyes, the love in her heart. Watching her love die would destroy him, as well.

And there wasn't a darn thing he could do about it. Or was there?

He stood and watched her walk away, then pulled the cell phone out of his pocket and made a call. Words of love and promises of forever wouldn't do a bit of good, but he refused to let Kara slip away without a fight.

After putting his plan in motion, he strode down the beach to catch up with the woman he loved.

* * *

The ride to the hotel had been quiet, the air filled with despair. Kara had expected Michael to argue his point. Instead, he'd kept his thoughts to himself.

A part of her wished he could come up with some way to make a marriage between them work, but he couldn't, because it was impossible. And apparently he knew it as well as she did. Being right didn't make her decision any easier.

As they pulled into the long, tree-lined drive that led to the lobby of the New England Garden Towers, she gazed out the window of the limousine. Several different news vans lined the curb, and she had to squelch the bile rising in her throat. She hoped those vultures hadn't followed her, looking for a story about the shameless temptress who intended to bilk Michael Harper out of his fortune.

As they entered the lobby, Kara headed toward the elevator that would take them to the top floor, but Michael grabbed her hand and pulled her to a stop.

"What's the matter?" she asked.

"Come with me."

"Where?"

"I've called a press conference, and I want you to attend."

A press conference? Kara's heart dropped to her stomach. "You did what? I thought you hated the attention."

"I do, but I've got to announce Eric's upcoming surgery. I think it's the best way to quell the media's curiosity and keep them at bay."

Her cheeks warmed, and she felt her temper rise. "I don't want to be there. My presence is only going to give this press conference a focus it shouldn't have."

"Trust me," he said, all but dragging her down the long walkway toward a conference room at the end of the hall. Voices murmured from inside open doors.

Oh, good grief. He wouldn't do this to her. Would he? She didn't want to be subjected to the embarrassing questions, the accusations.

As Michael strode into the room the chattering stilled, and was replaced by the flashing bulbs of cameras and the bright light of a rolling video camera. A microphone had been set up at a podium, and Michael led her to the front of the room.

She thought about kicking him in the back of the leg, something to appease her anger, something that would stop him from making her a laughingstock on the national news. Instead, she allowed him to play out the embarrassing scene he'd set in motion.

With his free hand, he pulled a chair from the front row and set it to the side of the microphone. "Have a seat, Kara."

"No," she mouthed slowly, trying to pull her hand from his.

"Please?" His eyes, warm, rich and earnest, tugged at her heart.

Against her better judgment, she took a deep breath and sat in the chair he'd provided.

She wasn't going to like this. Not one little bit. Michael had never seen her angry before, but he was in for a humdinger of a confrontation when this debacle was over. It was bad enough knowing everyone would be talking about her, but why did she have to be present? She didn't want to experience it in person.

"I'd like to thank you all for coming on such short notice," Michael began. "I called this press conference to announce Eric Campbell's upcoming surgery."

"Doctor," a man in front began. "What seems to be Eric's problem?"

"He has a misaligned growth plate, but Dr. Cunningham believes it will be easy to correct. Surgery is scheduled for the day after tomorrow."

"Are you going to pay for the surgery?" a woman asked.

"Yes. I've grown very close to the Campbell family."

"Does that mean you'll stay involved in the boy's life?" the man in front asked. "It's been suggested that you're romantically involved with Kara Westin, the young woman who wants custody of the children."

Michael cleared his throat and gripped the edge of the podium. "There has been a lot of speculation about my life—both past and future. For the most part, I've avoided interviews, dreaded the questions many of your colleagues have asked."

A camera flashed from the side of the room, and Michael continued. "I've always been a private person, consumed by my medical practice and the seriously ill and injured patients I treat. My job required it, so I thought. And in a sense, that's true.

"I don't have to remind you of the recent trial of my ex-wife and her lover. You're all aware of the incidents that led to their arrests and conviction. Needless to say, I didn't want to discuss the deceit or betrayal any further. As far as I was concerned, the past was over.

"I found the overzealous attention the media and tabloids focused on me disconcerting. Why me? I wondered many times. I'm just a man, like any other who had a wife cheat on him. Is it my fame as a surgeon? The wealth of the family into which I was born? Surely there are other men more deserving of public attention than I. For the past six months, I have avoided cameras and reporters like the plague, hoping to maintain my privacy."

Kara, her anger diffused by the words Michael shared with the world, the feelings he'd held close to his chest, relaxed her pose.

What was he doing? Trying to appease the media's curiosity?

"I successfully avoided you people for a while. Then,

while taking some much-needed time to sort through my plans for the future, I met a wonderful woman in Harbor Haven, a spot of heaven near the beach in southern California. That lovely lady, with her nurturing spirit, healed my heart and touched a secret place in my soul.''

A tear trickled down Kara's cheek, and she swiped it from her eye. She had no doubt Michael loved her, that she'd affected him in a special way, but proclaiming his love before the nation wouldn't work. There'd still be those, like Jason Baker, who would belittle Michael's profession of love, who would say she had financial motivations for marrying a wealthy doctor.

''I had no idea that the woman I grew to love would be the focus of media coverage, that the precious children she introduced to me would draw such enormous public attention. I tried to maintain my privacy, to avoid the spotlight, but my involvement with Kara Westin and the Campbell children has put an end to that.''

Yes, Kara realized, his association with her and the kids had thrown him back into the public arena. She was sorry for that. Sorry for Michael, and if truth be told, she was sorry for them all.

''I love Kara, and I've asked her to be my wife.''

As the cameras changed their focus from Michael, numerous bulbs flashed in her face. Kara dug her nails into her palms and tensed her lips. How dare he try to pressure her into making a commitment? She looked the cameras straight on and shook her head. Then she glanced at Michael, shooting him daggers of ice meant to quiet him.

''As you can see,'' Michael said, turning to Kara, ''she refused my proposal.''

Kara crossed her arms and glanced away, yet the cameras continued to flash. She was going to clobber him. It was as simple as that. Right on television. And he'd get more public attention than he'd anticipated.

''Does that surprise you?'' he asked those present.

"That a woman who has very little money would turn down the offer of a wealthy surgeon who loves her?"

This time, Kara couldn't keep her head turned away, couldn't avoid listening to what he would say.

"If you knew Kara Westin, it wouldn't surprise you at all." A camera flashed, this time catching Michael in its glare. "There has been a lot of unfounded speculation about Kara Westin's integrity, as well as implications that she might be easily swayed by the lure of a financial carrot."

The cameraman turned his lens toward Kara. This time, her stiff demeanor had softened. She was pleased to know Michael would defend her, but she doubted any man or woman in this room would believe him without reservation. He was wasting his time.

"You have no idea how badly I wish that Kara's motives were selfish, that she actually intended to snag a rich husband. Because, if her motives were based on securing a sound financial future, I'd stand as good a chance or better than any man in becoming her husband."

Kara caught her bottom lip with her teeth, her concentration no longer on her anger or displeasure at this news conference, but instead on Michael, on what he was saying. And on the love glowing in his eyes.

"If anything," Michael said, his gaze locked on Kara's, "my wealth has hampered my plight to secure her hand in marriage."

A tear trickled down Kara's cheek, but this time she didn't brush it away. She was too intent on keeping her lips from quivering.

"But it's not Kara's hand I want. It's her heart. I'd give anything in the world to have her love. She's the best friend I've ever had, and I know she'd make a perfect wife and mother.

"Some would say I've had a charmed life, perfect by

many standards. But that's not true. I never experienced life to the fullest until I watched Kara play Frisbee on the beach and nurture a child. I hope my character is substantial enough to convince her how much I love her, how far I'd go to make her happy.''

Michael, his eyes pleading, reached out a hand toward her. ''I'm laying down my pride to tell the world how much I value your integrity, your stubborn pride, your loving heart. I'm not worthy of you, Kara. But I'd be honored if you will agree to be my wife, to allow me to be a father to Eric and Ashley. Please, give us a chance at being a family.''

Had any woman ever received such a proposal? Did any woman ever deserve such a man? Life might not be easy, and people might not believe Kara's only motive for marrying Michael was love, but she'd risk the criticism.

With tears in her eyes, Kara stood and strode toward him. He opened his arms, and she stepped inside, where she belonged—close to his heart.

As flashbulbs popped and video cameras rolled, Michael and Kara shared a loving, bonding kiss that would be televised throughout the country.

The depth of Michael's love for her and, she hoped, her love for him would become public knowledge.

When the kiss ended, Michael answered more of their questions.

''When will you marry?'' one woman asked.

''As soon as possible. If Kara is willing, we may have a private ceremony before we return to California.''

''One more question, Dr. Harper.'' A reporter Kara believed to be a television newscaster stepped closer, along with a video cameraman. ''We've heard that Elizabeth Campbell, the children's grandmother and current guardian, is in poor health. What is to become of the children?''

"Kara and I will adopt them," Michael said. "And Mrs. Campbell will live with us, assuming she's agreeable."

Happiness surged through Kara, and she leaned against the man she loved.

"Now, if you'll excuse us," Michael said. "Kara, the children and I have some celebrating to do."

Kara swiped a tear from her eye, then smiled for the camera before basking in the love she saw in Michael's eyes.

"Let's get out of here," Michael said.

"I'll follow your lead."

As they made their way through the throng of reporters, Kara held tight to Michael's hand. He'd said she had healed his heart, but he'd healed hers, as well. And together, they would make a home for the children. Joy and love filled her soul and lightened her steps.

Michael paused before the elevator door. "After we give Eric the good news, I'm going to ask Kathy to take the kids to the zoo."

"Today?"

"Yes. I've got some making up to do."

"What are you talking about?" Kara asked.

Michael gave her a clever smile that made her heart sing. "I'm going to make love to you again, and this time, we're going to enjoy the afterglow."

"I enjoyed it before," she said, as they stepped inside the elevator.

"Not like you should have." He squeezed her hand, then punched the top button.

"I'm so happy," she whispered, as the elevator doors closed them in privacy.

"And I'm the luckiest man in the world."

Michael pulled her into his arms, and they kissed their way to the penthouse suite where their family awaited them.

Love had healed them all.

Epilogue

Kara stood on the porch and surveyed the backyard that had been prepared in celebration of her graduation from UCLA, a feat she'd managed to pay for by herself, in part with the money she'd received for telling her story to *Mother's Mentor*.

Magazine sales had increased dramatically, and Kara had agreed to participate in a special Christmas issue. And just recently, she'd been offered a job as a regular columnist. Writing for *Mother's Mentor* proved to be a perfect outlet for her creative side because it allowed her to work at home. Her first article, "Raising Unselfish Children In a Privileged World," was well-received by the editing staff as well as readers.

The caterers swarmed around a buffet table while the musicians warmed up in the gazebo by the lake. Kara had wanted a small party with close friends and family, but both Ashley and Eric had insisted they had a great deal to be thankful for and had set about making such heartwarming plans that Kara couldn't possibly object.

The kids wanted to celebrate the blessings of the past two years—their adoption into a loving family, Lizzie's good health, Kara's graduation and the new baby brother or sister who would be joining their family soon.

How could Kara possibly say no? Eric had carefully penned the invitations, and Ashley had added bits of crayon and colored marker to individualize each hand-made card. The kids insisted there be five guest lists, one drawn up by each member of the family.

Kara glanced at her watch. In just a few minutes the first of an eclectic group would arrive. The diverse list of invitees included doctors and medical professionals who were friends of Michael's, a few of Kara's fellow graduates, several retired people Lizzie had met at the senior citizens center, Eric's soccer teammates and Ashley's entire preschool class.

The baby, an active little thing, moved, skewing Kara's swollen belly to one side. She wondered whether the new child would be a boy or a girl. They'd had several ultrasounds, but she'd wanted to be surprised and wouldn't let the obstetrician tell her the baby's sex.

A hard knot formed under her rib cage, and she rubbed it gently. "Are you just about ready to join your brother and sister?" she whispered to the precious little one she carried under her heart.

Michael stepped onto the porch and slipped an arm around her once thin waist. "How are you holding up?"

Kara smiled and leaned into his embrace. "My feet hurt, and my back aches. Other than that, I'm ecstatic. It's going to be a lovely party."

"My father just called from his cell phone. He and Mother are nearly here. He'd hoped to arrive before the clown and magician showed up."

"The clown and magician?" Kara asked. "Who included them?"

Michael laughed. "Mother was afraid we wouldn't be able to keep the children occupied without entertainment. I suppose they were on her guest list."

Kara grinned and shook her head slowly. Michael's stodgy parents had really loosened up since that first dinner party. She was glad they'd flown in and more than happy they felt comfortable enough to take an active part in the festivities.

"I've done everything in my power to make sure there won't be a medical emergency that calls me away from this party," Michael said. "Carl Rodgers has agreed to take my calls for the afternoon."

A strong cramp nearly took Kara's breath away, but she rubbed her tummy and tried to ignore the discomfort. She only had two more weeks until her due date, and from what her books said, the last days were full of aches and pains. Still, this one was stronger than the last. She glanced at her gold watch, deciding to time them.

"Look up there." Michael pointed to a bright yellow helicopter in the sky. "Isn't that the chopper from Channel Nine?"

"Yes, I think so," Kara said, craning her neck to get a better view. "Do you suppose we'll ever be yesterday's news?"

"Not as far as I'm concerned." Michael pulled Kara into his arms and kissed her, lovingly, possessively. "When you agreed to marry me, it was a miracle. I still feel like shouting news of my good fortune from the rooftop."

"I'm the lucky one." Kara ran her hand along his cheek and cupped his strong, angular jaw. "I love you so much."

"And I love you."

Another cramp tightened low in her belly, and this time she winced.

"What's the matter?" Michael asked.

"You might be able to guarantee no medical emergency, but I'm not so sure I can promise the same thing."

"Are you kidding?" Michael suddenly looked more like an expectant father than a doctor. "Are you in labor? How far apart are your pains?"

"I'm not sure. I only decided to time them after the last one. I've been having cramps and contractions all morning, but I just assumed it was my body practicing for the real thing." She glanced at her watch. "This contraction was closer than the last one."

Michael ran his fingers through his hair. "I wonder if we should call the doctor or just wait for her to arrive? It's a good thing we sent her an invitation."

Kara laughed. "This is definitely going to be one of the most memorable parties any of our guests have ever attended."

"There you are," Beatrice Raleigh-Harper said from the sliding glass door. "Lizzie said you were both on the porch."

"Mother," Michael said. "How do you feel about being the hostess today?"

"What do you mean?"

"I've got to go to the hospital, but this time Kara's going with me."

"Oh, dear," Beatrice said. "Are you all right?"

"I may be in labor," Kara said.

Beatrice clapped her hands. "What a lovely surprise. Charles, come quick. We're going to have a baby."

Charles joined them on the porch. "Today? This isn't why you decided on a party, is it?"

"We didn't plan it this way," Michael said, kissing Kara again. "But the best things in life are never planned."

* * * * *

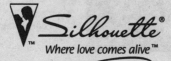

Silhouette Books

is delighted to present
two powerful men, each of whom is
used to having everything

On His Terms

Robert Duncan in

LOVING EVANGELINE
by *New York Times* bestselling author
Linda Howard

and

Dr. Luke Trahern in

ONE MORE CHANCE
an original story by
Allison Leigh

Available this February wherever Silhouette books are sold.

Silhouette®

Where love comes alive™

magazine

♥———————————————— **quizzes**

Is he the one? What kind of lover are you? Visit the **Quizzes** area to find out!

♥———————————————— **recipes for romance**

Get scrumptious meal ideas with our **Recipes for Romance**.

♥———————————————— **romantic movies**

Peek at the **Romantic Movies** area to find Top 10 Flicks about First Love, ten Supersexy Movies, and more.

♥———————————————— **royal romance**

Get the latest scoop on your favorite royals in **Royal Romance**.

♥———————————————— **games**

Check out the **Games** pages to find a ton of interactive romantic fun!

♥———————————————— **romantic travel**

In need of a romantic rendezvous? Visit the **Romantic Travel** section for articles and guides.

♥———————————————— **lovescopes**

Are you two compatible? Click your way to the **Lovescopes** area to find out now!

Silhouette —

where love comes alive—online...

Visit us online at
www.eHarlequin.com

SINTMAG

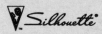

Silhouette®

COMING NEXT MONTH

SPECIAL EDITION